SHADOW HUNT

MICHAEL PEDICELLI

Sentium Press

CONTENTS

DEDICATION

To all who have served

***

ACKNOWLEDGMENTS

Thanks to Mo and her team for guiding a new author thru the long process of getting their first novel published. Thanks to Mike for being there to motivate and to listen to my crazy ideas during those early days.

And to my family, I will always be grateful for your support..

***

Edited by Monique Happy Editorial Services
www.moniquehappy.com

Cover art by David Mickolas of Universal Book Covers

PROLOGUE

Bosnia 2004

The tires of the American military Humvees chewed up the windy dirt road beneath them as the three lightly armored vehicles traveled along the well-used road surrounded on both sides by steep, densely forested hills, making the men inside nervous. The members of the early morning recon mission stayed vigilant as they navigated thru the Bosnian hillside.

BOOOOM

One minute, the lead Humvee was cruising along the road toward the border town of Lozinca. The next minute, the truck disappeared in a cloud of smoke. Specialist Boyd, driving the second Humvee, had been focused on keeping the proper dispersion distance between the lead vehicle and his own when he saw a red flash ahead of him. The lead of the convoy vanished. The young man hit the brakes hard, peering forward to figure out what the hell happened. He watched the smoke begin to clear, revealing a surprisingly still intact vehicle.

Soldiers in the affected Humvee began to spill out as the vehicle's highest-ranking soldier spoke. Lieutenant John Hanna's voice crackled over the radio reporting they must have hit some sort of improvised explosive device, or IED, but that everyone was okay. Lieutenant Max Barrett, the leader of the security element and riding in the third vehicle, immediately ordered his men to secure the small convoy. His men deployed to take up defensive positions on both sides of the road.

Barrett made his way up to the front of Specialist Boyd's Humvee to meet with Hanna.

"She's going nowhere." Hanna's frustrations came across to his fellow officer and friend. Both men had graduated from Military Intelligence School at Fort Huachuca together two years prior.

"You sure everyone's okay?" Barrett couldn't help but stare at the smoking vehicle.

"Looks worse than it is." Hanna's Texas drawl flowed out while he tried to clear the smoke out of both his eyes and nose; they itched like hell. "Must have hit a body popper, which destroyed the transmission. Nobody saw the damn thing."

"That's why you're supposed to ride behind the recce team." Hanna didn't respond, ignoring Barrett's advice … again. "Okay, let's clean her and move out." Barrett took command since he led the security element. Hanna, who ran the intelligence element of the mission, proceeded to instruct his men to "clean" the vehicle. This meant getting rid of any classified information so it would not fall into the enemy's hands, in this case the Serbian paramilitary elements who continued to thwart the peace talks. The rest of the soldiers would then cram inside the two remaining Humvees to continue their mission.

The process seemed like an eternity to Barrett, especially after Sergeant Kufts informed the young lieutenant that, per Barrett's orders, he had radioed in the situation to Command and had been advised two Apache gunships would be deployed to destroy the damaged Humvee and provide cover for the remaining men. Barrett loved his quick-thinking NCOs. The problem with this otherwise good news was that it would be at least twenty minutes before the helicopters arrived. Being in a non-secured zone known for high levels of enemy activity, Barrett knew a lot could happen in two minutes, let alone twenty. It was imperative that their little convoy get moving.

Barrett scanned the horizon to the south; he didn't like surprises. Hanna approached him from behind. Having just finished passing the order to evacuate the damaged vehicle, he also got the update on the inbound gunships.

2

"Figures …" Hanna, the six-foot-four rock of a man, towered over the just barely six-foot Barrett.

The shorter officer smiled and was about to face Hanna when a sharp hiss interrupted him followed by "Fire … fire!" Specialist Craven, lying prone on the east side of the road, shouted the alarm. Barrett dropped to the ground, looking for the closest available cover. One more shot rang overhead as he low-crawled toward shrubs on the roadside in front of him, stabilizing his Kevlar helmet on his head with the fingers of his left hand while clutching his M-16 with his right. The lull between shots could only mean one thing: a sniper.

Barrett used his knees and elbows to propel his body into the bush line. Once in position, the lieutenant pulled the cocking mechanism back on his M-16, letting the metal slide forward, causing a reassuring slapping sound. Set to engage, Barrett searched the hilltops overlooking the road. He focused in the direction of his men, who were returning fire. Unable to identify a target to shoot at, he turned around to signal Sergeant Kufts in the front seat of the second Humvee. "What the …"

Shocked, Barrett spied Hanna's body lying contorted and motionless in the middle of the road. Without thinking, Barrett crawled out of the bush line and sprinted out to him, completely exposing himself to the sniper. He reached down to grab the upper neck portion of Hanna's body armor, pulling his friend over to the parked Humvee. His eyes were gray and rolled back. *Not good.* Barrett pulled Hanna under the vehicle and called out for his team's medic. Barrett examined his fellow officer, who appeared to have been hit at least once somewhere in the neck. Dark blood flowed from the wound, gurgling when mixed with the oxygen in his throat.

The soldiers continued to return fire, doing their best to suppress the sniper. Barrett administered first aid until the medic arrived. Sergeant Carlson got there in good time considering a sniper lurked out there. Carlson knelt next to Hanna, his hands a blur of motion as they crisscrossed the wounded officer's body. He finished his assessment then made eye contact with Barrett, shaking his head. Barrett turned away; he had to refocus on the mission at hand. He peered down at his uniform, noticing a hole for the first time. What Barrett hadn't realized was that once he broke concealment, the sniper fire had increased dramatically. One of the rounds had torn through his pants as he ran. He had been real lucky.

The young officer surveyed the scene in front of him. The men continued to return fire toward the hill to their east. Once he realized the sniper no longer shot at them, he ordered a ceasefire and demanded a headcount. If the sniper was a pro, then he would be firing from a position out of the effective range of his men's rifles; also, he'd move after a couple of shots so the Americans wouldn't be able to get a bead on him anyway.

Barrett learned two others had also been seriously wounded, but Carlson got both soldiers stabilized. The mission was over.

Now, Barrett had a choice; the young intelligence officer could abandon the two operating vehicles and wait twenty minutes for the cavalry or jump in the remaining Humvees and use whatever protection they offered, high-tailing it out of there. He chose the latter. Waiting to see if the sniper had more friends out there did not appeal to him. Besides, if they used the Humvees, the soldiers would run into the gunships a little earlier, and if anyone dared to pursue them, they would be in a world of hurt.

"We're filling in the Humvees." As the men packed into the remaining vehicles, a thought occurred to Barrett. "Is the lead victor completely clear?" He directed his query toward his first sergeant. The stocky Sergeant Fienz responded by simply grabbing a LAW that PFC Watts had on his back, aimed, and fired at the damaged vehicle. The anti-tank round broke the rear windshield and detonated inside the vehicle. While the explosion did not obliterate the Humvee, there would be nothing of value left inside.

"The victor's clear, sir." Sergeant Fienz gave the LAW back to the private. The men climbed into the two vehicles, which made very abrupt u-turns before racing back along the main road. The men remained alert, scanning the terrain for any other surprises. The stress level had escalated. After what the soldiers had been through, they anticipated something else to happen. Barrett worked the radio, trying to get a fix on the two Apaches in relation to the convoy's current position. He had been informed someone in command had the foresight to send a Blackhawk with a medical team on board along with the two gunships. Barrett pulled out his map and decided on a location to meet the helicopters where he could safely transfer his wounded, along with Hanna, over to the Blackhawk. He and the rest of the men would then ride back to their base in the Humvees.

The lead gunship noticed the convoy first and raised Barrett on the radio. The young lieutenant was grateful to see the incoming helicopters, though it did reinforce the severity of their situation. Barrett and the pilot of the Blackhawk decided on a landing zone two kilometers south of their current position. The spot, near a fork in the road without being surrounded on all sides by hills, had enough room for the large helicopter to land.

While the Blackhawk flared to land, the two Apaches started circling above to provide security for the transfer. Barrett coordinated the smooth handover of the wounded personnel between the ground and air assets. Before the convoy and helicopters headed home, one of the Apaches headed north to destroy the abandoned Humvee. The helicopter disappeared from view as the rest of them headed back in the direction of their base. A few minutes later, "Smoke 1," came over the radio—the Apache pilot's call to let everyone know that the abandoned vehicle was now an unrecognizable heap of burned metal and scattered debris. A victim of one of its ultra-lethal sidewinder missiles.

The crammed Humvees continued to speed back to base with the lone Apache to provide air support if needed. When the ground convoy finally came within sight of the base, the built-up stress was replaced with an overwhelming emotion of anger and frustration for the young lieutenant.

***

Barrett lay across his bunk, staring at the ceiling, wondering why he was so lucky to have made it out of the ambush in one piece while three others didn't. The young officer enjoyed his current solitude, especially since his "quarters" was basically a mobile home sleeping six junior officers. Barrett had spent most of the afternoon along with his men in debriefing, relieving the ambush over and over

5

with investigators and his superiors. He still couldn't forget the look on his friend's face as Hanna lay in the road in a pool of his own blood. He envisioned the scene every time he closed his eyes. Barrett blamed himself, and the resulting frustrations built by the minute.

Colonel Cole, Barrett's battalion commander, entered the drab, green-painted mobile home, searching for his young charge. The colonel straightened his graying red hair while surveying the young officer with a mixture of envy and sadness; Barrett was just now getting to experience being an officer with a long career in front of him, but Cole remembered what it had felt like the first time he'd lost a good friend in battle.

After a few minutes of niceties, the colonel led Barrett back to the briefing room next to the makeshift command center. The command center sat across an unpaved road from where the Intel officers lived and was housed in a large, steel structure surrounded by sand bags. The good thing about being in Intelligence was that you were always close to where the decisions got made. The bad thing was that most of them spent their entire time in-country inside the command center. That was why Hanna and Barrett had been so keen on performing their intelligence-gathering mission. The two junior officers had begun going stir crazy always being cooped up; it wasn't why they had joined the Army in the first place.

The men entered the building and headed straight toward the secured section. Cole stopped at the door to the briefing room and motioned for Barrett to go ahead. "They're waiting."

"Aren't you coming, sir?"

"I'm not invited." The colonel walked away. Barrett went through the door with his head spinning. *What's going on?*

The briefing room looked like a typical college classroom with a projection display system up front and a series of tables and chairs lined up behind it. Maps and pictures of the break-away countries of the former Yugoslavia adorned most of the wall space. Awaiting Barrett inside and sitting at a long table at the front of the room was General Halton, Colonel Bishop, Major Sunden, and another man who only introduced himself as McKenna. The setup reminded Barrett of a board inquiry he had seen in old war movies.

6

Facing the "board" sat twelve Special Forces soldiers, an entire A-team.

Barrett sat, trying to remember what he knew of the senior officers. General Halton, commander of the American sector, was an old-fashioned artillery officer, spit and polish all the way. Colonel Bishop, sitting to his right, headed the 19th Special Forces group out of Fort Carson. He was known for being level-headed and calm during both training and in battle. Major Sunden needed no introduction; nicknamed "Sandman," he was one of the most well-known Green Berets in the Army, or as well-known as a member of the quiet professionals can be. He'd led special operations teams in Panama, Afghanistan, and Iraq. It was also rumored that he had been sheep-dipped to lead a CIA team into North Korea back in the '90s.

Sheep dipping was when the CIA recruited active soldiers to perform specific covert missions. The major was obviously a man who had everyone's respect in the room. What Barrett did not know was that "Sandman" now served as a senior officer in the Army's tier one special mission unit, the super-secret counter-terrorist unit here to assist in the planning of certain 'sensitive' special operation missions.

Barrett had no clue who the man named McKenna sitting next to the war hero was, especially since the man didn't even wear any insignia on his uniform.

What am I doing in a room with these guys?

General Halton stood up, adjusted his jacket, and began the briefing. He went on to explain the area near Lozinca where Hanna had been killed had become a trouble spot. A number of reports had filtered in about villagers being tortured and killed, with Serb terrorists coming in and out of the area. Also, men had been shooting at relief workers and helicopters as they passed overhead. The killing of an American soldier was the last straw. The Pentagon had decided they were going to do something about it.

The plan was to insert a Special Operations team, in this case an Army Special Forces unit, clandestinely at night into the area. The team's primary focus would be to gather intelligence and, if needed, perform search and destroy missions on approved targets of opportunity. The A-team would be split into two groups of six, dividing the area of operations into geographical zones. The A-team's commanding officer, Captain Rowan, would take his team to cover the northern area and Chief Warrant Officer Paul Sensi would be leading the southern group. Barrett would be assigned as an Intel liaison to Sensi's group. The team needed on-the-spot intelligence analysis and, after Hanna, he had the most knowledge of the area. His basic language skills might come in handy too. While Barrett outranked the chief, he wasn't Special-Forces-qualified so Sensi had operational command while in the field.

Barrett, being a relatively young intelligence officer, was still honing his craft, so he studied the senior officers intently, trying to decipher their speech patterns and body movements. This might also give him a better idea of what was really going on. Barrett perceived rather quickly that while the general had the highest rank in the room, the person actually running the show was Major Sunden. He provided the most details and answered almost all of the questions. The second most important man seemed to be the enigma named McKenna; he didn't say a word through the whole presentation but there had been a few instances where Sunden would look at McKenna before proceeding with a statement or answer to a question. The others attended most likely just to baby-sit the proceedings. Brass politics. The general wrapped up the briefing by addressing them all, saying, "Good hunting, gentlemen."

With the meeting adjourned, Barrett observed Sunden walking out of the room in a deep discussion with the mysterious McKenna. The other senior officers followed, leaving Barrett and the Green Berets behind.

The Special Forces operators did not appear happy. Having been training and working together for years, the men knew each other's movements and reactions without thinking. Now, they were being asked to work with someone new. To compound the problem, the individual was not only a conventional soldier but what they considered "green," a novice to combat. Sure, he'd performed admirably during the ambush—all the team members had been briefed on the earlier incident—but to operators like the Green

Berets, that was to be expected. What the young officer did had been a one-time occurrence; he could now possibly be in continual combat for days or even weeks. This was what always bothered them about "conventional" thinking from the Army.

Barrett had the opposite response. The young officer looked forward to going after these guys; being a typical young soldier, he wanted payback. The consequences of his wishes being fulfilled did not even cross his mind.

As the rest of the operators headed out of the command center, one of the SF troopers, Sergeant Thomas, approached Barrett. "How good do you shoot?"

"Okay."

"Are you busy right now, sir?"

"No. What do you have in mind, Sergeant?" Barrett's expression added to his somewhat quizzical response.

"Let's go to the range, sir." Thomas intended to gauge the level and proficiency of the young lieutenant's marksmanship. Barrett agreed; the idea of squeezing off a few rounds pleased him. He still had a lot of pent-up anger.

Brad Thomas, the weapons specialist on the A-team, was a stocky, laid-back man in his mid-twenties who had spent a quiet existence as a youth in Wisconsin before joining the Army. After enlisting, he'd volunteered for Airborne training and the Rangers. At the time, he found life in the Rangers a little boring, all training and no playing, so he gravitated toward Special Forces. Thomas quickly found himself in the jungles of Colombia and the deserts of the Middle East. This was definitely more to his liking.

Thomas led the young officer past the outdoor shooting range and over to an adjacent wooden structure. The armory, located a short walk from the Command Center, sat in an old converted barn. They entered, not from the front entrance as Barrett usually did, but from a side door. Barrett had never been in this part of the building before, since this section housed the weapons for the Special Forces troopers. Here, Thomas had the Special Forces' armorer issue Barrett an M4A1 carbine, a Special Operations modified variant of the M4 Barrett and the rest of the conventional army used. Barrett liked knowing he had full auto capability if needed.

After an hour of shooting and target recognition exercises that Thomas put Barrett through, the other SF team members joined them to rehearse close-quarter tactics and other tactical firing scenarios. At the conclusion of the short but highly intense training session, Chief Sensi reminded the team not to shave, shower, or eat anything not indigenous to their target area. Once they finished cleaning their weapons, the soldiers headed back to collect their gear and forty-eight hours of pre-mission quarantine.

**

The Blackhawk lifted off shortly after sunset, using the darkness to cloak its mission. The normal flight time to their destination was just less than two hours, but the roundabout route, which the helicopter took in order to maintain optimal operational security, increased the transport time to over three hours. The night was cold and calm. It appeared the whole country slept as the blacked-out helicopter flew low over the Bosnian countryside, skimming the border with Kosovo, or Kosova as the Albanian minority called it. Barrett leaned back, resting on his pack while thinking about Hanna and rerunning the road ambush in his mind over and over as he had almost every waking moment since the attack occurred. Thomas tapped Barrett's shoulder, bringing him back to the present. Go time.

The group fast-roped down. Barrett watched each man before him grab the rope with two hands then slide quickly out of view. He went out fourth, speeding down the rope before his legs pounded into the ground, knocking him off balance. Barrett recovered quickly, moving to get out of the way before the man behind him crashed down on his head. Once everyone was on the ground, the team moved swiftly into the brush. Sergeant Reeves, the most senior man on the team, stayed close to Barrett as they moved toward their objective.

Greg Reeves, a tall and well-built twenty-year grizzly veteran, had served everywhere from Africa to South America during his time of duty. At forty, Reeves had the dubious distinction of being the oldest team member, and this meant he had the most experience as well, which was why he got tasked with keeping an eye on the "green" officer.

Before they launched for the mission, the team decided to base their ops from a tree-lined ridge north of the village; their new home away from home. From that vantage point, they would be able to recon the small village and the surrounding area. The team moved out as silently and quickly as possible.

Barrett's heart raced. He wanted to start this mission and do some good. As they ascended the hill, Reeves asked Barrett if he needed help. The young lieutenant dismissed him with a wave of his hand. "Keep moving," he said in an officer sort of way in an attempt to hide his impatience.

The group moved in on the ridge and searched for a good hiding place. They found a spot between two large trees and dense underbrush, which provided cover from the village and the air. The soldiers got right to work preparing their hide site. With a dugout big enough for the men to lie in, they began pulling down some of the loose foliage to camouflage their handiwork. The team planned on leaving no signs of their residence, such as newly strewn dirt from recently dug up and refilled earth.

The team spent the daylight hours in their makeshift hideout waiting for nightfall. As soon as the sun began to set behind the hills to the east, the men started preparing for their busy night ahead. The first night on a mission like this was always the toughest, since the members of the team needed time to adjust to their new surroundings. Reports and pictures never told the whole story, never mind the accuracy questions that accompanied them. The operators needed to get a feel for the terrain and the environment they would be operating in.

Once ready, the men covered up their temporary home and moved stealthily toward the village. It was getting late in the evening, and the place seemed deserted. The team moved out in a predetermined fashion with Smith on point, followed by Thomas, Sensi, Reeves, Barrett, and Jones. Barlow would be pulling rear security. The seven soldiers settled in a row of trees just on the outskirt of the village. Using their night vision goggles, or NVGs, the team surveyed the town, looking for anything that would lead them to the Serbs responsible for fighting the UN peacekeeping mission and the sniper who'd killed Hanna.

After two days of observation and limited forays into the village, Barrett noticed a pattern of rough-looking men coming and going each night from a barn-like structure on the west side. After conferring with Chief Sensi, they decided that the chief, Reeves, Thomas, and Barrett would conduct recon on the building, the X, as it was the location of the new mission. They planned on going in teams of two, with each team responsible for one-hundred and eighty degrees of observation on the target. The rest got tasked with providing enemy movement updates and sniper cover if things went wrong on the X.

They deployed earlier the following night, giving themselves plenty of time to get into their respective positions in order to recce the Barn, as they were now calling the objective. Sensi and Thomas approached from the south side, while Barrett and his chaperone Reeves took the north side. Barrett and Reeves made their way as quickly and silently as possible. Their side of the Barn lay opposite to the team's approach, so the two moved at a quickened pace. The north side also had a corner section visible to a few homes. The two men had to be extremely careful not to get exposed. They used pieces of underbrush, trees, and shadows to mask their movements.

The team watched and listened as men streamed in and out throughout the night. Both teams used long-distance listening devices along with their night-vision-equipped monoculars. The visitors were always armed with AK-47s, sidearms, and some were even spotted with RPGs. After observing this, it became clear to the Special Forces soldiers that these men should be on top of the list of suspects causing the UN trouble in the area.

The team surmised the men were picking up instructions as well as weapons; they paid special attention to a middle-aged man with long, dark hair and a mustache. He reminded the soldiers of a member of a Mexican Mariachi band, so they nicknamed him Mariachi. After three additional nights of surveillance, the troopers returned to their hide site. Sensi and Barrett decided to report in. The team was ordered to enter the structure, capture Mariachi, and exploit the site for as much intelligence as possible before being extracted by a Blackhawk helicopter. The team members in the field conferred then agreed among themselves on an assault plan. They planned "bottom up," not like the rest of the Army's "top down" approach. Everyone on the team had a say in the plan.

Barrett's intelligence expertise would be needed once inside forced his inclusion in the assault force. He would enter the target building from the back with Reeves. The men moved out quietly. They deployed as they had before with two teams and two snipers. Jones and Barlow took up their sniper positions along the treeline overlooking the Barn and readied themselves to provide cover for the assaulters. The operators waited as men came and went throughout the early evening hours. Sensi decided the best time to enter the Barn was when Mr. Mariachi began cleaning his desk for the night. That usually meant that he was preparing to go home. Plus, he was almost always alone at this time.

Sensi would have preferred to take Mariachi at his home and have an additional team take down the meeting place, but the lack of available manpower prohibited this. Besides, his job was to do the difficult tasks the rest of the Army shunned, and he took a lot of pride in his work. The team got into position and waited. Finally, after an hour, their target was alone in the Barn. Barrett checked his Casio G-shock watch … *Go time.*

The front door made a crunching sound as Thomas kicked it open. Sensi moved through first, sweeping the corners with his rifle. Reeves crashed in the back door, followed by Barrett. The two teams quickly swept through the large, open space. Mariachi looked stunned at the sight of the fully armed and camouflaged SF troopers in his sanctuary. He began to mumble incoherently as Sensi put him on his knees. He didn't stop mumbling until Sensi stuffed a gag in his mouth. With Mariachi secured, phase one of their operation ended. Reeves took his position covering the back door with Thomas doing likewise at the front.

The rest of them began the site exploitation phase, collecting any intelligence they could find. Barrett looked around and tried to figure out what would be important to them. He put aside the bag the suspect had held for a look-through later. Then he attempted to discern what else was of import in the room; there was a lot of stuff that would be useful to the analysts back at the base.

The room itself was a large, open space with a bathroom in the back; the walls were adorned with pictures of local Bosnian leaders. Half had big red X's on them. Barrett knew some of the marked men had been killed, so he deduced that the others with the mark must also be dead or on Mariachi's hit list. *Guess these guys had a lot of enemies.* He snapped off some pictures before moving on to the large table next to the wall covered by maps and letters, most of them written in a Serbian dialect that he couldn't read. This made him miss Hanna even more. *He could read this stuff.*

They also discovered a large cache of weapons locked in the cage in the north corner of the room. As Barrett put documents into his pack, he noticed lights shining across the wall. He looked up and out the open window. A car had just pulled up: an old, beat-up Peugeot that looked like it had seen its share of tough times.

"We have company." Thomas kept his voice low. Three men exited the car. Never before during their recons of the headquarters had men come this late. Barrett glanced over at Mariachi, noticing a large burlap bag under the desk. Barrett realized why they had visitors. "I think he's taking a trip, and these guys are his ride."

"Great." Sensi went to the front door as one of the men approached the Barn. The other two remained outside, lighting up cigarettes.

Barlow and Jones saw the car pull up and were ready to provide support if needed. Inside the Barn, Sensi directed hand signals to Thomas. The ex-Ranger nodded, backing behind the front door. It opened, and the newcomer nonchalantly walked through. He didn't get very far.

Thomas grabbed him from behind, kicking his right knee out as he snapped the newcomer's neck ninety degrees to the left, breaking it. Thomas dragged the dead body to the weapons locker.

The Americans now prepared to take out the two remaining Serbs. Before they could move on them, a truck pulled up near the back. Barrett made out at least five guys inside. The situation went from bad to worse in a hurry.

"Chief," Barrett whispered, making his way next to Sensi. "Take him out the front. Reeves and I will take care of the guys in the truck. That should buy you some time." Sensi peered at Barrett, and while he didn't like the idea of leaving anyone behind, he knew the young lieutenant was right. Their objective was to capture Mariachi and gather as much intelligence as possible.

"Okay. Rally point, one hour." Sensi dragged the prisoner up and moved out toward the front door with Thomas in the lead.

Barrett moved stealthily to the back door, joining Reeves as he studied the truck. Some of the men in the back had gotten out of the flatbed and were stretching. An electronic lantern provided the Americans with silhouettes of even more passengers in the back.

"I count two in the front, four in the back, and three others roaming around." Reeves pointed them out. Barrett's anger had dissipated; he felt like he had a huge hole in his stomach as he began to realize that he was about to get into a firefight. His hands shook as he checked his ammo. *Watch what you wish for.*

"Any suggestions?" Barrett adjusted his night-vision goggles. Though Barrett technically held the higher ranking of the two, he knew he would have to rely on Reeves' expertise if he wanted to get out of this alive.

"You take the two in the front cab, and I will handle the four in the back."

"What about the others?"

"We play those by ear. We should get some sniper support, but I wouldn't count on it. Mr. Murphy has already made one appearance tonight." Reeves grinned. Barrett thought he had gone crazy.

Barlow prepared himself to provide cover for the Americans at the Barn's rear. Just then, another truck pulled up, blocking the sniper's view of Barrett and Reeves' position. He used the night-vision scope on his sniper rifle to count an additional four men in the truck. Oh well; he had enough targets of opportunity in his sights. Besides, success now determined he needed to eliminate them all anyway. For now, Barrett and Reeves were on their own.

As soon as Reeves and Barrett heard gunfire emanating from the front of the building, the two soldiers engaged. Sensi and Thomas appeared to have made contact on their way to the brush. Barrett sighted and fired on the driver. The body jerked, but since the windshield cracked, obscuring his vision, he couldn't tell if the driver died. He did not have time to wait. He immediately shifted his rifle sights to the left … focus … breathe … fire. The rifle butt kicked against Barrett's shoulder as the round exploded out of the barrel. The passenger's head slammed backward thanks to the bullet ramming into his skull. In the same amount of time it took Barrett to get off those two shots, Reeves had eliminated all four targets in the back. The differences in the men's training and experience became apparent.

The Americans now began their run to the brush and the total darkness it provided. The enemy soldiers from the first truck had been stunned by the Americans' surprise attack; some dropped to the ground and readied themselves to fight back, while the others headed for the safety of the forest. Reeves, in the lead, slowed just as he passed the first truck and took out two soldiers lying prone who were attempting to locate their assailants.

Then the night exploded. The unnerving hammering noise of multiple AK-47s filled the air along with the even scarier *crack* as rounds came dangerously close to the two Americans. There were more enemy soldiers than Barrett and Reeves had previously thought.

Barrett watched as it seemed like a whole platoon of Serbian soldiers arrived on foot. *Great. Mr. Murphy did indeed decide to make another visit.* This explained why the second truck had showed up empty.

With twenty yards of open space left before the edge of the forest, Reeves' leg suddenly kicked out from under him. Just as the pain began to register, he felt like someone took a sledgehammer to his shoulder, the pain screaming through his body; the wiry old sergeant fell forward, crashing to the ground as rounds continued to fly above him. Reeves' lower right leg was shattered by the first bullet, and his shoulder now lay limp due to another round.

Reeves used his good arm to grope around for his assault rifle when he noticed movement beside him. His night-vision goggles went dark. Something blocked his optics. Reeves ripped his NVGs off to see what was going on. Barrett, on his knee and shooting, had placed himself between Reeves and the incoming fire!

"Fire in the hole." Barrett tossed two grenades, one after the other, toward the area where the most intense barrage emanated. The two combined grenades exploded, lighting up the night sky. Barrett remained prone on the ground to wait out the ensuing blast and for the enemy fire to subside.

When the firing slowed, he grabbed the sergeant's webbing and half-carried, half-dragged Reeves into the safety of the brush. Barrett hoped the chaos going on around the Barn would buy them time while they trudged through the forest.

After moving a few hundred yards deeper into the woods, the pair felt safe enough to briefly stop so Barrett could address Reeves' wounds.

"How you doing?"

"I'll live." Reeves tried to hide the pain in his response. "Won't make my wife happy." Barrett could tell, even with Reeves' best efforts to hide it, the veteran soldier was clearly in a lot of pain.

"We need to keep moving." Barrett helped Reeves up and put his arm under the sergeant's good shoulder to keep him steady. The men needed to hit the rally point soon. Barrett figured with the injuries, the trek would be a painstakingly slow process.

After a short while, they stopped again for a brief rest to allow Barrett to take another peek at Reeves' wounds. He glanced at his watch and realized they had only thirty minutes to transverse about two miles. Between the hilly terrain and the Serbian paramilitaries still lurking about, he had real doubts about making the time. This was the Serbs' turf, and they had the home field advantage. Barrett checked his map to make sure they were going in the right direction, and both men started out again.

***

Sensi and Thomas, along with their prisoner, had made the rally point in good time. After the brief, initial firefight with the two remaining men from the car, they had encountered no one else on their trek to the rendezvous point. Jones welcomed them; he had gotten there first and secured the site. Barlow showed up a short time later. Jones gave the area a quick look over. "Where are Reeves and Barrett?"

Barlow's frustration came through in his voice. "I lost contact with them after they exited the Barn. I engaged as many tangos as possible before exfil."

"Okay, if they don't show when our ride gets here, we'll stow our friend here on the bird and go find them," replied the chief, pointing to their prisoner. Sensi then sat down and pulled out his pre-mission briefing packet and map. Time to work out a search plan.

***

Barrett and Reeves were moving at a grudgingly slow pace when they heard movement in the trees to their left. Both men stopped, and Barrett helped Reeves position himself seated with his back against a tree stump. Barrett cautiously crept toward the noise. As he got closer, the young soldier dropped even lower and crawled ever so slowly.

He peeked through a shrub and noticed two armed men conversing calmly with each other. Unfortunately, the men stood on the high point of a well-used trail that led to and from the village with a great view of the surrounding vicinity; they were in a perfect position to see who came and went regardless if on the trail or off.

The young lieutenant saw no way around these men if they wanted to make the extraction on time. He had no choice but to eliminate the men without giving away their position. Barrett went back to inform Reeves of the situation and his solution. The older soldier concurred, offering some helpful instructions on close-quarter combat.

Barrett made his way back to the shrubs behind the two men. The soldier knew what he had to do. Barrett picked up a fallen branch and threw it a couple of yards behind some trees just to the left of the men. Cliché, but the deception worked; both Serbs abruptly stopped talking and started looking around. One raised his rifle and wandered over into the brush to search for what caused the noise. He disappeared from sight. Barrett, letting the rage over Hanna's death take over, snuck up on the remaining man and cupped the soldier's mouth tight while driving his knife into the man's body as Reeves had instructed. The blade severed the man's spinal column, killing him instantly. Barrett dragged the limp body behind some shrubs and waited for the other soldier to return. The young officer remained crouched as the other Serbian soldier came toward him, calling out to his comrade. When the man got close enough, the young officer leapt up and grabbed the Serbian's face and attempted to kill him the same way as the first one.

This time, it was not so easy. The other man's defenses were up. The Serbian spun his upper body before Barrett got a solid grip, and they made eye contact. This threw Barrett off. Barrett's opponent was no small man either; he stood around six-foot-one and resembled a tank. The Serb threw a roundhouse punch at Barrett, which barely missed. Barrett connected on a straight kick to the man's sternum, dropping him to the ground. Barrett followed with an uppercut. With his opponent stunned, Barrett grabbed his rifle and swung at his enemy.

The loud crack signified that the Serbian's jaw had broken. His eyes rolled upward then the man slumped to the ground. Barrett stashed him in nearby bushes. The man lay unconscious but alive; no longer a threat, so Barrett left the Serbian alone. By the time he regained consciousness, Barrett and his team should be long gone.

Barrett returned to the spot where he'd left Reeves. The older soldier did not look good. He had lost a good amount of blood and was going into shock. The cold air didn't help either. Barrett knew he had to get Reeves back to the rally point fast so he could evac him to a proper medical facility. He helped Reeves get back on his feet and had the veteran soldier lean on his shoulder again as they resumed their slow trek through the dense forest.

***

Worry crept in on Sensi's thoughts. The chief prepared to have his men move out to the actual LZ a few hundred meters away to meet the incoming chopper. There'd been no word from Barrett or Reeves. *Where are my men?* The pilot had recently radioed to inform him they should be at the station within minutes. He ordered Jones to move out first to secure the landing zone. The point man would be followed by Thomas and Barlow, who guarded the prisoner. Sensi himself planned on remaining as long as possible before heading out, thus he would be bringing up the rear.

The team moved out as planned. Sensi fought the urge to use his radio to contact his missing men. He knew the radio signals might be intercepted by the Serbians, thus giving away their position. They had proved adept at doing this in the past to other units operating in the region. The chief hated having to send the Blackhawk back without them, but he didn't have much choice. He needed to know what happened to his guys.

Suddenly, the forest came alive to the east of Sensi as the sound of footsteps crashed through the brush. Sensi knelt next to a tree and raised his rifle, attempting to range his monocular attached to his night-vision goggles. His view focused on two figures making a beeline in his direction with one practically carrying the other. Then he noticed their gear, and his heart jumped. Americans!

Sensi assumed the wounded man had to be the inexperienced young officer. As they approached, he gave out his half of the pre-arranged challenge greeting. "Tastes great."

"Less filling." Sensi got a close-up view of the pair and was surprised for the second time when he realized Reeves was the one hurt, not Barrett. Reeves also appeared to be fading in and out of consciousness. *Not good.*

"How is he?" Sensi held up Reeves' opposite side.

"Not sure." Barrett was relieved they had made the rendezvous in time.

"Let's get him to the LZ and have Barlow take a look at him."

The men moved faster now with the chief's help, but still not quickly enough. The roar of the massive turbine engines signaled the Blackhawk's approach. Sensi, feeling time slip away, finally gave in and grabbed his radio. *What the hell. We'll be out of here before anyone gets a fix on us.* "Fox three, this is Fox one."

"Fox one, Fox three. Over." Jones wondered why radio silence had been broken.

"Fox three, hold position. I repeat; hold position."

"Affirmative, Fox one, we'll hold position. Fox three out."

The three men negotiated their way into the clearing; the sight of the big helicopter sitting there was heavenly. Like Christmas morning to Barrett. Barlow and one of the helicopter's crew chiefs came over to help with Reeves. The men fought through the rotor wash to the open side of the Blackhawk, where they laid the wounded warrior out on a stretcher, tying him down to the floor. This kept the injured from moving too much as the Blackhawk weaved its way back into safer airspace. With Reeves secured, the rest of the men boarded the chopper and prepared for takeoff. Thomas looked over at Barrett, giving him a thumbs-up as the big bird lifted into the air.

The soldiers on board the Blackhawk kept vigilant for any possible threats as the big helicopter navigated out of the danger zone. The exfil seemed to take forever, but eventually the helicopter crossed back into friendly airspace again.

Chief Sensi put his hand on Barrett's shoulder and leaned closer to be heard over the roar of the engines. "Good work." The young officer, too exhausted to appreciate what he and the team had just accomplished, only nodded. All of the adrenaline and rage that had carried him for the past couple of days left, and he succumbed to a level of exhaustion he'd never known existed.

The soldiers later learned the man they had captured, Mirko Tolvich, a Serb general and mastermind of many atrocities against the other ethnic groups in the region over the years, had been operating clandestinely out of the small isolated village in order to avoid being discovered by the UN and NATO forces. His luck had finally run out.

CHAPTER 1

Prague, Present Day

The late-evening fog bullied its way over the capital city of Prague. It swept across the Charles Bridge, almost hiding the Grand Castle with its magnificent Gothic steeples and sloping, diamond-patterned roof. Max Barrett watched this fall phenomena from his seat against the window in the Slavia Café. The café, which sat next to the Vlatava River in the Stare Mesto or Old Town section of the city, normally provided panoramic views of the riverfront. Unfortunately, the weather was not cooperating tonight.

Barrett endured another sip of strong Czech coffee while stealing glimpses at the other patrons, who were enjoying the Art Deco-inspired café's wide variety of beverages, including the ever-present pivo. The micro-brewed beer was all the rage in Prague.

The American was doing his best to blend in—or "go gray" as it was known in his tradecraft—with the local crowd that frequented the establishment. His short, dark brown hair had a messed-up look about it, and his six-foot athletic frame was hidden under charcoal pants and a black, turtleneck sweater. Barrett sat in the popular café, waiting to meet a new contact.

He ran through what he knew about Lin Foresky in his mind. The two had never met before. Foresky, a Polish intelligence agent currently on loan to the International War Tribunal at The Hague in the Netherlands, was charged with the ongoing search for indicted war criminals still on the loose in the Balkans. Recently, he had been investigating the mysterious deaths of six suspected war criminals in Eastern Europe. Most of the war criminals were part of Bosnian Serb

Paramilitary Units that had been indicted by the court for crimes that included genocide, rape, torture, and murder committed in former Yugoslavia during the 1990s Civil War. Their bodies had been turning up all over the region.

With the search for war criminals in the Balkans considered a low priority, the responsibility got pushed on the U.S. State Department. The State Department was working with the Tribunal to discover who was behind the deaths and to try and bring them to justice. When Foresky's primary contact with the State Department was killed in a car bombing in Budapest, and his alternate contact with the American agency had been found dead in his apartment of an apparent suicide, the Polish agent requested a meeting outside the normal parameters. Hence, he wanted nothing to do with official government representatives, meetings at the U.S. Embassy, or with any of its attaches.

Barrett didn't mind the assignment. He had spent the last few months on an intelligence-gathering mission in Eastern Afghanistan, doing his best to avoid becoming a trophy for the resurgent Taliban. This job was to be a short detour on his way back home and what he believed to be a much deserved vacation. The trip gave the American an opportunity to visit some of the one-time capital of the Holy Roman Empire's most renowned sites. As someone with a bachelor's in history, he enjoyed visiting the Prague Castle with the famous St. Vitus cathedral in its center, the ninetieth-century Rudolfinum, where the Czech Philharmonic Orchestra had held a concert featuring Mozart in its grand hall earlier in the evening, and the majestic Strahov Monastery.

He visited the monastery more for tactical reasons than for its famous library or his indulgence in old-world architecture. There, on top of leafy Petrin Hill, surrounded by 800-year-old Baroque and Gothic-styled buildings, sat the best view of the city, a good place to orient himself and get to know the ground he was operating on. Plus, it allowed the American to map out any escape routes he may need if anything went wrong. He was a firm believer in Mr. Murphy of Murphy's Law fame.

Barrett seated himself at a corner table so that he could observe both the kitchen door and front door. These were the only two ways in or out of the café. He kept scanning the door for any sign of his contact as the place began to empty, many of its patrons heading home after some late-night fare. Foresky was not making a good first impression on Barrett. The Polish agent had missed the scheduled time for their appointment.

Barrett felt impatient and anxious since he was never fond of meeting under these circumstances. Contrary to popular belief, fearlessness in Barrett's line of work was tantamount to stupidity, and stupidity led to failure or worse: death. He stared down for the umpteenth time at his silver Tag diving watch and observed the fluorescent dials slowly creeping around the black dial of the Swiss timepiece. Looking up, he caught the eye of a pretty brunette. He reflexively matched her smile in return. Then he immediately looked back down at his coffee mug. *Discipline, Barrett.* He knew it would be a challenge since there were a lot of good-looking women in the Czech Republic.

The waiter stopped by to refill his cup, Barrett's fourth. Now he knew why it was standard procedure to pop a Vesicare pill before an op.

He looked up at the doorway as someone entered: a disheveled man in his late forties with a graying goatee, hair to match, and a long, brown coat. The newcomer appeared worried and made a beeline right for Barrett's table. Barrett observed the newcomer's approach. *Not very subtle.*

"Sie Herr Brady?" the disheveled man asked in German, not bothering to sit down.

Barrett never used his real last name on operations such as this one and he preferred keeping English to a minimum abroad for cover purposes. He had been told that he spoke German with almost no accent, and what little existed could be passed off as Bavarian. Foresky also spoke fluent German.

"Ich Bin." Barrett wondered about the lack of protocols in their greeting.

"We must go." The Polish agent switched to heavily accented English.

"Könnten Sie das bitte wiederholen." Barrett politely and calmly asked Foresky to repeat himself.

"Go now." It dawned on Barrett that this was no act.

"Where are we going?" The operative switched back to his native tongue. Foresky prodded even more to get Barrett to leave the restaurant. The American decided it was best to follow the man's lead.

"Somewhere else." Foresky kept his voice to a whisper while he looked around. Both men started for the door.

In the rush to leave the café, Barrett barely had time to grab his black leather coat off the back of his chair. They stepped outside, and the night air hit Barrett. It seemed a lot colder now than earlier in the evening as the men took a right, heading east on the sidewalk toward the Charles Bridge.

Foresky put his hand on Barrett's back to guide the young agent forward. The American had had enough. Barrett began to turn around so he could confront Foresky about his incessant rushing when he heard some rustling. Two fairly good-sized men were trying to manhandle the Polish agent, who was doing his best to resist. Before Barrett could intercede in the unfair battle, he was suddenly grabbed by someone from behind.

His left arm was pinned to his back while another arm reached around his waist. Barrett had his guard up after seeing the attempt on Foresky, so he didn't hesitate. He threw his free right elbow back, toward where he hoped his assailant's head would be. He felt it connect with something hard, freeing both his arms. Barrett didn't want to waste time or expose himself to further attack by turning around, so he bent down between his own legs and seized his opponent's right leg. He quickly rolled forward over his right shoulder, holding the other man's lower leg tightly. It wasn't a perfect rolling kneebar, but it worked. Both he and his mysterious assailant ended up on the ground with their bodies forming the letter T. Barrett now had control of his opponent's right leg. With his adversary's right leg straight and locked at the knee, Barrett pulled back both his body and the trapped leg. Using his leverage, the agent continued to pull backward with all his might until he heard a cracking noise followed by a scream as his opponent's leg snapped with a muffled crunch. Barrett scrambled to his feet. He finished off his attacker with a hard kick to the head, rendering the assailant unconscious. With the initial threat over, Barrett looked around for Foresky.

The Polish agent stood only a few feet behind him, still tussling with one of his attackers. The other attacker lay on the ground, out cold. Foresky was tougher than he looked! Barrett watched as the older agent lost his footing and fell. Barrett intervened. He stepped between the two men and took a shot to his midsection for his efforts. He recovered in time to block a blow intended for his head with his elbow. Barrett then grabbed his attacker's hand and tried to apply a wristlock, but just as he was about to exert pressure with his forearm, the other man twisted out of it and countered with one of his own. Barrett turned his body so his opponent's attempt would be just as unsuccessful. It appeared both combatants were trained professionals and evenly matched.

Barrett countered with a palm heel strike to the face, which his opponent parried away. His adversary used the momentum of his parry to throw a horizontal elbow strike to Barrett's head in return. Barrett sidestepped out of the way at the last second. His enemy missed, leaving his upper body exposed. The advantage would only last for a split second, but Barrett capitalized on it. He followed through with a haymaker from his right fist that caught his opponent directly in the temple. The other man's eyes rolled up and his knees buckled as he crumpled to the ground. Sometimes, luck was better than all the training in the world.

"Friends of yours?" Barrett asked, helping Foresky to his feet. The two men hurried down the street in an effort to get away from their assailants.

"Take this." Foresky handed the American a jump drive.

"What is it?"

"It is why you are here," Foresky answered, still gasping from their confrontation and hurried walking. Barrett had trouble hearing the Polish agent, his accent now mixed with heavy breathing. The American slipped the small device into his inside jacket pocket as they made their way down the street.

Suddenly, Barrett and Foresky heard a hissing sound. A suppressed round had come within inches of their heads. The bullet crashed into a nearby bench's padded backrest with a thump. Both men dove for cover behind a column as Barrett pulled his compact SIG Sauer P250 from its ankle holster. The Polish man also brandished a handgun; a Heckler and Koch P2000 from what Barrett could tell.

The men were hiding, huddled behind one of the Romanesque-styled columns that fronted an old mansion that had been converted to shops on the first floor and apartments on the upper floors. A common type of conversion in the historic section of the city.

"Your friends must really like you," Barrett teased Foresky as he attempted to locate the shooter.

"I guess I underestimated my attraction."

Barrett smiled, starting to like the older man, who now seemed to be gaining in confidence. While searching for their shooters, Barrett observed in the midst of the fog two men moving in a very determined manner on the other side of the street. The men were heading in their direction with another suspicious man coming down on Barrett's side of the road. All three had the swagger of military about them. *Great, outnumbered and outgunned by either foreign agents or mercenaries!*

The younger agent knew they had to move since it was only a matter of time before they would be found. "This should be a nice break for you, Max," the American muttered to himself, mocking his boss as he pulled the slide back on his SIG. Barrett kept his gaze on the suspicious men but still couldn't tell if their adversaries knew where they were hiding. He knelt behind the column facing the street, keeping his knee closest to the column up and the other down. He kept his elbows tucked in, doing his best to minimize his exposure. No point in giving the bad guys an easy target. Their attackers were either very brazen or desperate to confront them like this in public, neither of which Barrett thought boded well for them at all.

The crowds on the street were beginning to thin. This didn't help the two hunted men either. Barrett had initially wanted to blend in with the crowd for their escape, but that chance was fading fast. It appeared the people left on the street were not aware of the gun battle that had just started around them, although that would all change once Barrett or Foresky shot back, since neither of their guns had silencers.

"I will go out and lead them away," Foresky stated. He started for the street.

"That's suicide."

"It's the only option. You must get that information back, and I must take responsibility for putting your life at risk." Foresky took off, not waiting for the younger man's reply. The Polish agent didn't get far when his body abruptly jerked back before tumbling forward. Silent rounds had found their mark. Barrett immediately opened up on the two men on the other side of the road in order to provide cover fire as Foresky, still alive, tried to crawl out of harm's way. The few bystanders left screamed and scattered as Barrett's erupting SIG awoke them to the gunfight.

The man on their side of the street opened up on the Polish agent as well. Barrett noticed another possible adversary carrying a pistol about fifty yards away across the street, jogging to join his comrades. The new guy would be joining the fight in a matter of moments. There were too many shooters for Barrett to pin down as Foresky continued to edge out of the firing line. The wounds on his back were taking their toll.

A gunfight on a public street was not Barrett's first choice. Barrett saw the two attackers from across the road posted behind the base of a street light for cover, but he couldn't locate the near side man since he had stopped firing. This made him uneasy. He knew it wasn't what you saw but what you didn't see that usually got you killed in a gunfight. Barrett also had to avoid hitting innocent bystanders as well. The American watched in horror as the Polish agent was hit two more times while crawling. Foresky now lay sprawled out on the sidewalk, motionless.

Barrett had his attention brought back to the gunfight thanks to a torrent of bullets slamming into the column he used for cover. "What the hell," he muttered aloud, looking back in the direction the storm of bullets had just come from. One of his attackers had fired an MP-9 machine pistol. The gun had a thirty-round magazine and was easier to hide than an assault rifle. It was also much more effective than the semi-automatic pistol the American employed. These guys weren't fooling around.

Barrett turned back to engage the men across the street. He was rewarded when one of his rounds hit the closest shooter in the arm and spun him sideways. Barrett fired two more times, with both rounds finding the man's chest and blowing him back against the base of the light pole. The shooter dropped his gun as his lifeless body fell to the ground. This left the mercenary's partner, the man with the MP-9, exposed. Barrett squeezed the SIG's trigger in quick succession. The American put three rounds into the man before the gunman could fire back. Two down, one to go.

Barrett needed to reload; he jammed in a fresh magazine after letting the empty one fall away and cautiously crept out from behind the column. He had moved to a more exposed position, but the change helped him locate the gunman on his side of the street. Kneeling, Barrett engaged the nearside threat. The man tried to react, but it was too late; both of Barrett's rounds hit center mass. The man fell forward on the sidewalk with blood from the fatal wounds to his chest now flowing off the sidewalk and down into the street.

Barrett looked around for any avenue of escape and saw a tram coming his way from the opposite direction of his adversaries. He retreated back behind the column to wait. As soon as the slow-moving vehicle was parallel to his position, he made his move. Barrett used the tram for concealment as he scurried behind the rear of the slow-moving vehicle, crossing the road to his car. He jumped into the Opel, fired up the engine, then backed it down the street to the spot where Foresky had fallen. Barrett hopped out to check the Interpol agent's body. No discernable pulse ... Foresky was gone.

29

A round sparked off the hood of the Opel. Barrett looked down the street, seeing more armed men moving toward him. He had the distinct feeling that he'd overstayed his welcome. With a renewed firefight becoming a real possibility, Barrett got back into the car and sped away, leaving the brave Polish agent's body still lying sprawled out by the curb.

Right before Barrett reached the first corner, he observed a black BMW pull onto the road after him. He floored the pedal to create a little more distance between the two cars before letting off the gas. It wasn't enough. He could only drive so fast through the narrow, cobblestone streets of the city. The fog didn't help him much either. The BMW, with its muscular horsepower and obviously skilled driver, began to close the gap.

Barrett regretted choosing his current car over something that, while standing out, may have had more engine power like the faster BMW that continued to gain on him. *Next time, screw blending in.* He glanced in the rearview mirror. Barrett knew that the BMW wouldn't just ram into him from behind like in the movies. The cobblestone streets and tight roads prevented this since any collision would probably wreck both vehicles. No, they could only try something when they had more room at turnoffs or intersections, so he kept that in mind by downshifting right before he encountered any of these areas in order to give his meager engine some extra reserves.

Barrett's car squealed through a tight corner by the dead-end that led to the Old Town Square and under the shadow of its famous Astronomical Clock Tower. The square was permanently closed off from motor vehicle traffic for the safety and convenience of its patrons. Barrett wondered what those same city leaders would think about a car chase through the streets of this beloved section of Prague. After another few minutes and a hair-raising turn later, he blew right past the Black Madonna house with its unique, cubist architecture on Celetna Street. His car slid a little; traction is never very good on cobblestone-made roads.

Barrett took a hand off the wheel and pulled out his phone. He then retrieved the data stick Foresky had given him from his jacket. He didn't know how this chase would end up, so he needed a backup plan.

He jammed the jump drive into the phone using his free hand and glanced at it just long enough to make sure the automated drivers kicked in to begin downloading the information that Foresky had given his life for. Suddenly, Barrett heard some popping noises followed by a whoosh of cold air as his back windshield cracked open after being impacted from a hail of bullets. "Man," Barrett muttered to himself. "This just keeps getting better and better." His frustrated pursuers sent more rounds that started to pepper his overworked car. Barrett focused on his driving since there was no way he could return fire while attempting to navigate through the tight-winding streets of the old city. After a few more quick turns and two ignored mandatory traffic stops, he realized the guys in the black car were not going to give up. Barrett would have to think of something to end this chase before innocent people got hurt or, more importantly to Barrett, himself. He needed a miracle. Barrett scanned both sides of the road as he pushed his car to keep distance between himself and his pursuers. Then up ahead, he saw them …

Barrett turned the wheel hard to the right and headed for the stairs. These were narrow pedestrian stairs never meant for modern automobile use, but it was his best shot. At that point, he considered this his only shot. Barrett braked to slow the car down and gripped the steering wheel so hard his knuckles turned white as the car lurched over and down the steps. The car, barely fitting in the tight space, bounced like a bingo ball with Barrett barely able to keep control of the wheel. Sparks and pieces of the undercar blew out in all directions as Barrett plummeted down the stairway. The Opel, after making a lot of ungodly noises, finally came to the bottom and stopped. *Thank goodness I disabled the airbags.* Barrett looked in the rearview mirror. He didn't see the other car following him.

Barrett pulled off the curb onto the one-way street, feeling the car vibrating as if it was still on the stairs and spewing some serious smoke from the hood. It wasn't going to last much longer. He looked again in the rearview mirror. *They wouldn't give up that easily?*

As if on cue, he saw the black car coming up on his position from behind. His pursuers had indeed not given up, but instead had taken the long way around, saving themselves from a pounding in the process.

Barrett decided that with the condition his car was in, he couldn't outrun his relentless pursuers, so he did the next best thing. The agent put the sedan in reverse and drove the wrong way down the street, straight toward the advancing vehicle. He pushed the Opel as hard as he could. Smoke now poured out of the hood. The engine screamed as if it somehow knew its own death was imminent. The BMW braked to a stop. Barrett didn't and used the alley-like size of the road to his advantage since the other car couldn't get out the way. The Opel's back end rammed straight into the BMW. The sound of metal on metal and shattering glass replaced the engine whine of the Opel in Barrett's ears as he ducked in the seat, bracing himself against the impact. Barrett's back hit the dashboard, knocking the wind out of him before shooting him back into the driver's seat. The two cars had become one piece of unusable metal.

Barrett took a few moments to catch his breath then shook his head, trying to clear the cobwebs. Once recovered, he crawled through what was once his windshield. Outside the car, he drew his gun with shaking hands and began to climb over his car to check on the state of his adversaries. He crossed over on the BMW's hood and jumped down by the driver's door, scanning the interior of the car. The occupants of the BMW had all been rendered unconscious by the impact. He cut away the driver's airbag to get a better look at his adversaries: two white males in their late twenties, by his guess. He searched their pockets but found no IDs. They had even cut out or marked over any identifying manufacturer's labels on their clothes. These guys were trained pros. Barrett didn't have much time for a thorough search, so he quickly looked over the interior of the car then back at the men. He noticed something interesting: a tattoo on the inside forearm of the driver: a black scorpion. Barrett didn't want to wait around to see if any of their friends would show up, so he decided now was the best time to leave.

SHADOW HUNT

Barrett grabbed his phone and backpack as he planned on abandoning the severely damaged Opel. While looking at all the damage inflicted on the rental, he laughed to himself, trying to remember if he had signed the insurance disclaimer at the rental car agency. He could worry about that at another time. Barrett took off on foot down the one-way street for one more block then cut over the next narrow street and found what he was looking for: the metro station. Barrett stole a glance behind him to make sure no one was following then disappeared down the steps into the station.

CHAPTER 2

The concrete mixing truck snaked its way down the thoroughfare on Moscow's west side. The truck blended in with all the early morning rush-hour traffic passing through the heavy construction zone that seemed to swallow up this side of the Russian capital. There were plenty of infrastructures that needed to be repaired. Of course, only the infrastructure deemed important by Putin's government got any attention. The truck continued down the road before turning into the five-level parking garage that sat adjacent to the Moscow Bank's new thirty-story, glass-encased office building.

Mikail Semin, an investment banker, stood defiantly on the curb, waiting to cross the busy thoroughfare in order to get to his office located on the top floor of the Moscow Bank. This was the normal morning routine for a banker who preferred to park his car across the street from his office in the municipal parking lot. Parking his new Mercedes M-Class there cost him a little bit more than the building's garage, but the convenience of getting in and out made up for it. Semin liked getting out quickly after a long day at the office. Since the economy started doing its impression of a roller coaster, his customers were taking a beating, and he was getting tired of all the angry phone calls from his clients. He felt capitalism had made most of his clients greedy.

The investment banker hadn't noticed the concrete mixing truck that had just disappeared into the garage a few moments ago. His main focus was on not getting hit by someone rushing to work while he attempted to cross the street. Semin barely made it to the opposite curb, cursing as a tiny Fiat almost sideswiped him. He stopped to take in a breath. Suddenly, Semin felt a punch in the gut

34

before lifting off the ground. His ears filled with the loudest sound he'd ever heard before everything went dark …

***

Inspector Sergei Petrov solemnly looked around his dilapidated office, waiting for the coffeemaker to finish its task. The police station was old, and nothing in it seemed much younger. It was as if time had stopped in the precinct itself. Nothing had been replaced since the late eighties.

It had become numbingly frustrating for the men in the precinct. Of course, if they were the FSB or in the ruling party's offices, everything would be nice and new. The lack of funding for the precinct was because the government did not deem the local police officials' work important. Petrov and his compatriots chased criminals for a living, and since the fall of Communism, which he'd liked, most of the criminals simply became politicians and took power or bought the politicians who already were in office, which he didn't like. *Some things never change.* Petrov was old school; he preferred enemies he could see and chase. The politics of the new Russia depressed him.

The coffee machine buzzed, waking Petrov from his early morning trance. As the inspector removed the cap from his flask to add his version of Russian cream, or Vodka as it was better known, the whole room shook. Actually, it felt like the whole building rocked. Petrov also heard a loud thunderclap in the distance. The shaking only lasted for a few moments then stopped as abruptly as it had started. Petrov shot off a querying look to his partner, Oleg Litenko, a junior detective sitting in the corner of the office. The younger man had an air of shock about him and just responded with a shrug. Then the phones started ringing … all of them. At least they still worked.

The senior detective turned his gaze to the window on his left, watching a dark plume of smoke billowing into the sky from a few blocks away. He motioned to Litenko, and both men grabbed their jackets and hurriedly exited the squad room. The stairwell was empty as they made their way down the stairs to their car. Only one way to find out …

35

Petrov got off the most modern piece of equipment that he had: his mobile phone. The precinct commander had called to give him the general location of the smoke. From the frantic calls the precinct had received, it appeared to be some sort of explosion. With the siren blaring, Petrov navigated for Litenko. The younger detective really didn't need much help; a blind man could have found their objective. When the inspectors' unmarked car got within a block of their destination, they were met with unrelenting chaos: people running around, fire trucks attempting to navigate their way through the hordes of people, and vehicles in their way. There was smoke everywhere.

Litenko stopped the car in the middle of the street, the road now blocked. Both men abandoned the vehicle and jogged toward the commotion. Neither had any idea what had happened. The detectives placed scarves over their mouths to provide some protection from the smoke and continued working their way through the throng of people. Litenko's eyes were burning from all the dust and smoke in the air as the two men pushed past crowds of people on the street. Then, through a thin section of smoke, the detective saw the burning remnants of the blown-out building. His mouth fell open. He had thought he had seen it all before today …

"What did the Chechens do now?" The senior inspector stood beside Litenko, closing his own eyes and lowering his head.

CHAPTER 3

Alexandria, Virginia

"Nice work." The complimentary words of Barrett's boss, Colonel Lance McKenna, didn't do much for Barrett's mood. The lean senior officer, in his late forties, looked approvingly at his young operative from behind the desk. The two men were meeting in McKenna's office on the top floor of a two-story, non-descript brick building on the outskirts of Fort Belvoir. "You did the best you could. It appears the bad guys were two steps ahead of us on this one."

"Didn't help Foresky much." Barrett shrugged. "Think the info on that drive I brought back was worth it?"

"Foresky seemed to think so."

"Any ideas on who the party crashers were?" Barrett felt stiff: the effects of flying all night from Europe.

"No. We forwarded some of the data over to crypto for analysis. The info had deep encryption protocols, so hopefully they will come up with something soon."

"If not, sir?" Barrett's voice pitched, frustrated with the previous mission's outcome.

"Well, Max, sometimes you just don't get an answer."

Barrett didn't appreciate the response. *There should always be a reason or what's the point?* The men sat in silence for a moment.

"I see you passed the psych review." McKenna looked over a short brief on his desk.

"Yes, sir, first thing I did when I got back. Always fun."

"Good. I have a new assignment for you."

"What, no vacation time?"

***

With the public pull back on "the war on terror" Barrett had noticed his unit's operating tempo had increased dramatically. At first, he didn't think that was even possible, but he quickly learned that he was mistaken. It now became too public to use the regular military, and the civilian agencies had either proven ineffective or were perceived to be too politically sensitive. These agencies also had to fight layers of internal bureaucracy before they could be effective battling any outside adversary. The unit Barrett served with was being stretched to its limits as they silently searched out the enemies of the United States. He looked up at the motto behind McKenna's desk: "*Send Me.*"

Officially, Max Barrett was assigned to the United States Army Studies and Activity unit. Unofficially, he was a member of an elite intelligence unit that was so covert its name was known only to a select few. Like a chameleon, the unit's name changed constantly in order to protect itself. The unit's names, born after the failure of Operation Desert Claw in the Iranian Desert in 1979, had ranged from the Intelligence Activity Unit to Centra Spike, Gray Fox, and later, Black Wolf.

One of the fundamental issues with the operation that was supposed to rescue American hostages held at the U.S. Embassy and the Iranian Foreign Ministry Office in Tehran was the availability of quality "on the ground intelligence" in Iran. The Central Intelligence Agency either had no intelligence of their own or they were unwilling to pass any information on to the military units in desperate need of the vital intel.

The decision was made that U.S. Special Operations needed to have its own version of the CIA. So in 1981, the U.S. Army created the Intelligence Support Activity. The name had officially been changed so many times to keep it secret that those in the unit did not even bother to keep up anymore, so most just referred to it as the Unit.

The covert group performed two types of missions: intelligence gathering and direct action. Intelligence gathering included agent-run teams or "spooks" for human intelligence, electronic surveillance or "knob turners" using the newest and most sophisticated means of electronic monitoring warfare, and the intelligence analysts. The direct action mission component was used when mission time parameters did not permit the involvement of other Tier One military units like Army Special Forces or Navy SEALs, or if the mission was considered too sensitive to involve these units. What separated it from other intelligence agencies was that all of its personnel were experienced members of the U.S. military: experience, prior performance, and specialized skill sets won the men and women their chance to apply for the covert unit. Graduating from an Ivy League college or scoring high on some aptitude tests would never be enough. Unit personnel specialized in operating in hostile or denied areas. Those who ultimately made it as field agents were the total package, unlike any other unit in the U.S. arsenal. They not only collected the intelligence, but if needed could act on it as well. The truly elite.

Black Wolf, which continued to evolve, reported directly to the Secretary of Defense. After the events of September 11, many of the unit's constraints had been taken away. Gray Wolf had finally begun to be used to its fullest extent. Even as the overt war on terror had receded to the background in recent years, it meant that the super-secret unit would be used more than ever as the U.S. military's best weapon against terrorism.

The covert unit utilized an arduous selection process that was open to all branches of the U.S. military. Most members were ex-intelligence or special operations personnel who had passed training considered to be one of the most demanding and intensive in the world. The training included a battery of psychological tests, parachuting, diving, advanced shooting methods, and other forms of spy tradecraft. Barrett was considered a full-fledged operative.

***

He was pulled from his reverie by the colonel's next words. "Sorry, Max, but this is a high priority right from the old man," McKenna stated with an informal reference to the Secretary of Defense. He wanted to get Barrett back out in the field as soon as possible to keep him focused. McKenna knew that despite the younger agent's cavalier attitude, he always took his job seriously, and, more importantly, Barrett had a knack for thinking outside the box, an extremely vital trait in their line of work. This made him one of the best assets that McKenna had at his disposal. "You're tasked with providing additional security to a UN delegation in Nigeria. They are there on a fact-finding mission in conjunction with the WTO regarding the link between poverty and the oil situation in the country."

"Or lack thereof. If there was a link between the two, then no one would be poor, right?" Barrett said, shifting in the leather chair. "Besides, didn't anyone tell them there was a civil war going on over there?"

"You know the UN; they think they are untouchable." McKenna sighed. "Unfortunately, there is a high-ranking U.S. official among them, and the security contingent is now considered inadequate for the task."

"Isn't this a job for the DSS or the Marines?" The DSS was the Diplomatic Security Service, which reported to the State Department and was responsible for the security of diplomats in the U.S. and abroad.

"The DSS are spread too thin, and as for the Marines, they would make too much noise; being subtle is not part of their training."

"Babysitting?"

"You know we bring the most with the least to the battlefield. No one else comes close with our compact effectiveness. You will get more details and link up with a couple of shooters who I have assigned to you as a support package down at our Joint Operations Center in Florida." McKenna stood. "Your flight to McDill leaves at zero seven hundred. Good hunting, Max." The experienced operative reached out to shake the younger agent's hand. Barrett stood up and returned the shake, his mind starting to focus on the next mission.

Barrett headed out of the director's office, stopping briefly at the door. "You do realize, Boss, that it is the 'favors' that always get us into the most trouble." Barrett closed the door behind him, shaking his head.

Before Barrett left headquarters, he paused to pick up a few things from his locker then retrieved his beloved new Mustang GT from the parking lot. The growl of the black car's engine was music to his ears; he loved the feel of the retro sports car when it took the tight corners on the back roads in the Virginia countryside. Unfortunately, he didn't have time now for one of his favorite pastimes. Still, he kept the V-8 engine revved up as he navigated the streets of the crowded Alexandria suburb, working off some steam as he headed toward home. His townhouse development sat in a moderate section of the city between two much higher-priced neighborhoods. Barrett liked the location; it wasn't too close to work but still near enough that when he got called in unexpectedly, he wouldn't have to spend much time in traffic.

He eased the black sports car into the garage that made up the bulk of the first floor. He ran his hand down the curves of the hood, wishing he had more time to play. Once inside, he tossed his pack down, took a breath, and looked around his sanctuary. The agent had spent very little time at home lately and was starting to feel like a nomad; he had yet to find the right balance between globe-trotting and a home life like the other, more experienced members of his unit.

The townhome's décor leaned toward a bachelor's pad with the best entertainment system a government salary could buy alongside art and souvenirs collected from his many trips. Barrett did his best to make the place as homey as possible, but he was told numerous times that his townhome needed a woman's touch. Too bad he never kept one around long enough to do the job. Barrett kept telling himself it was because he was always busy with work and never home, but it was more likely due to the scars he carried from growing up in a broken home. He paused to look at a framed copy of an original American flag from the Revolutionary War hanging on his wall. His dad had given it to him for his tenth birthday, and it still gave him goose bumps.

Barrett headed over to a small cabinet to peruse his small collection of liquors and decided on a single-malt Glenlivet Nadurra. He took it neat, savoring every drop of the golden nectar. With the relaxing effects of his favorite Scotch taking hold, Barrett enjoyed a lengthy shower and then something quick to eat. He dropped himself down on the sofa to watch some TV, but nothing kept his attention for very long. He even attempted to read a new mystery novel he had picked up at the airport in Frankfurt on his way back from Prague. But he had trouble concentrating on the book as well. Barrett couldn't get Foresky out of his head. He strolled outside to his porch and proceeded to work his punching bag over as if it was one of the mercenaries responsible for the death of the Polish agent.

Exhausted, he followed the impromptu workout with another shower. Drying off, he parked himself in the townhome's other bedroom, which doubled as his office. Barrett settled in at his desk, fired up his laptop, and trolled the web to pull up information on Nigeria, getting a head start on the next day's briefing.

CHAPTER 4

The unit maintained a small operations center at McDill Air Force Base in Tampa, adjacent to the home of the U.S. Special Operations Command. It was there that the intelligence unit's personnel conducted a lot of exercises with other units of SOCOM in preparations for joint missions around the world. The geography and weather also provided great year-round training for the soldiers.

The flight aboard the C-130 cargo plane to McDill was brief and uneventful. Barrett smiled to himself as he disembarked and walked over to a waiting SUV. Being a native Floridian, Barrett loved coming home and enjoying the fall weather. Today was no different, though he would have preferred to ride in a convertible.

Barrett tossed his bag in the back seat of the Ford Expedition and climbed into the front passenger seat. The vehicle, assigned to the Unit's motor pool, was being driven by one of their new analysts, a younger man with cropped, red hair. He seemed intimidated by Barrett and avoided small talk with the older agent as they drove past the first couple of buildings on the way to the operations center. The sight of two F-22s taking off in the distance added to Barrett's euphoria as he watched them streak off into the sky.

The Expedition pulled into the parking lot of a three-story, light gray office building. The structure had no identification signage or additional security on the outside to signal that it contained one of America's most covert units. If anyone asked, it served as an administration center supporting various units under SOCOM command.

At first, the inside of the building looked just as inconspicuous. Barrett walked down the short hallway and entered the last door, simply marked "Records." He cleared another security post before passing through a set of double doors that finally allowed him to enter the inner sanctum of the unit's joint operations center. Barrett made his way to the briefing room on the first floor.

Due to the security content of the information that got passed around inside, the briefing room was actually a SCIF, or Sensitive Compartmented Information Facility. The secured area contained soundproof walls and a transmitter for black noise, which would prevent any of the modern, sound-penetrating devices from being used to listen in on the small, classroom-like space.

Inside the SCIF, or "vault" as it was referred to by Barrett and the others, he met with the rest of his team for the new assignment. It would be a four-man squad. The first two were Tom Reirson and Greg Bellows, whom he'd worked with numerous times before within the regular service and in the unit. Both men were ex-Special Operations, with Reirson specializing in hostage rescue and the muscular Bellows in waterborne operations. These men were the "shooters" and specialized in the unit's direct action missions.

Reirson, nicknamed "Cruise" since he had a laid-back demeanor, quick wit, and somewhat resembled the famous actor, had enlisted in the Army after high school. After serving with the Rangers, he volunteered for and became a part of the U.S. Army's elite Tier One Special Mission Unit known officially as the Combat Applications Group, or CAG. This was where he first encountered members of his current unit. He loved the autonomy that Black Wolf worked with and the type of missions they performed, so once he received an invitation to apply, he jumped at the chance. After he passed the vigorous indoctrination test, one harder than any he'd had to pass before he got assigned to the shooter squadron, Cruise would get more seasoning in the squadron while continuing to train in the finer parts of espionage before becoming a full-fledged agent of the Unit.

Bellows, on the other hand, reminded others of a dark and deadly Mako shark with his prowess in the water and focused personality. He arrived after serving with the Navy SEALs for six years. Even though he was in SEAL Team Six, Bellows also wanted to expand the type of operations he could perform, so he filed a request to join the Unit. After almost two years of waiting, he finally got invited to apply. He made it through the process and got assigned to a shooter squadron as well. The two men had become like brothers since joining the unit and had served on many operations together.

The black-haired, blue-eyed Ron Kale filled out the team. Kale, who still looked like a teenager, had started his military career as an Air Force Combat Controller, or CCT. Kale's first love, like many of his generation, lay in video games and computers. He jumped at the chance to delve into the covert unit's abundance of hi-tech gadgets. He had been sent to various communications and electronic courses available, making him a de facto electronics expert. All three men were very experienced and professional operators.

"Good morning, boys," greeted Janice Dooley, the unit's senior intelligence analyst and the person who would conduct the briefing. The mother of two had served in Army intelligence for ten years after graduating from Boston College and had spent the previous eight years with the elite intelligence agency as one of their top thinkers and planners. "The packet I will brief you on today is for Operation: Cloaked Shield." All four men rolled their eyes.

Standing next to a large LCD monitor in the front of the room, she briefed the men on their pending mission. As she spoke, she moved her fingers across the face of the monitor, manipulating the large smart screen with her hands like a symphony conductor; the monitor responded by showing images of Nigeria and scrolling potential threats across the screen.

She described their area of operations before moving on to what the ROE, or rules of engagement, would be in case anything happened. The ROE was vital standard for soldiers on any mission. The standard told them when they could or couldn't use their weapons if something happened. She went on to explain that the United Nations sanctioned project was focused on a study of the disparity between the country's wealthy and poor and how the oil money was distributed. She kept the delegation's reason for being there short since their mission focus was on protecting the delegates, specifically one of them.

Barrett inputted some notes into his phone as she spoke. The sleek, black device looked like the new version of the iPhone; it contained all the same features of the smartphone with a few extras added by the Unit's R&D department. The phone, keyed to Barrett, activated via a biometric security system done with a finger print on the touchscreen and voice analysis for calls, allowing only him to use the high tech device. The phone was wrapped in a hardened titanium case, contained a GPS tracker, and operated on a reliable, private military satellite network.

The hand-held device was also programmed to perform a data dump into a remote, secure server if it wasn't used for five continuous days. This ensured any obtained intelligence stored in it would not be lost if an agent were captured or killed. If the information had a virus or Trojan in the file, the phone also had a compartmentalized data storing section where questionable and possibly unsafe files could be stored temporarily without affecting the rest of the device. The modified phone served as Barrett's lifeline on missions.

Dooley finished up her briefing by pushing a button on her laptop, which e-mailed the list of names of the delegates with a brief background to each team members' cell phone. The senior analyst had saved this part of the briefing for last and with good reason. Dooley then turned her attention back to the large monitor. She moved her hands and fingered a picture of a file folder marked "Delegates," dragging the file to the center of the screen. She double-tapped the icon. "Now, for my personal amusement." She turned, grinning, and waited to see the reaction from her audience. Out flowed the delegates' pictures and bios, covering the monitor in two neat rows, but Barrett didn't notice at first.

"Oh crap," he exclaimed, his eyes widening as he glanced over the list now appearing on his phone.

CHAPTER 5

A Gulfstream G4 with Falcon Airways labeled on its fuselage touched down at Port Harcourt Airport in the southern region of Nigeria. The plane, a transoceanic aircraft registered to a front company, allowed the operators to travel the globe in a hurry without attracting too much attention. The jet taxied over to a private hangar Falcon Airways had rented for the duration of the operation.

The plane's crew consisted of two; pilot and co-pilot would stay aboard and secure specialized communications gear on the aircraft while Barrett and his team conducted their assigned mission. Barrett put on his Oakley sunglasses to ward off the afternoon sun's harsh glare as he stepped off the airplane. The blistering heat hit him hard; it was the middle of fall, yet it felt like August back in Florida. No easterly breeze or light rain that was the norm this time of year. Instead, it was "Africa hot" as many who have experienced the summers on the continent refer to the heat. Welcome to Nigeria …

Port Harcourt lies on the coast of the Bonny River near the Niger Delta. The city was an extremely busy merchant port but, more importantly, it was the center of Nigeria's oil industry, the country's greatest source of money and the source of most of its problems.

The port city did have a stark contrast between the beautiful, concrete-walled, ultra-luxurious residential areas for the wealthy that encircled its modern, downtown section of high-rises and the squalor settlements that comprised most of the rest of the city and its outskirts. This caused many of its people to believe there was serious mismanagement and corruption in the government, which led to the inner strife that had been ongoing since Nigeria gained its independence from Britain in 1960.

Barrett and his three-man team were unloading and double-checking their gear to make sure everything had survived the Cross-Atlantic trip.

"How did it go with that girl you met at Ybor City the night before we left?" Bellows asked Reirson. Bellows was still groggy since he'd slept through the whole flight.

"She shot me down," he answered.

"How bad?" asked Barrett, joining the conversation once he had all his gear accounted for and in front of him. Now the fun part; he had to inspect every piece.

"Both guns." Reirson shook his head. Everyone else laughed.

"Speaking of women, I hear Kale's taking the plunge," added Bellows, nodding toward the recently engaged man who was sitting on one of his bags while fiddling with some of his electronic gear. They all stopped laughing and looked at the younger agent. Kale gulped.

"Is that true?" Barrett became serious.

"Yes, Boss."

"He's your battle buddy now," declared Barrett, pointing at Reirson.

"What?" Kale looked over at Barrett. Being the newest member as well as the electronics expert, he was supposed to be assigned to the senior man on the team: in this case, Barrett.

"Don't you know the Golden Rule?" asked Barrett.

"No." Kale seemed uneasy by the sudden reassignment, not sure what to make of it.

"Never have a married or engaged man cover your flank," Reirson piped in.

"Why?"

Reirson looked at Kale as if he was a child. "Because they have nothing to live for." The group erupted in laughter with Barrett walking over and patting the ex-Air Force man on his back. *The team is bonding nicely.*

Two gray Range Rovers pulled inside the hangar next to their plane. The men immediately stopped laughing and became serious. It was one thing to joke around between themselves when they were

48

alone, but to outsiders they always projected an air of absolute professionalism. The team watched as a large man dressed like a tourist with a short-sleeved, button-down shirt, linen pants, and sandals got out the driver's side of the first SUV and walked over to them. Barrett recognized him immediately. Standing at six feet four inches with the build of a rugby player, the newcomer Stan Linford whistled to himself as he strolled toward the men.

The old bloke, as the very large man usually referred to himself those days, was once a member of the elite Australian SAS, who'd left the service of his country to join the famed mercenary group Executive Outsource in South Africa. He'd joined the private military outfit after he fell in love with the continent while on a peacekeeping mission in Rwanda, and he figured quite rightly that he would see more action in the African outfit than with the Australian Army. Linford became a veteran of numerous campaigns in the 1990s, including operations in Sierra Leone and Angola.

He was currently known as a handyman in Africa, working with some of the foreign agencies between times when he enjoyed relaxing on his ranch in South Africa. Most of the time, the Americans didn't seem to have much interest in Africa, so he was seldom bothered. This was one of the few exceptions, and Linford was always ready to provide information or services when needed.

"Nice of you to join our little soiree, mate," greeted Linford with his ever-present smile and bright blue eyes.

"Nice of you to invite us," responded Barrett with a smile of his own as he shook hands with his friend. Barrett looked him over, noticing that the man appeared to be carrying a little more in the middle these days along with a strain of gray mixed in with his blond hair. *Well, Time, the only undefeated force in history, catches up with us all.*

The two men first met a few years ago when Barrett was still serving in the regular intelligence branch of the Army. He had been part of a small task force sent to Algeria in order to gather intelligence on Islamic fundamentalist groups and their ties to terrorists operating in the Middle East and Europe. Linford had been one of the men who provided information to the researchers about his experiences with these people while living in Africa.

Afterward, the Aussie offered to give the task force members an up close and personal tour of the locales where a lot of those terrorists came from. The Algerian slums were extremely dangerous, and only Barrett and one other from the task force volunteered to go. They spent the next couple of harrowing hours traveling through some of the worst ghettos Barrett had ever seen, with Linford acting as a guide; he was so collected and entertaining throughout you would have thought they were on a tour at Disney World. The two men from the task force witnessed firsthand the despair and brutality of one of the world's worst slums. An informative excursion the American agent had never forgotten.

"So who are we today, lads?" Linford asked, smiling. He enjoyed working with the professionals from the unit even if he didn't have a clue as to who these men really were.

"We are a documentary team," smiled Barrett, spreading his hands to encompass the group and their photographic equipment.

"What are you supposed to be documenting?" asked Linford, still grinning as the men began to load their gear and "production equipment" into the two gray Range Rovers the Aussie had provided for them.

"The usual," responded Reirson, straight-faced, as he checked over his rifle. "Animals that wander out of their habitat and get into trouble."

This gave Linford and the others a chuckle.

Pretending to be a documentary crew did present some challenges, since the team members would not be able to overtly carry any weapons, so the R&D department had supplied them with modified, handheld, digital video cameras that in addition to actually working as video recorders gave the men thermal and night vision capability. The guys also wore vests that were very common among hunters and photojournalists alike, but these were made of a light Kevlar material that helped provide some protection against ricochets and flying debris. The vests also had a concealed compartment with a quick-release mechanism for a sidearm and extra magazine. Barrett and his teammates also wore customized EarPro sound suppressors with voice-activated radios. The hidden earpieces kept the men from receiving ear damage or going deaf in a combat situation while allowing them to communicate covertly with one another. Even with all these goodies, the men would still have to keep their rifles and other equipment hidden away in their backpacks.

On this deployment, the team members were employing the FN SCAR Mark-17 rifles developed specifically for U.S. Special Forces instead of their usual HK-416s. The futuristic-looking assault rifle with multiple sighting options and a bottom-fed magazine was a big improvement over the M-4 carbines the men and most of the rest of the U.S. military had been using. The SCARS were more reliable with less recoil and required a lot less maintenance to keep them working. The operators chose them for this mission due to the ease of modifying the weapon's size for stowing purposes, the additional stopping power of the 7.62 rounds, plus the "battlefield pickup" feature that allowed the rifle to accept the ubiquitous AK-47 type magazines that were in use all over the Dark Continent. This would be a significant help to the men if they ever found themselves in need of ammunition behind enemy lines.

As the team members began piling into the vehicles, Linford leaned toward Barrett, who sat next to him in the front passenger seat, and lowered his voice. "Can't wait till you meet the bloke in charge of the Americans."

"You mean Agent Gratton?" asked Barrett while Linford put the truck in gear.

"The bloke's a book, my friend. Not good in Africa." Linford backed the Rover out and led the two-truck convoy to the delegates' compound. The drive over gave the Americans their first taste of the notorious Nigerian driving experience. Most people in Nigeria drive more as if they are competing in a rally than simply going to and from their destinations. This was why Nigeria consistently had one of the highest accident rates in the hemisphere.

Linford drove the team to the Hotel Presidential, located in the heart of the city's downtown district. The white and blue, ten-story, contemporary-looking building was pulling double duty as the UN delegation's temporary headquarters. Barrett studied the building and its surroundings as the Rovers approached the complex.

The hotel appeared not as "hardened" as Barrett liked, but then again, this was not his show. Being hardened referred to the amount of safety measures in place in order to deter or stop any possible attacks. The hotel's safeguards seemed to contain no real physical barriers to a possible terrorist attack. There were just a few armed Nigerian military soldiers and security agents coming and going from the main lobby doors, but nothing else of substance for defense. Barrett would have preferred some motor vehicle barriers and a temporary checkpoint to control the flow of incoming and outgoing traffic. If anything, these actions would have acted as a deterrent to anyone thinking about attacking the hotel while the delegation was staying there. A United Nations' delegation should have been reason enough to warrant some better security measures be implemented, particularly, he thought, with the current internal situation in Nigeria.

The two Range Rovers rolled to a stop in front of the hotel's entrance. Barrett got out of the vehicle and started to stretch a little; he'd been sitting around way too much over the last two days. Linford, who had also worked with the UN over the years and therefore had assisted with some of their personnel on this trip, led Barrett into the hotel's lobby then over to a small ballroom off to the left, where the delegation held its meetings. Barrett's men stayed behind to check in, stow their gear, and begin their own subtle security work. The men knew their jobs and didn't need Barrett to micromanage them. Barrett and Linford entered the conference room just as the delegates were wrapping up their latest meeting.

Once the session ended, Linford started introducing the American agent to the delegates. There were the typical doctorate-educated people from countries Barrett had never heard of and a few from the majors. Linford introduced Barrett first to the leader of the delegation, Dr. Graham Tyre from England. The tall and balding anthropologist from Leicester attempted to clean his glasses while he asked Barrett his thoughts on the delegation's mission.

"Well, we are here to film it, Doctor," answered the American agent, not knowing what else to say. He couldn't tell the professor that he and his men were only there because of their orders, and he had serious doubts about the UN's ability to accomplish much in the divided country.

"Make sure you do not miss anything; this mission is vital." Dr. Tyre's self-importance came through loud and clear.

"Yes, sir." Barrett smiled, thinking he was glad he wasn't a part of the delegation that came under the doctor's supervision.

He then met Dr. Wanda Jones, a native from Toronto and, being African-Canadian, appeared to be very enthusiastic about their purpose here, though her optimism seemed a little overwhelming for some other members of the delegation, like Dr. Isbeza Kahn, the Indonesian psychologist, and Mary Ngong, the Cultural Affairs Minister from Kenya. Both women seemed to be a little wary of the Canadian's constant goings-on about this particular delegation's possible impact on the Nigerian people. The two ladies had much more experience in this part of the world than their Canadian counterpart and knew how things worked in Africa, especially how fickle and temporary the West's attention could be on internal issues.

Barrett did not have a chance to meet the fifth member of the delegation, Dr. Albert Moanda from Gabon. The delegate seemed engrossed in a conversation with some female members of the hotel staff in a distant corner of the conference room. Barrett didn't mind; the agent was only concerned with one delegate, and her name was Sara Hanson.

Barrett finally saw her: the real reason he was in Port Harcourt instead of on a much-deserved vacation. Barrett gave her a serious once-over, deciding that she was much more attractive in person than on TV or in pictures. In her mid-twenties with amber-colored hair, green eyes, and a friendly smile, she expressed the girl-next-door image. It was not what he'd expected from the only daughter of the President of the United States!

CHAPTER 6

The city of Moscow came to a virtual standstill after the terrorist incident. The bombing's death toll had not been as steep as numerous talking heads around the world expected: twenty-seven dead, thirty-eight wounded, and fifteen missing in yesterday's blast. Not nearly as many as could have happened if the terrorists set the bomb off later in the morning, when the building would have been full.

"We are lucky the Chechens are so incompetent. A few more hours, and it would have been a catastrophe," exclaimed Senior Inspector Markov as he addressed his two subordinates: Petrov and Litenko. Markov had just finished reading the initial report given to him by the fire department chief while the three men stood outside the once grand entrance to the Moscow Bank. The front bottom portion of the modern high-rise was a mess of concrete and steel. Its ruins were still smoldering, sending out enough heat to warm the men in the street while rescue workers were still rummaging through the debris of the burned-out hulk of a building that remained. As usual, the Russian government refused any assistance from other countries or the Red Cross. Pride played big in Russian politics.

"Did they say anything about the bomb?" asked Petrov, thinking this situation was already a catastrophe. He also didn't believe the numbers; nothing is ever as it seems in his native country.

"They haven't been able to get to ground zero yet."

"Where is it?" Litenko looked out over the smoke-filled street at all the vehicles and people roaming around the site. He had never seen anything like this in his ten years as a policeman.

Markov glanced back down at the file. "From the blast pattern, they believe the explosion emanated from somewhere in the garage area. We will know more when they get down inside."

Petrov smirked, having been around long enough to know how these investigations sometimes got handled.

***

On this trip, the President's daughter used an alias for the benefit of the local media. Not until after the trip concluded would her presence be made known to the general public. Right now, her security detail had been explained away as a precaution from a wealthy, powerful, and overprotective father. There is always some truth to a lie.

While greeting the President's daughter, Barrett met the head of her protection detail. Special Agent Shane Gratton of the Secret Service stood around six-two; he was blond, well-built, and looked more like a model than a bodyguard. He was her shadow, always close by.

"Can we speak in private?" The Secret Service agent made it sound more like an order than a request. Barrett politely nodded, and the two moved over to a corner in the room. They were far enough not to be overheard, but close enough for Gratton to keep an eye on his principal.

The Secret Service agent addressed Barrett in a supercilious tone, reminding him of how a parent speaks to their child. "I just want to make sure that your team understands that I am in charge. This is an official Secret Service operation in conjunction with the UN and Nigerian Security. While I appreciate your assistance, I consider you and your men merely observers. Between the Nigerians, UN, and my own people, we have plenty of security. Do we understand each other?"

Barrett forced a smile. "Of course; we are only here to help." Gratton's was the typical response from someone who hadn't been totally briefed on the individual backgrounds of the Black Wolf team sent and thus felt a little insecure. This was what Barrett had been afraid of, and he'd expected nothing else.

***

The UN delegation spent most of the next day in the hotel meeting with various groups and holding a dinner at the very red-decorated 4-5-6 Chinese restaurant for another obscure local charity. Barrett did notice the influx of Chinese in the city and learned from Linford that this was happening all over Africa. The Chinese needed the oil and other natural resources the continent offered for their modernizing economy and were willing to invest heavily for it. So while the West focused on the Middle East, the Chinese had begun to flex their financial muscle on the Dark Continent.

Barrett spent some time in a first-floor hotel room the Secret Service had converted into a command center, reviewing the current threat assessments prepared by Nigerian Internal Security and the U.S. Agency. Inside, the cramped room was filled with computers and communications gear. He didn't find anything new or worthwhile after scanning thru the documents. The men in the room were not very friendly to Barret, but did provide him with whatever he asked. This animosity toward Barrett and his men stemmed from the security personnel of the various countries being extremely wary of the production crew, while those few who were privy to them being part of the security apparatus didn't like the intrusion. Gratton had explained Barrett's presence in the command center to the others as simply them providing background information for the filmmakers to use in their documentary.

There was not much Barrett didn't know before he looked over the threat assessment the security detail had prepared. Most documents they furnished focused on the main militia group causing trouble in the region, the Movement for the Emancipation of Niger Delta, or MEND. Dooley had already briefed his team on them back at McDill. MEND wasn't a centralized organization but more of a collection of loosely connected independent militia groups fighting for a greater share of Nigeria's oil wealth. The militia group had claimed responsibility for kidnappings, assassinations, and violent attacks on the oil fields. It was believed that they were responsible for thousands of deaths during the ongoing conflict. There was also info on the Islamic extremist group Boko Haram that operated in the northern part of the country. This group had been picking up a lot of publicity lately by kidnapping young girls and running rampant through small, defenseless villages. The Nigerians' assessments actually diminished the effective threat from both groups. Barrett always found it ironic that most host countries liked to downplay their internal issues, since he found that it was these same issues that always caused the most problems.

Barrett followed Gratton on a brief tour of the top floor of the hotel, where the delegation members had their rooms. He was informed, not to his surprise, that he and his men would not be permitted on the floor unless escorted by members of the security detail. He also got a chance to meet some of the other members of the delegation's security team. All of them appeared to him to be competent and professional. While the security detail appeared cordial to Barrett and his men, they didn't go out of their way to assist them either. That was okay. Barrett and his team were here to do a job, not to make friends.

The rest of Barrett's team passed their time by going through the motions of a documentary crew, all the while studying the existing security procedures already in place. The men were restricted as to where they could or couldn't go, which was part of the problem of being undercover, so they dealt with it. The men secretly planted tiny cameras in the lobby, elevators, and even on the floor the delegates were staying on, Bellows using the ruse of needing some additional shots for their documentary. Kale patched the videos through to their laptops and cell phones. Each team member had instant real-time access if needed. The team members also used their highly developed relationship-building skills to befriend a number of the hotel employees. The men were looking for any nugget of intel that might help them.

The men didn't need any advanced skills to keep an eye on Dr. Moanda. The French-speaking economist from the tiny Central African nation kept pestering the crew for air time. He felt it was time for the world to hear about how great his country was and how the culture of Gabon was in fact more French than the French themselves. He used his experiences while studying at the University of Paris to illustrate the point. The only reprieve that Barrett's men got from the short, bald Gabonese delegate occurred whenever his attention was drawn—frequently—to women who crossed into his line of sight.

***

Barrett rejoined his men outside the conference room where the delegation was still holding a meeting.

"Learn anything?" asked Reirson, who pretended to be working on some audio equipment while actually listening in on the delegates. The men had bugged the conference room the delegates used as a meeting room just in case. The Secret Service did sweep the room daily, but their monitoring devices were not sensitive enough to pick up the team's bugs. Their failure stemmed from the fact that the unit used the Secret Service's procedures and equipment as a starting place for their own eavesdropping program. This gave them an advantage not only over the American agency but over everyone else since the Secret Service prided itself on having the best expertise and equipment in the business.

Barrett shook his head. "No. Is Kale all set up?"

"He has his kingdom set up in the room and has patched us all in." Cruise rubbed a kink out of his neck.

"I wish we had one of our own in there," added Bellows, referring to the Joint Secret Service-Nigerian communications center. The team would be able to do their job better if they were kept in the loop every step of the way, not always having to play catch up.

Reirson gave a small laugh. "Ain't gonna happen. We're just babysitters on this one." The others nodded in agreement. Barrett just hoped these babysitters would never be needed.

***

The following morning, the delegation planned a visit to a large school that also housed an orphanage and clinic near the small rural town of Bakana not far from the river delta. The delegation's convoy consisted of Nigerian military jeeps, armored Suburbans, and two Range Rovers used by Barrett's team. They departed the relative safety of the hotel first thing in the morning.

Barrett observed firsthand the poverty of the area as the convoy left the center of the city and got off the East-West highway near the city's edge. He watched as unemployed Nigerians congregated in groups, wandering the streets aimlessly while malnourished children played on top of a landfill. The men in the convoy saw the buildings on the side of the road change from concrete construction to those made of cheap metal and wood. They also began to see the ever-present, hastily constructed wooden lean-to. The structures got their name because they were built so fast and cheap that they looked like they were about to fall over at any moment. Building codes and zoning rules were rarely enforced in Port Harcourt, which led to the lean-tos showing up overnight and the entire city suffering from major sanitation problems. Even with all of the oil money flowing into the country, this was still the Third World.

"The level of neglect for such an oil-rich country is amazing," Kale declared while riding in the back of Barrett's vehicle after observing the sad conditions.

"You know they have to export most of their oil for refinement," Linford said.

"Why? Wouldn't local refining create more jobs and a better infrastructure?"

"Yes, but it would not be worth it to the rich here. Too small a return for a lot more effort," responded Barrett, who obviously didn't agree with the present system. Kale just shook his head, looking back out the window, thinking about how lucky the people back home in the States really were.

Heading north toward Bakana, the UN convoy passed a number of agricultural farms, including some of the new fish farms that the government was keen on developing to help diversify the economy of the region. Traveling down the slightly elevated, narrow road that sat between two slender canals, they came upon a sight that surprised Barrett. Among the web of waterways and lush, green landscape of the Delta region lay the "black water." This condition existed where the tributaries and streams had absorbed oil spills, which caused their water and banks to be stained black by the runaway crude. Unfortunately, this ecological tragedy was a common sight in the delta region. *Another shame*, thought the Americans in the vehicle.

The convoy came to a stop at a large plantation located just outside Bakana. The orphanage and school, housed in an old, worn-down, two-story Victorian home on the property that was once inhabited by a wealthy English family during the colonel period, overflowed with children whose parents had either killed or were too wounded to care for them. The house's large living room and sitting room served as the classrooms both for the children from the orphanage and kids living in the nearby villages. This visit had been scheduled as a typical photo op for its members, where the delegates performed their normal routine of meet and greet with the teachers and kids while some of the local media took pictures.

Barrett and the rest of the delegation next visited the medical clinic located only a few hundred yards behind the home, based in what appeared to be the old servants' quarters, which had been renovated with some additions. It didn't have much in the way of modern equipment, but the staff appeared to be extremely resourceful with what they did have. The clinic had three doctors: one, a local from nearby Bakana, and two from Port Harcourt, all volunteers and, by the looks of it, all overwhelmed.

The facility reminded Barrett of an army field hospital or triage clinic. Its patients suffered from gunshot wounds, missing limbs from being tortured, and burns from various types of incendiary devices. At least there were no current injuries being attended to as the entourage made its way through the small treatment center. Most of the critical patients were sedated in their beds behind closed curtains. Barrett wondered how the members of the delegation would have reacted to seeing someone screaming with blood spurting onto the floor and walls.

Though it appeared that the clinic personnel did everything they could to make the reception somewhat comfortable for the visitors, one thing they couldn't cover up was the smell. The odor hit them as a slight tinge in the air when they pulled up to the orphanage then got exponentially worse as the delegation got closer to the clinic. The combination of burnt skin, the coppery smell of blood, rubbing

60

alcohol, body odor due to the lack of enough clean water for daily bathing, and other bodily fluids mixed together with the natural humidity of the region created an indescribable aroma that permeated everywhere. Even for the experienced members of the unit, the stench was disconcerting. Thankfully, the tour through the inside of the clinic was extremely brief, and everyone walked back to the school, where the smell became more tolerable.

Barrett kept a sharp eye on those who approached Sara Hanson. Though she always wore a baseball cap when out and stayed in the background, he was still able to see her smile and the tilt of the head that usually preceded it. It got to him. *Focus, Max; she's just the mission ... nothing more.* Barrett pushed her smile out of his mind. He was normally very good at keeping his distance when on a mission. He felt he operated better that way.

Bellows and Reirson mixed in with the delegates. Bellows pretended to film while Reirson played with the audio boom. Kale remained back in the Range Rover, monitoring the command net, which the men of the unit were not supposed to have access to, according to Gratton. The agent provided a radio frequency that allowed Barrett and his team to talk only to him. This meant that if anything went wrong, the only person the team members could contact would be the Secret Service agent. With the mission and quite possibly the lives of his team at risk, Barrett didn't much care for that idea, so he had Kale work his magic and break through the encrypted radio signals of the whole security detail. They were now allowed to hear what everyone else was saying, which meant they were somewhat in the loop.

In the event of an incident involving the President's daughter, the team's primary action would be to eliminate the threat first, knowing that the Secret Service people, who were closer to the young lady, would move to physically protect her. This much had been agreed upon between Barrett and Special Agent Gratton. Barrett looked around at all the hoopla concerning the photo shoot. The delegates were taking more time for pictures than actual research of the facilities. He couldn't help but wonder if this UN mission would accomplish anything.

After a brief lunch with the staff from the orphanage and clinic along with more press time with local dignitaries, the delegation prepared to move out. The convoy filed out from the estate in the same manner as it had arrived. A Nigerian military Jeep led the way with three Suburban SUVs filled with the UN representatives and their security contingents. Barrett and his team followed in their two Range Rovers with another Jeep bringing up the rear.

Ms. Hanson sat in the first Suburban between Tracey Berns, a young, pretty Secret Service agent who, being female, was never far from her principal, and Sam Evans, a twenty-year veteran of the Service. Special Agent Gratton rode shotgun as he coordinated the convoy's movements with the Nigerians. Because of its high value cargo, the Suburban had additional armor plating and run-flat tires courtesy of the Secret Service. It was basically a tank on wheels. The ride back to the hotel was to take around two hours.

The beginning of the return trip proved to be uneventful and maybe even a little boring. Boredom was one of a soldier's greatest threats, but the experienced men of the unit knew to stay vigilant. There wasn't much for them to look at as the convoy drove through the endless green landscape. They passed some more farms while traveling on the main road back to Port Harcourt. This was a road in name only, since it consisted mostly of mud, pot holes, and rocks. The road was so bad that even with the sophisticated shock-absorbing system, the Range Rovers were rocking so much that the men inside quickly tired of all the bouncing and sudden jarring that their bodies were being subjected to. Barrett knew what it felt like to be in a salt shaker.

The convoy entered the city's outskirts, where the two-lane road narrowed as it crossed into one of the older sections. The road was now a little smoother, and this eased the beating the members of the delegation were taking. As the convoy edged through the city, something caught Barrett's attention.

There didn't seem to be many people on the street, and those that were started to head inside as soon as the convoy approached. They had crossed into a more moderate but still poor area of Port Harcourt. The rag huts and metal sheds faded away as the street became lined with one-, two-, and three-story buildings of various colors. Some had shops on the ground floor and either offices or apartments upstairs. There were also some of the shabby lean-tos spread out between the more modern buildings. The so-called modern buildings were actually all built in the '50s or '60s, the last remnants of British imperialism.

The late afternoon sun still shone brightly, so there should have been a lot more people around. This was a concern for Barrett since the Nigerians leading the convoy were too predictable; they did little to vary their routes. Barrett, like most soldiers who had experience operating in high-threat areas, had learned quickly to watch the locals since their actions would be the best indicator if the streets were safe or not. The fact that there was hardly anyone out on the street at all was not a good sign. *Where is everyone?*

"Let's close the gap," Barrett said through his earpiece before lifting the separate radio connected to the convoy.

"You getting that feeling, Boss?" Kale muttered to Barrett from the backseat of the Rover. He too watched the few remaining locals on the street walking quickly to get indoors as the convoy neared them. Kale picked up the pace, flipping through frequencies on his portable scanner and trying in vain to pick up any chatter that might help them, but he found nothing. The small scanner he used had a limited range, and both Kale and Barrett knew if someone was about to attack, they may have already initiated radio silence if they used radios at all. Barrett grabbed his radio.

Gratton answered, "Sierra One, go." This was the Secret Service agent's call sign.

"Sierra One, we need to get a move on. Something's not right."

Gratton responded with slight irritation, "Please elaborate, Sierra Nine," but before he could get Barrett's explanation, his radio went dead. "What's going on?" he asked aloud as he fumbled with the device. Out of the corner of his eye, he caught a glimpse of a speeding food truck slam into the lead Nigerian Jeep just when it made it into the intersection. Immediately, an RPG, or rocket-propelled grenade, streaked from an overhead rooftop toward the

Nigerian Jeep bringing up the rear. The military Jeep exploded on impact, sending its occupants and most of the vehicle itself airborne in a fiery explosion before slamming back to the ground. The burning wreckage blocked off their only chance of escape. The convoy was trapped!

CHAPTER 7

"Contact left," said Kale, reacting to fire from a large building which slammed the convoy vehicles from their left. It was the same building that the RPG had come from. He returned fire, doing his best to silence those muzzle flashes coming from his side of the vehicle. There were a lot of them.

"Contact right and rear," added Bellows over the radio as another RPG round streaked over their vehicle and hit the downstairs pottery shop in the building to their right. The men inside heard the whoosh as it passed dangerously close to the roof of their Rover. The explosion caused glass and ceramics to rain down on the street. Thankfully, other than feeling the heat of the blast, their vehicle escaped that attack with little damage.

"Talk to me, Kale," ordered Barrett while he fired at some muzzle flashes from a second-story room on the right side of the street.

"All coms except ours are out," Kale informed him while laying down some serious lead.

"How?" Barrett shouted over the sounds of his rifle firing. He didn't need to since Kale could hear him through his earpiece.

"Jammed." Kale kept busy with shooters who appeared to be really well dug in inside a first-floor room.

With gunfire erupting all around them, Barrett quickly assessed the situation. They were taking fire from both sides of the street with heavy concentrations on the two corners in front of them and on the roof to their left. It was a well-planned, L-shaped ambush.

Barrett grabbed the radio that Kale had programmed to hack into the command net and listened. Nothing but empty air. The radios were still jammed. Worse, the other vehicles were just stopped in the middle of the road. Barrett could only imagine what was going on inside those vehicles; there would be casualties for sure.

"Can you get anything?" asked Barrett. Kale let his rifle dangle while he fiddled with the team's master radio.

"I have something," Kale shouted. "Sierra Nine to convoy … Sierra Nine to convoy." No response. "We can listen but still cannot get through to anyone," Kale said, frustrated.

"Good enough."

Kale handed Barrett the radio before lifting up his rifle again. Barrett listened as convoy security operators drowned each other out over conflicting orders amid an underlying layer of confusion. The fog of war had made its appearance. He was thankful that there seemed to be no evidence of panic from the rest of the convoy. Even though these men were over their heads, they were still trained professionals.

Normally, once an attack began, the Secret Service immediately removed the principal from the danger area and then attempted to contain the threat. This was a completely different threat scenario. They were in an urban war zone. This was the Secret Service's worst nightmare. Lucky for them, Barrett and his men had come along.

Their attackers, at least the ones Barrett saw, were dressed in jungle camouflage. They looked to be local militia employing mostly the ubiquitous AK-47s and RPGs. "Third world candy" as they were known to members of the U.S. military. This was probably one of the rebel groups trying to send a message. *But what about the jamming of the radios?* Nowhere had he read that MEND had that type of technology. Barrett knew there would be a better time to answer that question as he became painfully aware that the convoy would not last long in this situation.

"Cruise, Mako, clear the building to the left corner and provide cover for the convoy," commanded Barrett.

"Copy that," responded Reirson, grabbing his equipment.

"Moving," added Bellows as both men abandoned the last Range Rover and started for the yellow, three-story building that dominated the west side of the street.

Barrett knew that the convoy had to head west or left to get back to the safety of the highway. He needed to reduce the incoming fire from that side, or they would be torn to shreds before any of them made it to the corner. He wanted the two men to eliminate as many hostiles in the building as possible, but, more importantly, they needed to get in a position to provide sniper cover if the convoy had any hope of trying to escape. That was if they could get the convoy moving ...

As soon as Bellows and Reirson opened their doors, the sounds of war exploded in intensity in their ears. The whoosh of an RPG streaked by with its trail of smoke staining the sky black as it missed its target. The second Suburban exploded behind a lean-to a good ways behind them. The hammering of AK-47s and the hisses of bullets flying all around them, not to mention the *cracks* they heard, reminded them of how close they were to cheating death. The two operators forced all this to the back of their minds, focusing solely on their objective.

The Americans crossed the road in a semi-crouch with their rifle butts squeezed firmly against their shoulders, heading toward the target building while rounds were hitting all around them, kicking up enough dust that the men could taste it. They avoided getting too close to the concrete walls of the building so that they wouldn't be hit by any walking bullets or other types of debris.

Once at the doorway of the apartment building, the operators stopped to check the heavy, wooden door that led into the apartment building. It was unlocked. They looked at each other, nodded, and then quickly created a two-man standing stack where each man lined up behind the other and entered the building. They saw no one around the small entrance, so the men moved up the stairs as quietly as possible, the hammering of their boots on the stairwell kept to a minimum thanks to years of training.

On the second floor, the operators cautiously advanced down the empty, bleak hallway, still in their semi-crouch with their rifles at the ready. They stopped every few feet, listening in an attempt to locate where the greatest concentration of shooting was emanating from. The operators dared not talk and give away the element of surprise, so they communicated with each other via hand signals.

Reirson and Bellows didn't have time to eliminate every single shooter in the building. The men were going to focus on the highest concentration of shooters in a given area before progressing to the roof. They moved down the hallway, the air warm and stale since the building, like many others in the outskirts of Port Harcourt, didn't have central air conditioning. In fact, a lot of these places were lucky to have any type of air conditioning at all. Reirson, with sweat sliding down his face and stinging his eyes, identified their first stop; it was an apartment two doors down. Wiping his face and eyes, he motioned to his partner. The heavy volume of fire inside the apartment was unmistakable. The men could even smell the increase in spent gunpowder in the air near the door.

Bellows pulled a mini-flashlight from his vest to inspect the door lock and examine the rest of the door and its frame for any type of booby traps. The sounds of assault rifles and the echoes of explosions from down on the street reminded them that they didn't have a lot of time. The lock was made of cheap, corroded metal typical in this part of the world, and he couldn't find any evidence of explosives either. Since some light escaped from under the door, the men assumed there were no other obstructions to prevent them from entering.

The men prepared themselves to enter and got into their two-man breaching stack. This type of operation was very dynamic; violence of action brought about by speed was the key. Bellows tapped Reirson on the shoulder from behind, Reirson kicked open the door, and both men rapidly entered the room.

Bellows stepped in first and went to the left and took his hundred and eighty-degree field of fire, while Reirson did the same on the right. Both men moved and scanned through the entry door that led directly into the living room with the kitchen off to the right. The living room itself ran to the back of the apartment, where the windows to the street were placed.

Reirson noticed in his sector three men firing from all of the three living room windows. The room was fairly dark with the only light coming from the open windows the ambushers were using as their firing platforms. Still moving toward them, Reirson lined up the shooter on his right first, clearing from outside to inside. Bellows covered his flank, in this case a hallway to their left. Reirson squeezed the trigger of his rifle twice with both bullets finding their mark in what was once the back of the man's head. Reirson expertly shifted his aim and fired another two times. Again, both bullets found their intended target, slamming into the back of the Nigerian's skull. The man never even had time to turn around before he was dispatched to the afterlife. Reirson repeated his actions and sent the third man to his maker as well. All three men were down. Reirson discerned that they were dead, but was not about to get near the windows to verify. He knew from experience that was how friendly fire incidents occur.

After clearing the initial room, Bellows headed left down the hall. He heard firing coming from that direction. Unlike the hallway, the living room had no light at all. Bellows liked it. The darkness played like a personal shield against his enemies. He checked the first room. Nothing. So he proceeded to the next one at the end of the hallway. The operator wished for a concussion grenade at this time, but the agent knew wishes were for the future, not the here and now. He also knew that surprise would still be on his side. The door was closed, and the operator could clearly hear movement behind it.

Bellows didn't bother with the door handle; he took a step and ferociously kicked it. The door flew open, breaking from its hinges with Bellows right behind it. He immediately noticed two men; one was firing out the window, while the man closest to the doorway was bent over, rummaging for what looked like more ammo. When the operator stepped into the room, the man nearest him looked up and rushed him. Bellows fired two shots into the man's chest, but the assailant didn't go down right away. The Nigerian just stumbled and incredibly remained on his feet, blocking Bellows' line of fire to the second gunman. The wobbling man was too far away for Bellows to push over, so he stepped closer. The second shooter heard the American's initial volley, turned around, and prepared to fire. Bellows was out of time. He hurriedly dropped his right hand from his rifle, letting the sling help to hold it up to his chest, grabbed his pistol from his thigh rig, and rapid-fired the Berretta twice. The 9mm rounds tore through the Nigerian, causing him to fall backwards against the window and crash to the ground below. The first gunman finally fell over, with Bellows sidestepping out of the falling body's way. Bellows and Reirson finished their sweep of the apartment and stepped back into the hallway.

The operators, heads down, listened for a few moments to hear if there was any more shooting coming from an apartment on the floor. There was intermediate firing coming from the next apartment, possibly a sniper. The lag time between shots became easier to distinguish with the other shooters silenced. The operators went through the same procedures as before, only this time when they entered the apartment, they saw only one gunman in the living room firing a high-caliber rifle. Bellows finished him off before Reirson even entered the room.

The Nigerian in the apartment was using a table as a sniper perch and shooting an old Remington rifle that was not very effective. The long-barreled rifle looked like a holdover from the British colonial days. The weapon itself was covered in rust, and the men were surprised it hadn't blown up in the man's hands when he fired it. This guy was by no means a professional and a direct contradiction to how the ambush had been planned and executed so far. Reirson wondered if he was just an opportunist. He filed the information away as the two men completed clearing the rest of the apartment. With the apartment empty, the two men headed toward their next and most important objective: the roof.

***

Gratton's searching had paid off; he had found an opening. The firing from the left corner had suddenly decreased. *It's now or never.* The experienced driver stomped on the gas and, with the engine screaming, raced the Suburban through the carnage in front of him and began the left turn that would get his vehicle and occupants ultimately to safety. All of a sudden, he caught a fast-moving blur in his peripheral vision followed by an enormous blow and the hellish sound of metal on metal. Then the world went dark.

CHAPTER 8

The UN convoy that Gratton's SUV had left behind was in a furious firefight. The other two SUVs with the rest of the delegates on board were being constantly hammered by small arms fire. Barrett's Range Rover was also taking its share of hits. The vehicle was not armored like the Suburbans, so the penetrating rounds had made impact holes that allowed light to shine through like lasers throughout the vehicle, constantly reminding its occupants that it was a miracle no one inside had been hit yet.

Linford, with one hand on his personalized, commando-style M-4 assault rifle and the other on the wheel, did his best to make them a more difficult target. He continued to drive forward and backward while weaving in the limited space provided on the narrow street. The Suburbans in front of the team's Range Rovers were taking the bulk of the attack. Barrett watched as the one directly in front of him rocked back and forth due to a barrage of heavy fire. *Thank goodness they're armored ... but they're still not going to last much longer.*

"You got eyes on the PD's victor?" asked Barrett, referring to Sara's Suburban. Sara was known to Barrett and his team as the code word PD. The First Daughter was still the mission and, besides his men, his first priority.

"Negative," responded Linford. "Think help is on the way?"

"The Nigerians were taken out quick. Without radios, I doubt any of them had a chance to call it in." Barrett was looking down his sight, leading a rebel who had tried to sneak out from a building and approach the second Suburban. He sighted the man, giving him a one-pace lead. Barrett slowly took a breath then let it go while depressing the trigger. Barrett watched as his round hit the man center mass. His target dropped. He moved the rifle back toward the buildings, looking for another target, keeping the rifle tight against his body. Barrett also made sure to keep his support hand well forward on his weapon. This developed a natural inward pull on his rifle, which steadied it and took off some of the strain. He might be using it for a while.

"Bollocks," muttered Linford to himself, still stuck on Barrett's answer.

"Don't worry; I'm sure somebody called nine-one-one."

The first Suburban carrying most of the delegates was getting raked. Round after round poured on it. The delegates crouched down in the back. Some prayed while others simply screamed in the chaos.

Barrett then ordered his friend to try and move the vehicle up to the front of the convoy while he and Kale continued returning fire with their assault rifles. It was slow going considering the road made for a tight fit before the attack. Now, Linford had to make them a hard target and navigate all the debris that was piling on the road as the fight continued.

Barrett noticed during the firefight that while some of their attackers were exposing themselves like amateurs, other shots seemed to be coming from places he could not get a good bead on. Those shooters were really well concealed, which he considered interesting since rebel militias were usually not that well-trained. Muzzle flash discipline was not something they cared about.

Peering forward, he observed that the two Suburban SUVs in front of them were not moving at all. "Kale, get those vehicles moving," Barrett ordered the ex-Air Force commando and current electronics expert.

"On it," answered Kale as Linford slowed down enough behind the lead Suburban for him to jump out.

It was a tight squeeze.

"Sierra One, this is Sierra Nine," Barrett called into the radio. He waited a few seconds, but a reply didn't come. Barrett repeated, but there was still no response to his hail. *What's going on up there?*

***

The front of Gratton's Suburban had been rammed by an old, beat-up Toyota Land Cruiser. The impact completely crumpled the front of the Suburban and rendered the vehicle useless. Moments later, a white delivery truck pulled up, and four men jumped out. The men were all were armed to the teeth like mercenaries. A fifth got out of the front passenger side and confidently walked toward the Suburban. He was a tall, muscular man with premature gray hair shaven tight to his skull. He also sported a large scar on his right cheek, a reminder of a mistake made in his youth. He strolled toward the incapacitated vehicle, watching one of the other men place a small explosive on the right rear passenger door. The door blew open with no further damage to the vehicle or its passengers.

These guys were pros.

***

Kale exited Barrett's Rover and sprinted up to the first Suburban. While doing his best to avoid being hit by all the bullets flying around from both sides, he noticed that the air was smoky with a mix of cordite and stirred up dust … an African cocktail. This was a concoction a sane person would think best to avoid. He reached the first Suburban and rapped on the driver side window in between returning fire with his SCAR. The vehicle was stuck in some nasty crossfire with bullets pinging the vehicle all around him. Kale noticed that while the security operative in the passenger seat returned fire, there was no movement on the driver side. He rapped the window again, yelling "Friendly" to warn the driver of his presence just to be sure. Kale really didn't feel like getting shot by a member of the security detail today. Staying crouched, he edged closer to the driver door but continued to keep his head below the window; he got a good look up at the window, seeing for the first time that it was riddled with bullet holes. It looked to Kale like some heavy-caliber rounds had penetrated through the bullet-resistant glass. *Not good.*

It was ironic since it was procedure for the driver to keep his window up when shots were fired, while the other members of the security detail had to roll down their windows in order to return fire. The driver was too vital to risk because if he got incapacitated, it usually spelled doom for the other occupants in the vehicle. He rapped on the window. No answer. Slowly, he opened the door, keeping his head down, yelling "Friendly" again. Kale saw the driver slumped over the wheel with blood running down the side of his head.

The security officer in the passenger seat turned to see who opened the door, pointing his assault rifle at Kale, trying to judge if he posed a threat, but he recognized him. "I think he's dead," shouted the man, who appeared startled at the appearance of the documentary crewmember now sporting a state-of-the-art combat rifle. Kale quickly checked the driver's pulse … nothing. Sure the driver was dead, he cut the man free from his seatbelt and told the back occupants to pull the body through the opening between the front seats to the rear of the SUV. He wasn't going to leave anyone behind.

This took a little doing on Kale's part as the delegates, who all understandably appeared in various stages of shock, were a little slow in responding to his commands. Dr. Kahn, who sported a slight wound from when one of the high-caliber bullets grazed her shoulder, helped guide the dead man's body into the back, but Dr. Tyre seemed unresponsive. The delegation's leader sat there, doing nothing with the exception of incoherent mumbling. Some people didn't respond well to gunfire. Kale settled himself in the driver's seat then told the security operative next to him to get the attention of the driver behind them and have the Suburban follow. *Here we go …*

***

As the men outside the wrecked Suburban were approaching the vehicle, Gratton began to stir. Blurry-eyed, with a splitting headache, he looked over at Graham slumped behind the deflated airbag and, with pained effort, he turned to get a look at the rear occupants. The three rear passengers were sprawled all over the backseat, unconscious. *Damn.* He was about to reach for a pulse on Graham when the backdoor blew. He tried to locate his gun but to no avail. "Who are you?" Gratton asked, flustered because he was still groggy and couldn't find his weapon. He would never get an answer. The only reply was a retort from a G36 assault rifle as it sent a burst of high velocity rounds point-blank at Gratton. The man who

75

had fired into the Suburban then pulled a picture from a combat vest pocket and showed it to his leader, the scar-faced man. The man's lifeless, gray eyes seemed to look right through his subordinate while he waved the picture away without a look. He had no need for it since he'd memorized every feature of their targets.

One of his men checked Sara Hanson's vitals and determined that other than being unconscious, she was alright. He nodded the go ahead for her removal. After his men removed the President's daughter from the vehicle, the large man signaled again, this time at his subordinate with the picture.

The subordinate proceeded to raise his rifle and fired another burst into the unconscious agents still in the back seat. The storm of rounds ripped through the defenseless bodies of the Americans, tearing through the upholstery and showering the rear of the Suburban with pieces of cloth, plastic, and blood.

The two men carried Sara to the truck and secured her to a seat in the back. Once the other gunmen returned, and with all passengers accounted for, the truck sped off.

***

Reirson and Bellows cleared the final stairs and prepared themselves to go through the access door that led to the roof.

"Reloading," Reirson quietly called out as he pulled out the almost expended magazine from his rifle and reached for a new one from his vest. He slammed the new one into place with a loud clap. "I'm up," he said. Once again, without a word, the men moved onto the roof and progressed rapidly to their respective fields of fire. The element of surprise was still their best weapon.

There were four men on the roof firing down mercilessly on the convoy.

Using the noise from the gunmen's weapons as cover, the operators went unnoticed. All four were rewarded with two bullets each without ever having the chance to turn around. Within moments, the shooting on the roof ended.

Both men called, "Clear," practically at the same time, signaling the end to any threat up on the roof. Reirson now moved to the east side to provide sniper cover for the stuck convoy, while

SHADOW HUNT

Bellows headed to the north side to make sure their escape route was secured. Reirson quickly replaced the barrel on his modular SCAR to the longer sniper version and then set up his position. The roof had a four-foot wall on its outside edge which he propped his weapon on to use as a stable firing platform. He placed a small, non-reflective mirror on the ledge facing behind him. Reirson really hated it when his enemy tried to sneak up on his rear.

The sniper leaned against the wall for cover, wrapped into his rifle by twisting the sling around his arm, and began to scan for shooters on the other side of the street. He could see a lot of muzzle flashes coming from across the street, pounding the convoy mercilessly. Reirson immediately got busy since there were ample targets of opportunity.

Bellows got to his position and surveyed the street below. "What the fuck?" he exclaimed to himself as he noticed what looked like a car accident involving the principal's Suburban and an old delivery truck. The scene on the street also included a group of armed men getting into a white truck. The armed men, some of whom had shemaghs wrapped around their necks, didn't strike Bellows as the cavalry come to save the day.

CHAPTER 9

Heavy rounds pounded Kale's SUV. He tried to keep the vehicle's movements unpredictable as they crawled through the kill zone. "Fuck." Kale felt an ax hit his shoulder.

"You okay?" The security officer sitting next to him looked like he had had enough.

"Yeah." Kale assessed his injury. Round, clean in and out. The Air Force operator shifted in the seat, pulling his belt free. He wrapped it under his armpit and over his shoulder as a tourniquet. "What's the status on the rest?" He didn't need the security officer to reply. He looked back as he asked and saw that the back occupants were in a bad way. Two looked to be breathing, but not Dr. Kahn, or what was left of Dr. Kahn. Two rounds, one to the jaw and one to the scalp, had completely ripped her head open. Kale didn't even recognize her anymore.

***

Barrett and Linford had expended a heavy load of ammunition in a very short period of time, evidenced by the number of empty casings that filled the floor of their SUV. They were engaged with the two forward problem spots, receiving a heavy volume of incoming fire from both corners. Until the fire could be suppressed, the rest of the convoy couldn't get free.

"Reloading," Barrett barked, changing his magazine as he looked toward the far corner, trying to figure out how best to suppress the fire coming from it. He noticed the wrecked Nigerian Jeep. "Sit tight," he shouted, jumping out of the vehicle and running toward the original accident site that had blocked the convoy. He dove behind parts of the wreckage just as an intense barrage of fire exploded all around him. Barrett peeked around the burned carnage briefly to return fire toward the east corner. Rounds were bouncing off the twisted metal all around him. Barrett ducked into the upside down Jeep and confirmed that the Nigerian soldiers had made the ultimate sacrifice.

Barrett frisked one of the dead soldiers and found what he was looking for: a grenade. He'd noticed that the Nigerian soldiers carried at least one of them on their ammo belts at all times. Barrett did have a concern about injuring any innocent bystanders left on the corner or inside the building, but figured if he tossed one in the street between his position and the bad guys, the resulting explosion wouldn't kill many of their attackers, and it also wouldn't cause much collateral damage. It should, however, buy the convoy some valuable time. He pulled the pin, cooked the grenade a few seconds, then tossed it. Barrett ducked behind the wreckage and waited.

While prone on the street, he quickly glanced over at the food truck and noticed that the driver's body was also riddled with bullets. *Interesting.* The grenade exploded, sending shrapnel, flames, and smoke toward the rebels on the corner. Once the grenade blew and the incoming fire from the far corner stopped, Barrett sprinted back to the SUV and jumped in. "Go," he ordered, pointing toward the opposite corner.

"You're a crazy bugger, mate," Linford exclaimed as he got them moving and drove their Range Rover onto the curb near the left side of the building and right at the three militiamen holding the corner. Without the deadly crossfire, it would be easier to deal with them now that the men could focus solely on those threats. Barrett's ears were still ringing from the explosion, but he got the gist of the driver's comment and shrugged. As their vehicle approached the west corner, one of their attackers jumped out of the way while Barrett quickly engaged two other two shooters.

He nailed the first one with a head shot. The man went down quickly, but Barrett's other target took a round in the leg and tried to scamper across the road behind the crash site. The American finished off the hobbled gunman with a shot to the man's upper back. There were no more shooters, so Barrett used both hands to hold on as the truck bounced up on the corner and onto the intersection beyond the accident that had helped pen them in during the ambush. The convoy was now free.

By the time Barrett's bullet-riddled Range Rover pulled up to the First Daughter's accident site, most of the shooting seemed to stop. It appeared that once the convoy cleared the ambush area, the militia had given up and melted away, leaving behind damaged buildings, blown-up cars, bodies, and plenty of smoke.

"Kale," Barrett said into his radio.

"Kale here," he responded, trying to navigate one-handed through the white smoke billowing out of the Suburban's hood. He was amazed that the vehicle still functioned.

"Exfil the convoy back to the hotel," ordered Barrett.

"Roger that," Kale responded, leading the other Suburban through the last corner and into the intersection. The security operative in the passenger seat stared out his window at the surreal scene that passed by outside. With the shooting stopped and no other threats apparent, he now focused on the carnage going by. He saw dead bodies in the street riddled by bullets, half of a body hanging out a blown-out, first-floor doorway blackened by the explosion caused by an errant RPG that missed its target, and then the distorted corpses of the Nigerian soldiers that occupied the lead Jeep. Men whom he had just met and couldn't believe they were now gone. He was lost in the utter awfulness of the situation and was starting to feel nauseous. The security operative was barely able to stop himself from freaking out. He was also struck by how calm the driver was. *Who is this guy?*

***

Barrett hopped out of the Rover and, with Linford joining him, headed over to the mangled vehicles. The two men split up, each taking a vehicle. They approached the mangled autos with their rifles at the ready. No one was moving inside either vehicle, and no other immediate threat presented itself to the men. "Clear," Barrett called.

"Clear," echoed Linford.

Barrett inspected the Suburban. *Crap ... no PD.* "Any visual on the PD?" he asked Linford, who was exploring the other vehicle.

"Negative." Both of them were confused. Linford reached down and picked up three small, brown beads on the driver's side of the vehicle. "This could be interesting."

"What's up?" Barrett asked.

"I believe I found some pieces of a Misbaha."

"Muslim prayer beads?" Barrett wondered aloud.

"The very same." Linford held them up so Barrett could see them for himself.

The sound of engines coughing and metal scraping caused the two men to turn. Barrett and Linford watched as the beat-up remnants of the UN convoy limped by on its way back to safety. Barrett viewed the damaged vehicles closely for the first time. *At least some of them had made it.*

Barrett had no idea what the casualties were at this point. His main focus had been to get them out of the danger zone, and he had accomplished that. The UN and Nigerians could handle the rest. The pair returned their attention to the scene at hand. Barrett confirmed what Linford just told him; there was no driver left in the Toyota truck. Both men returned to look over what remained of the Suburban. It wasn't pretty. Everyone left inside was dead. Both men were repulsed by the manner in which all four Americans still inside the vehicle had been executed. Barrett felt for the agents in the vehicle. *You won't die in vain.*

Another thing that did get Barrett's attention was that other than the severely damaged front of the Suburban and the rear door, there was no further damage or pockmarks on it. *Interesting for a vehicle that just fought its way through an ambush ...*

"Boss, this is Mako." Bellows' voice sounded in Barrett's ear, breaking through his thoughts.

"Go, Mako," Barrett answered, reflexively touching his ear.

"Be advised, I observed a white delivery van with at least four Unknowns ... white males, some wearing shemaghs, at the PD's crash site. They loaded her up in the van and headed east. I tracked them to the highway before I lost visual."

"Copy that, Mako. Continue to provide security for the convoy's exfil, then return to the hotel. Out." Barrett looked back toward the east, hearing the wail of sirens in the distance as the local authorities finally responded. He knew the two operators stationed on the roof were extremely resourceful and would make it back to the hotel safely.

"Let's head east," Barrett told Linford as they both hustled back to their Range Rover.

"Where exactly are we going?" asked Linford as he turned the Rover around and headed east.

"My guess is the airport." Barrett wiped the sweat and grime off his hands before grabbing his phone.

***

Reirson and Bellows covered the remaining vehicles from their hastily prepared rooftop sniper perches until they were out of range. The operators then each took a coil of nylon rope out of their packs and, after setting up two lines that hung from the roof to the ground below, repelled down the side of the building. They hit the sidewalk in a few seconds, immediately scanning the area for transportation.

A Mitsubishi Lancer parked nearby appeared to be in good working condition. Bellows bypassed the lock and hotwired the car while Reirson wrote a note. *Please pick up at the Presidential Hotel.* He did his best not to smear the ink or ruin the paper due to the perspiration raining from his face. He placed his attempt at an apology under a rock next to the car's parking space, hopeful the car's owner would find it and retrieve the Lancer. Bellows looked up at him from inside the car, making eye contact. Both men laughed, relieving some of the pent-up emotions left over from the firefight. Reirson jumped in the passenger seat before Bellows pulled out and set off after the battered convoy.

***

"Tangos in a delivery van heading towards the airport?" McKenna repeated aloud Barrett's own words.

"I doubt they're locals, so I'm thinking they're moving her out of the country. Men lugging around a kidnapped white girl would not fit in well here," Barrett informed McKenna, who was mortified at hearing the news. But his response was why the guys under him absolutely loved him.

"What do you need?"

"First, we need to close the airport. We've got to keep them here or at least slow them down." Barrett figured these guys, whoever they were, were going to try and get her as far away from Nigeria as they could.

"It'll be impossible to keep them from leaving. Nigeria's borders are very porous as you know, but I concur. I'll get State on it ASAP," responded McKenna.

"I know." Barrett shrugged while still seated in the Rover. "That's why I am also going to need clearance to chase them down." He was painfully aware of how precious time would be.

"You got clearance, Max. I'll also get with the NRO to see if they have current imagery of your AO. If not, I'll have them move some of their satellites around." The NRO, or National Reconnaissance Office, was the department of the United States government that handled clandestine satellite surveillance. It was through them that the NSA, CIA, and military obtained most of their satellite imagery. "I'll get whatever else I can together and get back to you."

"Thanks. I'll get the boys to fire up the signal surveillance gear here as well. We'll be at the airport in forty mikes. Barrett out."

Barrett knew the limitations of keeping the kidnappers in country. He just hoped they would get an idea as to where they were headed or a clue to their identity. Any lead would be crucial. He looked over at Linford. One thing had been bugging him since he'd found out the President's daughter was kidnapped. "How did they know she was even here?"

CHAPTER 10

The President of the United States was a very busy man. The leader of the free world sat in the West Wing's small conference room, conducting a lunch meeting with a few members of his cabinet, when the phone carried by his Chief of Staff, Bob Glavine, began to rattle in his pocket. Glavine quietly walked out of the room to take the call. He returned a few moments later just as the President picked up the second half of his turkey on whole wheat sandwich. Glavine politely asked if everyone could excuse himself and the President. This was not an unusual request; the President had a lot of instances come up where privacy had been paramount, but something in Glavine's voice struck all those present that this was serious. The room went silent and, without protest, the others collected their belongings and prepared to leave.

While the cabinet members were filling out, President John Hanson, the one-time Navy helicopter pilot and Ohio governor, reluctantly put down his sandwich and looked up at his Chief of Staff. Glavine stood across the table framed by the portrait of George Washington, which dominated the wall behind him.

"What is it?" The President noticed the grave expression on his longtime friend's face.

If it wasn't for the persistent pushing by Glavine, Hanson would not have run for the presidency. He had been content to govern his home state and do all he could to help his fellow Ohioans. The Chief of Staff had met the President when he was an attorney working for the federal government during a probe of Ohio's governor. Hanson, then the state's attorney general, cooperated fully with the investigation and showed a willingness to clean up the corruption in the state's administration. He left a strong impression on Glavine, who had worked on a number of political campaigns before being in the Justice Department. As soon as the probe ended with the governor's conviction, Glavine resigned his post with the Justice Department and went to work on Hanson's gubernatorial campaign.

"I just received a call from Tim Conley," started Glavine. He knew the President always wanted his news straight, no sugar coating allowed. Hanson nodded, knowing that Tim Conley was the director of the Secret Service. Glavine continued, "He just informed me that he thinks Sara has been kidnapped in Nigeria." He paused to let the information sink in before finishing. "He's on his way here now to brief you personally."

The President felt the air rush out of him. *Not Sara.* He put his head down, folded his hands in his lap, and did his best to refocus himself, his old Navy training coming back. He looked up at his Chief of Staff with a steely gaze that Glavine knew all too well.

"What do you know?"

"Briefly, sir, only that the convoy she was traveling in was ambushed, and there were some casualties. Also, Defense Secretary Spencer informs us he has pertinent information on this situation and is also on his way here."

***

Defense Secretary Will Spencer was rereading the last brief he'd received from Colonel McKenna on his Blackberry. Secretary Spencer felt it best to see the President in order to personally brief him with the information McKenna had provided. Disbelief permeated his thoughts. *How does such a thing happen to the President of the United States' daughter?* The co-pilot of the Bell Iroquois helicopter transporting him to the White House motioned for him to put on the headset hanging in front of him.

The Secretary of Defense moved gingerly, trying to prevent the airsickness that occasionally afflicted him when flying in helicopters. He figured it was the straight up and down motion that got to him since he had no problems flying in airplanes. Today was not a day to be off his game. He pulled the bulky headset over his steel-gray hair then adjusted the mic over his lips before giving a thumbs-up to the co-pilot.

"They're asking you to hold for the President," said the co-pilot. His slight drawl, though digitized in the headset, still gave away his Tennessee roots.

"This is Secretary Spencer; I will hold," Spencer said into the microphone, not really looking forward to the conversation ahead.

***

Linford steered the Range Rover to the Nigerian military compound at the airport where McKenna had already made contact. The small military post was encased by a large, barbed wire fence and plenty of sentries patrolling three structures which made up the compound. The three buildings consisted of a hangar, a one-story building, and weapons armory in the back. The Range Rover passed the guard post and parked as directed in front of the one-story stucco building, which served as headquarters for the local military regiment.

Barrett and Linford were intercepted by the tall figure of Captain Huka in the parking lot. The guard post had alerted Huka to their arrival, and he had come outside immediately to greet them. Barrett recognized the slender officer after meeting him at the hotel on their first day in Nigeria. Huka motioned for the men to follow him into the building and directly to his office.

Captain Huka didn't stop or slow down, plowing through the first floor of the building, forcing Barrett and Linford to keep up with the tall man's brisk pace. The floor was a beehive of activity, forcing the three men to dodge equipment and other soldiers coming and going. Huka's rank did help in clearing a path. He also appeared to fully understand that time was of the essence. As soon as the men were seated in his office, the Nigerian officer closed his door and proceeded to get right to business.

Huka informed them that a white delivery truck had been seen entering the airport, but a white delivery truck at the airport was a common occurrence. Probably one of the reasons the kidnappers had used one. The exact one matching Bellow's description had yet to be found even though his soldiers were making a thorough search of the entire airport. Once they located the truck, he would have a picture sent to Barrett's man for confirmation.

The Nigerian explained that his superior, who happened to be the regional military commander, had been able to make the necessary calls, so the airport had been closed per their request, but not before three planes had taken off in the time it took for the airport to actually cease operation. "My friends, we cannot keep the airport closed for much longer. The closure is already raising many questions, and it will only be a question of time before the political pressure will overwhelm my superior no matter how hardheaded he may be." Barrett appreciated the attempt, but he had no time for jokes.

"I understand; the kidnappers probably planned for this contingency in the first place, so they are either already gone or have changed to a second exfil option. What can you tell us about the three planes?" Barrett realized his job had just gotten a whole lot harder. He still had the mindset that these guys would want to get her as far away as fast as possible, since that's what he would do if in their place.

Barrett listened while looking at a picture of a much younger Captain Huka out in the bush with his squad. The men all had this invincible look about them. *Ah, to be young again.*

The captain's slightly accented English interrupted his thoughts. "Two were commercial aircraft—a 737 and 757—and the other was an Antonov An-140 cargo plane."

Linford looked at Barrett. "Any ideas, mate?"

"It's too risky to try and get her on or off a commercial aircraft. Plus, those types of aircraft are limited as to where they can land. I'm thinking if they flew out, then it's the cargo plane." Linford nodded in concurrence.

"Do you know the specifics on the cargo plane?" Barrett began to formulate the beginning of a plan in his head.

CHAPTER 11

The whine of the twin turboprop engines was soothing to the plane's occupants, except for one. The large man, whose body had been honed into a dangerous weapon after years of combat, would not relax until he delivered his package. His plan had worked so far. The experienced soldier had used the locals as fodder with no casualties suffered by his own men, and he'd acquired his target.

No one outside the tight group of fellow mercenaries knew his true name or origin. Scarov, the name he now used to mark his rebirth after the incident that had left him disfigured, was a man born into the centuries-old Yugoslavian conflict between Christians and Muslims. Growing up in the mountains outside of Sarajevo, he'd watched his parents tortured and then murdered by a local militia. After barely escaping with his life, the young man took up the cause. His schooling comprised of guerrilla warfare and torture. His test had been the regional civil war in the 1990s, which he passed glowingly. He had led shock troops for the cause. He served his masters well, never failing to complete a mission, including those refused by the most extreme of the radical elements in his group. Others had taken notice. Killing and torturing came second nature to him. The pleas and cries from his victims only served to validate his existence.

With the war in the Balkans winding down, his skills were in high demand. He left and embarked upon his new challenge: a ruthless mercenary for hire. The man served as an instrument for others; that was all he ever remembered being and all he wanted to be.

Scarov took a look to make sure the package still lay unconscious in the back of the plane. She would be much easier to handle while in that condition. Besides, he liked his women this way. *It makes them more tolerable.*

***

Barrett had just finished checking up on his team. Kale had been attended to and should recover quickly. He ordered them to stay in country to await further orders. He still wasn't one hundred percent sure the President's daughter had left on the cargo plane. Part of his own contingency plan included having his men ready to follow up any other leads that might be uncovered in Port Harcourt while he was gone. It was enough for him to embark on a wild goose chase, not an entire team.

"Do you have a plan?" Linford asked as he drove Barrett and himself to the hangar where the Falcon Airways jet was kept. Barrett had called ahead to get the plane ready.

"Not really. More of a 'Develop the Situation' scenario."

"So you're gonna make it up as you go. Why am I not surprised, mate?" The two men sat in silence for a few minutes. "Think they're really going to Lisbon?"

Barrett checked his phone again. "These guys are good. They would know any aircraft leaving this part of the world that deviated from its flight plan is gonna send up too many red flags. Portugal would also not be on anyone's top ten list. They'd think we assumed that they took some other plane headed for another African country or the Middle East."

"Part of an Islamic terror group?" Linford still remembered the beads he had found in the food truck.

"Not sure … You have any ideas? This is your neck of the woods."

"Lad, this is all too high and mighty for me: President's daughter, UN delegates … I deal with the commoners." Barrett stared at Linford, knowing the ex-SAS soldier was more well-connected then he was letting on. "But I will make some inquires. See if any blokes I know have any information on this charade. Question is, what do they plan on doing with the lass?"

"Your guess is as good as mine, old buddy. Besides, these guys, whoever they are, did plan for everything perfectly … except for one thing."

"What's that?"

"Us." Barrett wondered whether the President's daughter was going to meet the same fate as Foresky. *Not if I can help it.*

***

Sitting around the grand table in the West Wing's main conference room for the hastily prepared meeting with the President and his Chief of Staff were General Calhoun, the head of the Joint Chiefs; Dan Shay, Director of the CIA; and Tim Conley and Secretary Spencer. Director Conley had just finished his briefing.

"So," President Hanson started, "besides Nigeria and the UN causalities, we have four dead Secret Service agents." He was looking over the table where his cabinet normally sat for their meetings.

"Correct," answered Conley dourly.

"And no one is missing but my daughter?" asked the President. His eyes briefly moved around the conference table as he waited for the reply.

"Yes," Conley responded. "All the other delegates, security operatives, and Nigerians are accounted for."

Chief of Staff Glavine broke in, "I talked to the Nigerian government and the UN. Both are offering any assistance they can and agreed to help us in keeping a media blackout on your daughter's situation, but we do not have long; this news is going to break sooner or later."

"Will," the President said, looking at his Secretary of Defense.

"Mr. President, our initial intel suggests a number of possibilities at this early stage. However, we do have a lead, though it is slim one." Spencer paused. "She has been taken to the airport and flown out of the country on a Russian-made cargo plane. We have an agent attempting to follow the aircraft. Once we can narrow down its final destination, we will get a better idea of what our next move might be."

"You already have someone on site?" Shay stared at Spencer.

90

Secretary Spencer looked at the President, since he felt it was not his place to answer the Director of the CIA.

The President waved his hand and spoke directly to Shay. "I asked Will for a favor, and he obliged." He knew her presence could endanger everyone in the delegation. He had felt duty-bound to send the team, though he never thought this would happen. *Not my Sara.* "Any idea as to where they are headed?" the President asked, doing his best to remain calm.

"Flight plan was filed to Portugal, but we are not certain whether that is their real destination yet." The President nodded in understanding.

"What if they want to use her as a bargaining chip?" asked the general in his Kentucky twang. All heads in the room turned toward President Hanson.

He looked right back at them. "We will not negotiate," he said without hesitation. He had been pondering that same thought for a while. "Any ideas on who is behind this?" he asked the group as a whole.

"No'" both Conley and Spencer replied in unison.

"I would put my money on a radical Islamic group: ISIS, AQ, Boko Haram, pick one." Shay was staring again at the defense secretary. "This is their cup of tea."

"It definitely fits with them or some of the other Islamic fundamentalist groups," added General Calhoun. "Our man did find prayer beads used by the Muslims."

"Yes, the … beads?" queried the President.

"They are like rosary beads but for Muslims, Mr. President," Glavine informed him. The President's eyes lit up in recognition.

"The fanatics would love to use this incident for propaganda purposes," Conley said. Of course, everyone in the room sensed if it indeed was Al-Qaida or some offshoot radical group, then they would love nothing better than to parade her on Al-Jazeera and possibly behead young Sara in some grand ceremony. Maybe as revenge for Bin-Laden or the many other leaders who had been killed by the U.S. and their allies. This would show the world the true impotence of the Great Western Devil! But no one felt the need to say this out loud. They all knew the consequences if she wasn't found soon.

CHAPTER 12

"We can't confirm its destination. It's not on our radar yet," Barrett told his boss from the co-pilot's seat of the Gulfstream IV jet. "Anything on the sats?"

"Nothing, Max. We had no assets positioned over the AO at the time, nor are we getting any new SIGINT, but we're still working. There is a lot of area to cover, but if Signals does pick up anything, you will be the first to know. About the cargo plane; the Antonov-140 is a top-of-the-line aircraft with a base range of thirty-seven hundred kilometers, but it could be modified with extra fuel tanks for longer distances. It also can operate on unprepared runways at multiple altitudes. Not a lot of groups or even countries in that part of the world can afford that type of aircraft."

"I know; I took a brief peek at the blueprints Dooley sent me."

"Preparing a one-person plane takedown?" McKenna's slight sarcasm came through the radio. He was well aware of Barrett's penchant for pushing the envelope.

"You never know. Any ideas on who owns her?"

"We are still trying to trace its registration. I'm told there are a lot of layers on this one."

"Copy. I'll contact you when I have something."

Barrett left the co-pilot's seat, going to the passenger compartment to check over his weapons and load up on extra magazines. He everything into his bug-out bag: a civilian style black Oakley backpack. So now besides carrying a change of clothes, back-up passport, some hard currency, emergency rations, and a few other items one might need if he had to scram in a hurry, it also contained his rifle with the butt disassembled from the frame to fit inside and extra ammo. Now he could pass himself off as someone backpacking through Europe rather than a military agent.

"We got something." Major Brad Wright pointed at the high-tech radar screen situated on the side console between his seat and the co-pilot's, one of the modifications made to the government-owned aircraft. Wright was the captain of the Gulfstream jet that brought Barrett's team to Africa, and the only crewmember left onboard. His co-pilot had agreed to stay behind in case the rest of the team needed to fly out before new transportation arrangements could be made.

"Is it our target?" Barrett headed back to the cockpit. Wright had been on the radio with international traffic control, declaring them as an Interpol plane following a suspected drug trafficker in order to confirm that the transponder signal of the airplane matched the one they were looking for.

"More than likely, though possible they could have switched transponders," he said in the typical calm and cool response of a pilot.

"Heading, Brad?" Barrett ignored the second part of the pilot's comment, getting back into his seat. If they did swap out transponders, there was nothing he could do about it. He needed to get a look at the aircraft.

"Confirmed. He is indeed going to Lisbon," Major Wright concluded after comparing the Antonov's flight direction with his charts. He then reviewed his own gauges since Wright had been pushing their own plane to the limits to try and catch up with the larger Russian jet.

"I'll make the call."

**

The Antonov's pilot told his passengers to prepare for landing as the aircraft began its final approach. After a smooth landing, the jet immediately taxied inside a private hangar away from the prying eyes of any curious onlookers or lurking satellites. Even though everything was going the way he expected, Scarov knew that the U.S. and its allies had tremendous resources available to them, so any little mistake or oversight by his men could ruin their operation. *Failure is not acceptable.*

He looked out one of the plane's windows, surveying the hangar. His eyes fell on a sleek, silver Dassault Falcon 50 private jet parked inside. The cargo plane pulled alongside the French-built, transcontinental capable aircraft. When the plane stopped, Scarov began directing his men to bring the package out. He had a timetable to keep.

***

"We need to get down there." Barrett looked down at the lights illuminating Lisbon's Portela International Airport, a little bit of frustration creeping into his voice. He looked beyond the airport toward the expansive coastal city from his seat in the cockpit. Barrett knew that every minute they spent circling gave the kidnappers more time to disappear.

"I know," replied the pilot as he waited for clearance from the tower. Finally, after what seemed like an eternity to the men in the plane, the tower order was given, and the Gulfstream received its permission to land.

***

"Have you told the First Lady yet?" asked the Chief of Staff as he and the President walked back alone to the Oval Office.

"No. I don't want to panic her if we can get Sara back before she returns." Hanson still held out hope. He was having trouble bringing himself to tell his wife, preferring to spare her the pain if he could.

"I understand, Mr. President. Just remember, the First Lady is scheduled to return from California in three days." The President already knew this but politely nodded his understanding. *In three days, the whole world might be aware of my daughter's fate.*

***

Two Americans and a member of the Portuguese Security Intelligence Service, or SIS, met the Falcon Airways jet as it rolled to a stop on the tarmac. Barrett saw through the façade when the Americans introduced themselves as members of the Diplomatic Corp assigned to the Embassy. They gave themselves away with how they moved and of course their eyes, which constantly scanned their surroundings. Permanent paranoia. The men had been trained well. McKenna had advised Barrett back on the plane that he would be meeting two local DSS agents on temporary loan to him.

The senior of the two Americans, Chuck Leary, a middle-age northeasterner with graying hair and a slight bulge in his waistline, looked like a typical American businessman. "You boys travel in style," he said, noting the G4 standing proudly on the tarmac.

Barrett smiled. "We were in a hurry." The fancy plane remark hopefully meant the men thought Barrett was CIA. His unit's secrecy, even to fellow American operatives, was paramount to their effectiveness.

"Is this a terrorist situation or something else?" he asked Barrett.

"Something else."

Roy Kramer, the younger man with piercing, green eyes, carried himself as if he was still in the military. In fact, Kramer still had his light brown hair in a high and tight haircut. *Marines*, thought Barrett, *they never let it go*. The Americans explained to Barrett they had been only ordered to find the location of the cargo plane and report to him.

The Portuguese agent Luis Costa advised Barrett that his superiors gave him the same information and authorized him to assist.. Costa went on to inform Barrett that the cargo plane currently resided in a hangar on the same side of the airport where they were currently holding the impromptu meeting. He pointed over to his right—Barrett's left—and said the hangar was within walking distance. The Portuguese agent also reported one of his men had just informed him over the radio that the cargo plane had not moved since his man got there a few minutes ago to conduct surveillance. Barrett ordered Wright to stay with their jet and to keep the engines running. If he recovered the girl, the agent wanted to be airborne as soon as possible.

The four men made their way over to the Antonov's hanger. The group stopped just short of it so Costa could point out their destination. The hangar was situated across the tarmac and two hangars to their left from where the group now stood. Hangar Row came to mind for Barrett as he peered down the apron, catching his first glimpse of the target building. The hangar's outward appearance was no different than any other in any airport Barrett had ever seen. The steel-gray, shed-like structure had a large, open bay for the planes along with what looked like offices in the back. Barrett didn't spy any sign or corporate logo to identify who operated out of the place. It was about as non-descript as you could get if you wanted to hide out in plain sight.

The quartet moved closer, meeting up with Costa's man. He informed them the plane still sat inside, and no one had come or gone since he'd taken up his station. Barrett knew he was operating on a seriously compressed timetable; he concluded he needed to take more direct action.

"Why are there so many workers inside at this hour?" asked Kramer. "The locals like late-afternoon siestas."

"This is not uncommon. Turnaround time for the aircraft is probably limited, so they do maintenance work on the planes regardless of the time of day," Costa explained.

Barrett turned to the Americans. "You gentlemen bring any toys?"

"Yeah," responded Leary, looking a little uncomfortably at the Portuguese agent. "We were told to be ready for anything."

"Well, this is anything," replied Barrett as he retrieved his SCAR and ammo from his pack. He put the weapon together and loaded it before placing it back into the bag. The American felt it was best not to walk in there waving an assault rifle around. After all, this was Lisbon, not Baghdad. The SIG holstered behind his back would have to suffice until he could retrieve the rifle from the bag. Hopefully, everything would go smoothly, and he wouldn't need either.

Agent Costa looked about to protest when Barrett cut him off. "We don't have time to wait. I'll take responsibility." Looking at the three others, he said, "We need to secure the hangar. I'm looking for a female with auburn hair in her late twenties who has vital information pertaining to National Security. She is a Tier One priority." The DSS agents had not yet been read in, so each would be operating on a need-to-know basis. Barrett then explained his plan to the group.

He and Agent Costa would enter the hangar under the guise that they were looking for a suspected criminal who had just stowed away on an arriving flight, which would initiate a thorough, airport-wide search of the airport, including the private hangars. Meanwhile, the two American agents would stay near the entrance of the hangar, keeping an eye on both the perimeter and the two men inside. Costa's man would remain at his station to run interference in case any of the airport's security showed up.

As Barrett approached the hangar with Costa, one thought kept nagging him; where is all the security? He was sure they'd picked the right plane to follow. Doubt began to set in, but he ignored it. *Doesn't matter now. I'm here.* When the two men entered the large open bay section of the hangar, a short, bald man in a shirt and tie quickly intercepted them. Agent Costa immediately got into his act by engaging the man in conversation. Barrett didn't know what was being said in Portuguese, but the bald man, whom Barrett scanned from head to toe, looked like some kind of office manager and kept shrugging with his answers.

Barrett surveyed the area. Parked by itself in the large bay sat only one plane: the Antonov! His heart jumped a little at finally seeing the aircraft. The American silently walked away from the pair and closer to the cargo plane. He felt the engine closest to him; it was still warm. The agent peeked into the plane's cabin, looking from front to rear. Empty. There also appeared to be no evidence inside the plane that could tie it to the kidnapping. Barrett continued toward the rear of the hangar, where he assumed the offices had to be located. *Maybe the girl is being held inside one of them.*

He moved to the back of the hangar, and instead of small offices, he found two large rooms with windows facing into the bay. These appeared to be maintenance areas as men in overalls worked over various pieces of plane equipment. Barrett kept walking, ignored by the laboring men. Thankfully, the hallway continued after the second workspace. It appeared that even though the open bay section ended, the parallel hallway didn't. Someone had built an extension on this hangar. He continued down past the workrooms and came up on the offices, which had been visually cut off from the open section of the hangar.

Barrett approached the first office. Peering inside it, he observed a big, muscular man fighting to get out of his tight-fitting shirt while sitting behind a desk with his feet propped on top. Barrett got an uneasy feeling. The man looked out of place in a civilian airplane hangar. The operative also noticed a tattoo of a black scorpion on his forearm, which seemed familiar, but he couldn't remember why. Then he saw a second man pacing in front of the desk. This guy was not quite as large but also had ripped arms and carried himself big, more like military than an office clerk or aircraft mechanic. The boots, cargo pants, the mannerisms—he felt in his gut the men had to be ex-military, probably some type of mercenaries. He seemed to be running into mercenaries a lot those days. Barrett couldn't spot a tattoo on the pacing man from his vantage point. He continued past the office with the two possible mercenaries to get a closer view of the adjacent one when someone called out to him from behind. Barrett came to a sudden stop and spun around.

Unfortunately, the man wearing overalls and covered in grease who now confronted him seemed to only speak Portuguese. Barrett had no idea what the newcomer had been saying; however, he did understand that this was making a scene and attracting way too much attention. He got a quick glance of the second office; the space looked empty. Barrett smiled at the man still berating him before starting back toward the open bay.

Then, out of the corner of his eye, Barrett noticed the two mercenaries from the first office coming out and heading in his direction. Their body language told him they would not be interested in talking. He also noticed they were bringing party favors.

CHAPTER 13

McKenna had never gotten used to riding an office desk while the agents under him continuously went into harm's way, though in most cases he could make decisions like what kind of assets should be deployed or what type of support was needed, which gave him some part to play. But now, he had to wait on Barrett or someone else to provide him with updates. He hated these types of missions the most. McKenna also did not want to be a burden to his people, so the unit's director refrained from constantly requesting situation reports from his people. He'd abhorred superiors who operated that way when he worked a mission.

So McKenna did the only things he could; first, he went over everything in the pre-planning mission reports to see if anything got missed. Then he reviewed all of the data they had accumulated after Sara had been abducted in Nigeria. Once McKenna finished reviewing the pre- and post-mission reports, he reached into his pocket, pulled out his keys, and opened the one locked drawer in his desk. He retrieved a small notebook, which contained a lot of the personal contacts he had made across the globe in over twenty years of service in the deep, dark world of covert ops. *Time to make some calls...*

***

Costa spotted the row going on between the mechanic and Barrett. He walked over with the office manager in tow to try to calm the situation down. The scene was attracting too much attention. The mechanics had stopped working, now staring at the man challenging Barrett. The Portuguese agent tried to explain to the mechanic the reason for their visit, but his efforts didn't appear to be working. Barrett had to think quickly.

The two guards approached fast with their guns at the ready, both men carrying HK G36 assault rifles. He took notice of the high-end rifles, realizing these boys did not plan on playing around. After his experiences in Nigeria, Barrett knew if these guys had been the same ones that ambushed the convoy, then they wouldn't hesitate to escalate the situation. Images of the slain Americans in the Suburban flashed through his mind.

Barrett seized hold of the man berating him in Portuguese and shoved him into the path of the incoming mercenaries. He called to Costa and grabbed the office manager, making them both run and dive behind some machinery and plane parts stacked on the bay floor. Costa followed. The three men barely made it as the two mercenaries fired.

Both guards opened up into the stack of spare aircraft parts and equipment that Barrett and Costa had dove behind only a few moments earlier. They crouched between the stacked pile of metal and the front of the Russian-made plane.

The mercenaries kept firing as they looked for their own cover. Keeping the strangers pinned down, the two mercs found another stack of strewn parts to hide behind on the opposite side of the bay. Barrett quickly retrieved the rifle from his pack and returned fire. Between shots, he looked around the hangar to see what options he had available. *This is not going to plan* ...

Leary and Kramer took up firing positions outside the hangar as soon as they heard the gunfire. Costa's man tried to rush inside, but Leary held him up. No need to add to the chaos. Leary tried to get a read of the mess inside, but to no avail. All the action appeared to be going on across the open bay. Both agents knew that the last thing they wanted to do was fire indiscriminately into the hangar.

Barrett experienced his own difficult predicament; he knew this would be a fight to the death, but he also needed valuable information. He still had to find the President's daughter. This was a definite advantage for the other guys, since they were only intent on eliminating the three of them. *Or maybe just the office manager. Did he know more than he was letting on?* Barrett pushed those thoughts out. *First things first.*

He looked to his left, seeing most of the workers escaping through an emergency exit in the back of the hangar next to the first workroom. No chance for them to make it out that way; they would more than likely be torn apart by the gunmen with all the open space between them and the exit. He turned back to the Portuguese agent. "Guess they're not in a talkative mood." Barrett's sentence was punctuated by a barrage of bullets zinging right above their heads.

"Why so quick to shoot?" queried Costa, returning fire with his pistol. It was not having much effect. The office manager next to him had his head in his hands, praying.

"These guys are wound really tight. There must be something major going on here." Then looking at the office manager, Barrett said, "Ask him where the girl is," as pieces of metal rained down from the mercs' rounds, impacting the equipment providing their precious cover.

Costa asked, and after the manager's reply, he turned to Barrett. "He says he doesn't know anything about any girl."

Barrett didn't have time for this. He drew his sidearm one-handed and pointed it at the man's head. "Okay, tell him that she's my wife, and if I do not get what I want, then I will consider him an accomplice and blow his brains out." Barrett played to the machismo culture of Southern Europeans. "Make sure he understands," continued Barrett. Even though the office manager probably didn't understand what the American was saying, his tone and body language could not be misunderstood. Costa again talked to the manager, whose eyes widened, and he started to speak fast. It sounded like babble to Barrett. He sent some more shots across the bay to keep the mercs from getting too comfortable.

"She's not here," Costa shouted over the gunfire, "but the men who came on the cargo plane left immediately on another jet parked in the hangar. He didn't see a girl, but he had been in his office when they first arrived."

Maybe she left on the other plane? "Grab him," said Barrett as he pointed to the office manager. "Get out. Use the cargo plane for concealment. I'll cover you." He pointed to the area between the hangar wall and the Antonov to their rear right. There was no point in sticking around if the girl was not here.

Costa nodded and pulled at the office manager, who didn't need much prodding to leave. He ran in a crouched position with the manager in tow toward the big cargo plane. Barrett shifted forward between two big, metal cylinders that used to be engine casings to gain a better vantage point; he got a bead on the smaller of the two mercs, who was focusing on the escaping pair. Barrett fired and the man's neck was ripped open by one of his rounds. The mercenary's blood splattered the wall behind him, while his body jerked back and fell over, out of Barrett's view. Now, he was down to one. But the American realized that he had a new problem.

If the girl wasn't here, then the only thing going for him at the moment was that the kidnappers didn't know how closely they were being tracked. If the remaining mercenary got away, then his advantage would be gone or worse; the kidnappers might cut their losses. This could be disastrous for the girl. He had no choice but to capture or eliminate the lone merc, a task getting more difficult by the minute. The larger merc dug himself in behind a large tractor normally used to pull airplanes in and out of hangars. It would be impossible to penetrate the tractor's metal construction. The mercenary also had a clear line of sight to all avenues of approach with the wall of the hangar a few feet to his back. Plus, he didn't give Barrett the impression of being the type of guy to give up either. With things looking dreary, Barrett started to scan the rest of the interior. Halfway through, something grabbed the American agent's attention. He got an idea.

***

Inspector Litenko reread the official report for a second time. He couldn't believe it. The report was not only done before he and Petrov had finished their investigation and provided their findings to their boss, but also stated the case had been closed. *How is this possible?* He looked over at Petrov, who, after handing the report to his junior partner, had spent the last fifteen minutes staring out the window in their shared office. "How did they find out who was

103

responsible so fast? I did not think we had even identified the body of the driver yet."

Petrov shrugged, taking another sip of his vodka-fueled coffee. At first, the experienced detective thought the Chechens might have actually been involved, but the investigation had gone too fast too smoothly. He had also heard the TV reports that the Chechen separatist group had claimed responsibility, but neither he nor anyone else he knew had actually seen the video they sent in taking responsibility. Everything about the situation from the bombing to the investigation made his gut twist.

***

Barrett continued to exchange fire with the mercenary behind the tractor in order to keep his attention, while Costa and the suddenly talkative office manager carefully made their way out of the hangar. Once he saw Costa and the office manager clear past the plane and outside the hangar, he stuffed a fresh magazine into his rifle and fired a long, continuous burst right above the mercenary to keep him pinned down. Barrett used the barrage to cover himself as he backed up, getting closer to the plane. He stopped firing and started sprinting toward the space between the plane and the wall.

It took only a few moments for the mercenary to realize where Barrett had gone. He immediately began to blast away in the direction of the plane, sending out a relentless volley of death. Barrett couldn't hear anything over the volume of rounds slamming into the metal airframe, shredding it as they tore through the fuselage in the vain hope of hitting the American. When Barrett got to the tail section of the Antonov, which was only a short distance to the outside of the open bay portion of the hangar, he stopped and looked back into the hangar.

He didn't see anyone other than the mercenary. It appeared that most of the other workers had been able to escape the carnage going on in the hangar. It was now his turn. He sighted his rifle back toward the mercenary, who had stopped shooting in order to reload; he heard the "slap" as the fresh magazine locked into place. The American fired into a pair of flammable fuel tanks sitting on a cart next to the wall behind the kneeling mercenary.

In their haste, the two mercenaries guarding the hangar had never noticed the two tanks of lethal liquid sitting right behind them, or they just didn't care. A big mistake, one Barrett wanted to cash in on. He had observed that the tanks were hit sometime earlier, leaking fuel and vapors. Barrett released a stream of lead into the tanks, hoping to set off the fumes, and then ran as fast as he could out of the hangar. The tanks hissed for a few seconds, calling attention to the merc in front of them. He turned in time to view the escaping vapors finally ignite the tanks with a flash before both tanks blew, taking half the hangar with them.

The explosion reverberated all over the airport. Fire alarms went off, signaling the impending response of the airport's firetrucks racing to the scene. Major Wright, sitting in the cockpit of the G4, looked up in awe as the plume of smoke rose high into the afternoon Portuguese sky. He smiled, knowing it probably had something to do with Barrett. Wright prepared the plane for takeoff, since he guessed Barrett would be in a hurry to leave.

Barrett flew through the air, arms and legs flailing as the pressure wave hit him. He hit the ground hard, causing him to roll along the concrete before disappearing into the smoke billowing from the hangar. The impact knocked the remaining air out of him, while he felt his bones rattle with every spin. His body finally stopped rolling. *When did I become a stuntman?*

Barrett stood slowly, trying to clear his head. It still rang from the explosion. He shook it a few times and worked his jaw over, trying to get his ears to start working again. The others had been farther away from the hangar entrance and thus had suffered less from the effects of the blast.

Once outside and recovered from the shootout and ensuing carnage, the group assembled a safe distance from the smoldering debris. Costa was now able to get the office manager to tell them everything he knew, including that the second jet had filed a false flight plan to Rome when in fact it was going to Sofia. The office manager was adamant he only ran the operations for the air freight company and had nothing to do with the armed men, who had left on the smaller jet. He also provided them with a description of the tattoos a lot of the mercenaries seemed to have, but he admitted he didn't know what they signified. He explained again that by the time he came out of his office, the small jet was already loaded and getting ready to taxi out to the tarmac. Costa, who was translating rapidly, almost had to shout at the group because their hearing was still impaired by the blast, especially Barrett's.

Barrett, after another attempt at dusting himself off, gave Leary an obscure email address to forward any additional information the DSS agents might gather during the local investigation. The email, after some intricate rerouting, would at the end be received by the Black Wolf's intelligence analysts at Fort Belvoir in Virginia, where they would start the process of sorting out the information.

Barrett's curiosity about the tattoos rose. *Do they mean anything? Why did they seem familiar?* Costa interrupted his thoughts. He would detain the office manager and anyone else connected to the freight company for questioning. Then, with a wink, the Portuguese agent told Barrett that he would explain to the airport authorities that it was an unexpected accident involving security guards that caused the explosion.

Barrett thanked the men before the sirens of the approaching firetrucks and local airport police overwhelmed them. He grabbed his gear and raced back to the Gulfstream. The chase was just beginning.

CHAPTER 14

"Bulgaria!" exclaimed the President as he made eye contact with his Chief of Staff. "Why there? He was on a conference call with the "Sara Seven," as Glavine had nicknamed the small group of men and woman who were involved in the search for the President's missing daughter. This call included the original six from their meeting in the conference room at the White House plus Carol Mayes, the Secretary of State, whose negotiating skills would be sorely needed during this sensitive situation.

"Sir, I disagree. We believe she is still in Africa. We are currently working on confirming this with some new intel," stated the CIA's Shay.

The President cupped his hands in front of his face and leaned forward. "What new intel?" His eyes begged for good news about Sara.

"Mr. President, I prefer to confirm the source before we go further. No point in getting your hopes up." Shay's firing of a subtle shot at the Secretary of Defense did not go unnoticed.

"I understand, but let us know the minute you have something."

"Understood, sir."

Secretary Spencer sat in his office at the Pentagon, shaking his head. *Politics.*

"As for the Bulgarian lead?" asked the President.

"The Bulgarians will not be very cooperative," General Calhoun chimed in. "And if she is there, finding her is going be like trying to nail jello to the ceiling."

Secretary of State Mayes interjected, "They will need solid proof before they do anything or even allow us to do anything. It's a no-win for them; they want to be accepted as part of the new Europe and NATO, so the last thing they need is for something like this to happen on their soil."

"So … Will," the frustrated President directed his next comment to his Secretary of Defense, "looks like it's up to your man."

***

The Dassault private jet started its final approach to Sofia International, Bulgaria's main airport. Sofia, even though its origins spanned over two thousand years, was considered the youngest capital in Europe. The city was best known as a notorious haven for drug smugglers and arms dealers. The country's status as a refuge for the criminally inspired went back to the days when Bulgaria was still behind the Iron Curtain. Back then, a company called Nemex, which was run by the Bulgarian Intelligence Service, was famous for assisting the Turkish and Sicilian Mafias in the narcotics trade by allowing Sofia to be a main transition site for drugs being moved from Turkey to the West. The communists loved nothing more than to help flood the West with addictive and debilitating drugs. They also provided Sofia as a safe meeting point for the criminal cartels and allowed many of the organized crime members a place to stay in order to avoid the prying eyes of the western law enforcement agencies.

Officially, Nemex made weapons like the ubiquitous AK-47, its replacement the AK-74, and other small arms for rest of the Eastern bloc. Over time, the company's directors discovered it was more profitable if some of those weapons found their way to Western Europe, Africa, and Asia.

After the fall of communism, Bulgaria's criminal barons were free to expand their operations and spend their money on once-hated western goods, which flooded into the city like rain during a desert monsoon. All of this turned Sofia into the "Wild East." There was no place better to hide valuable contraband, especially if it happened to be the President of the United States' daughter!

108

"Bulgarian connection?" Barrett quizzed Janice Dooley in between bites of a Clif bar he'd fished out of his pack. Dooley was updating the agent on the information provided by Leary and Costa after Barrett had left Lisbon. He had passed the time since departing from the Portuguese capitol washing the debris from the explosion from his body in the plane's small bathroom and putting on a new change of clothes. He then methodically stripped, cleaned, and oiled his weapons.

"Crestek Air, the company that owns the hangar in Lisbon and registered in the Canary Islands, traced back to an office that included over two hundred other registered firms."

"Love those off-shore agents," added Barrett. "Bet those companies are registered to other agents in different countries?" He had a feeling where this was going.

"Give the man a prize. Knowing we don't have months to back-trace all of these firms, we ran a cross search to identify companies that Crestek consistently did business with over a long period of time."

"These firms are notorious for being interrelated to the other companies that they do business with. Keeps more money in house and helps clean it as well."

"Right again. After discounting some firms for providing the obvious services, two came up. Both of them were listed as transportation firms registered in Liberia. The two are fronts as well because of numerous credit charges made in Sofia we can't validate." Dooley exhaled. "That's all we have. I even ran them through Yandex," she said, referring to Russia's version of Google. "Sorry, Max. We are still trying to put the pieces together, but this is a sophisticated chain of front companies to go through."

"Anything on those tattoos?"

"Not yet."

"Copy," Barrett replied. "Just give me the info on the two companies please." After receiving the front company names and addresses, he had another item on his mind. "One more thing; wasn't her presence on the delegation supposed to be a secret to the general public?"

"Good question. We need to find an answer," she responded before hanging up.

"Well." Barrett looked at Major Wright. "Not sure if I am ready for some more frustrating time waiting to land."

"I've been thinking about that," responded Wright, "and I have an idea."

As soon as the G4 entered Bulgarian airspace, Major Wright contacted Bulgarian Traffic Control and advised them in a very concerned voice that their plane was low on fuel and needed to land ASAP at the nearest airport. Barrett stole a nervous glance at the fuel gauge then looked over at the major and smiled. Wright responded with a wink as Sofia's air controllers came up on the radio, clearing them to land immediately.

***

"As usual, we are not getting much from the CIA," McKenna told the Secretary of Defense, who had placed a quick call for an update. He particularly wanted to know how the agencies were cooperating with one another. "They've advised us that they are running their own investigation."

"Shay," said Spencer, shaking his head, "he's still ticked off and playing his turf war."

"You'd think after all the publicity they've received recently thanks to our hard work they would be more cooperative."

"Use every other available resource." He took a brief pause. "It's not like we really need them; we can obtain faulty intelligence all on our own."

"Understood." The word had more than one meaning.

***

It was time for Barrett to do what he did best: hunt in the shadows. Since the kidnapping was still top secret, Barrett and McKenna needed to keep this operation off the Bulgarians' radar. Barrett's current mission in Bulgaria would therefore be conducted "off the books" as McKenna liked to say. Barrett liked the idea, especially since he had been growing weary of the possibility an insider had passed on vital intel about the President's daughter to her kidnappers. He couldn't think of a better way to explain the precision of the operation. The agent's experience told him they had to have had good intelligence to pull off that kind of mission.

The Gulfstream taxied over to a refueling station as directed by the Sofia controllers and rolled to a stop near a line of fuel trucks. Barrett waited for one of the trucks to pull up closer alongside the aircraft before he lowered the hatch and climbed down and under the plane, pretending to conduct an inspection. In the darkness, he painted a flashlight across the plane's belly as part of the charade. At the same time, Wright stuck his head out of the open hatch and yelled at the two fuel workers attempting to hail them.

The pilot called out to them in English, a language neither man knew. Both looked at each other and headed toward the door of the G4. One of them pointed a response to a small building just behind the designated refueling area. Wright assumed this was where the airport inspectors were due to be arriving shortly. He started asking them more questions. The two workers stood there hapless, both men now pointing back to the same building as before. As this was all going on, Barrett turned off his flashlight and walked out from behind them under the plane toward the truck. He headed past the vehicle, using the confusion of the moment as a screen for his exit.

Barrett decided to borrow a late-model Skoda sedan he found parked in a neighboring lot. The car looked common enough for his purposes, plus it had a turbo engine. *Just in case.* Barrett stowed his pack on the front passenger seat, keeping it close. The pack contained all of his goodies except for his rifle and sidearm. Back on the plane, he'd figured he would have to be more restrained in the Eastern European nation, so he planned on leaving the assault rifle behind. He'd switched out the chassis on the modular SIG P250 to put the pistol in the compact 9mm pistol configuration. Like in Prague, Barrett only carried the sidearm now concealed at the small of his back.

Once Barrett had the car running, he headed into the city proper. Though dark outside, Barrett did his best to check out his surroundings. He was initially surprised by the tree-lined streets and overall greenness of Sofia. He fully expected the typical dreariness of a former communist-controlled Eastern bloc capital. Instead, he drove into a city with a lot of trees, shrubs, and gardens sprinkled throughout. The other things Barrett saw, the fancy cars and high-end motorcycles blowing down the road past his own car on the deserted streets, were expected given the notoriety of Sofia.

Barrett stopped at a small row of boutique shops in one of the city's new upscale plazas. Dawn was still breaking, so none of the shops would open for a few more hours. Barrett parked in the far corner of the parking lot, where a large oak tree hid the Skoda from the main road. Barrett made himself as comfortable as possible in the small sedan before taking a much-needed nap.

***

"What?" McKenna couldn't believe what his boss was telling him. It was late, real late in the evening; maybe he'd heard wrong.

Spencer informed him the CIA reported they had a high confidence level of Sara Hanson being in Morocco. Reports surfaced of a female that resembled the President's daughter being led into a building that operated as a well-known safe house for Islamic militants. CIA informants picked up on the information and quickly passed the intel to their handlers.

The CIA had sent in one of their para-military Special Assets Division, or SAD, teams to back up the agency's man on the ground and assault the building in order to conduct a rescue. The President had authorized the rescue on one condition; the team could not put Sara in any additional danger while simultaneously minimizing collateral damage. McKenna had been invited to observe the operation, but his unit's assistance would not be needed. The CIA said they had everything under control. *Sure. They always have everything under control until something goes very wrong, and then the time comes for the military to bail them out.*

***

The sunlight slithered through openings in the mountains as dawn broke over the capital city. The light penetrated the Skoda, washing over Barrett's face, waking him. He stretched out as best he could in the car before heading out to the recently opened shops.

Looking out over Sofia, he now made out the impressive silhouette of the seven-thousand-foot tall Mount Vitosha in the distance.

Barrett used his Black Card, a backup, government-provided credit card with an obscure company name on it, at an ATM located outside a small bank that resided in the center of the shops to help augment his emergency money supply. This particular credit card pulled from a shadow account known only to the unit's leader and the assigned agent. This was the ideal situation for the card; Barrett did not want anyone other than McKenna to track his movements. Regardless of even that type of security, Barrett realized that because he didn't know where the leak came from, this might be the last time he used it.

Barrett always wondered how other agents operated in the past, like during the Cold War when ATMs were not placed on every corner and there were no smart phones or GPS trackers. He grabbed a much-needed coffee at a sidewalk café next to the bank before heading back to his car and driving to the first of the two locations provided by Dooley on his list.

Barrett arrived at the Zapaden Park Complex in the western part of the city. He stared at a modern office building in the middle of an executive center where a lot of people in suits paraded in and out. A hostage and armed men would definitely stand out in a place like this, but he still needed to make sure. He drove around the garage area below the building for a few minutes, and when nothing grabbed his attention, he parked. The information Dooley had sent him said the company resided on the fourth floor, so he rode the elevator for the short ride up. The trip up took less time than he used to figure out which button represented the floor he desired.

As expected, he stepped off on a very typical office building floor. He was in a nicely decorated hallway with doors containing signs in Bulgarian to identify the company that occupied the space. He could have been in an office building anywhere in the world. The agent used his phone's translation program to help him figure out what corporate sign he needed to find. He found the office on his list near the other side of the building.

The outside wall had a large, internal glass window and door, so Barrett had the opportunity to peer in and study the place before actually entering. He saw clearly into the small reception area, where there was only a single female receptionist behind the counter and no one occupying the chairs or sofa just inside the door. The receptionist, a young, well-dressed, stacked blonde, had probably been chosen as much for her looks as any other ability. She seemed calm and relaxed.

Barrett strode in and right up to the counter, smiling in an attempt to disarm the receptionist. He used the time crossing the waiting room in order to further study the beautiful young lady, who now waited to greet him. His trained eyes told him that she had no extensive muscle definition, noticeable scars, or calluses on her fingers. She was a receptionist and nothing more.

Barrett peeked behind the receptionist, and though he couldn't see much beyond the reception area, he did observe a few other people walking around. Again, they all appeared calm and going about their normal routines. *Nothing out of the ordinary happening here today.* He put his hand up and smiled, acting like he was lost, turned, and headed back out toward the elevators. *No way are they keeping her here,* he concluded. Holding such a high-profile person quiet in this type of a setting would be too difficult. Barrett mentally crossed the location off his list.

***

"It appears your man is way off the mark." Shay could barely contain his "I told you so" tone. His smugness irritated McKenna as both men stood next to each other, staring at the forward monitors in the Situation Room at the White House. It was the middle of the night, but the place buzzed like rush hour. The operation's command had been moved here due to the need for absolute secrecy and for the convenience of the President. McKenna knew the real reason was that Shay wanted an opportunity to show off in front of the Commander-in Chief.

The Situation Room of the White House was located right below the ground floor. The room was not as high tech as McKenna would have thought. It held a couple of computer stations along one wall and a few on a large, rectangular table that ran down the length of the room in the middle. The front of the room had two monitors topped with a row of clocks that showed various times around the world. In fact, most of the equipment currently being used had just been brought in by Shay's CIA people.

The reason for the sparse room was because it tended to be used as more of an observation area than a command and control center. The President used the center to observe emergency situations while places like Langley, Fort Meade, the Black Wolf's headquarters at Fort Belvoir, and the Pentagon had centers staffed with people to command and control military operations worldwide. Homeland Security had their own for domestic disasters. Since President Nixon's micro-management of military operations during the Vietnam War, most presidents had since only been observers, allowing the experts to handle the minute by minute decisions. Therefore, the sitting President only needed the ability to watch and listen in on what was going on and be able to communicate with the commanders in the other centers.

"I just want to recover the President's daughter." McKenna didn't give Shay the satisfaction by turning to look at him. He kept staring at the front monitors. The two were joined by Dave Kelner, the Deputy National Security advisor who worked with the various Intelligence agencies. Kelner stood out from the others because he tended to keep his black hair longer than most men in the conservative circles of Washington bureaucracy. He reminded McKenna more of an artist than a government official. It had become the man's calling card, fitting since he didn't operate like a typical bureaucrat.

The soft-spoken Kelner was one of the few in the Beltway Intelligence apparatus who actually got along with everybody. In fact, he had spent a lot of his time working as a buffer amid the different agencies, smoothing out potential issues, and being the peacekeeper between them all. Kelner had a straight-up personality with no hidden agendas. He always seemed willing to sacrifice scoring points for himself in order to further the mission. He became for all intents and purposes Hanson's right hand when dealing with the nation's intelligence agencies. The word around the beltway was that Kelner would be appointed the next DNI (Director of National Intelligence), the overlord of the U.S. Intelligence community.

McKenna took solace that Kelner had been read into the operation to rescue the President's daughter so that he could use his magic touch to clear any obstacles along the way. He also wanted him to head up the investigation for the administration after Sara had been recovered, alive, and he hoped in one piece.

The President was the last person to enter the Situation Room. The doors closed tightly behind him. Everyone inside became quiet. He marched directly to the front of the room and stood next to Shay. Chief of Staff Glavine and Secretary of Defense Spencer joined them up front.

The picture displayed on the forward monitors originated from two sources: the first an overhead view by a Global Hawk unmanned aerial drone, and the second by a car-mounted camera placed by the CIA agent to provide a ground level view. The clincher for Shay to believe this was the place Sara was being held had been when one of the informants described exactly what she had been wearing at the time of the kidnapping. This made McKenna skeptical. Wouldn't sophisticated operators like those who conducted the takedown at least make her remove anything that might contain a tracker, not to mention getting sloppy enough to be seen with her? These people knew whom they had kidnapped, of that he had no doubt.

"What are we looking at?" the President asked, staring at the grainy, green video on the two screens in front of them.

"The target building is the three-story one in the center." Determination and focus tightened Shay's facial features.

"What are those buildings it's next to?" The President pointed at the two smaller buildings that sandwiched the building where his daughter was supposedly being held.

"A dance school on the left and a small mosque on the right." Shay bent over a monitor, reading some of the incoming data from the man on the ground.

Spencer leaned his head toward McKenna. "The kidnappers couldn't have picked a better place to stash her."

Or a trap, McKenna thought.

"Mr. President, we need to move quickly," Shay said.

The President looked steely-eyed at Shay. "You have a go." He turned back to study the front monitors, rock solid. No emotion showed in his demeanor.

"Put the FLIR vid on the second monitor," ordered Shay. "Audio?" One of his men looked up from his station, shaking his head.

"Keep working." The tension in the room grew even more. The show was about to begin.

The video monitors showed a van pulling up. A small group of men jumped out, guns in attack mode as they moved into the target building. The people in the room turned their attention to the second monitor, which showed thermal images of the building, watching the red figures move toward the floor where the CIA believed the President's daughter was being held.

The men on the screen stopped at the stairwell entry to the third floor, paused, then moved in. The screen displayed white pulses in places where the CIA men had tossed flash-bang grenades in order to disorient the guards. McKenna studied the red images on the third floor where the supposed terrorists were holding Sara. None of the images seemed tall enough to be standing or moving as a reaction to the assault taking place. *Are they in the prone position lying in wait?* He involuntarily took a step closer to the monitor.

Then it hit him. The people on the screen laying or sitting on the floor were *praying*. Before he could say anything the whole screen went white. The seasoned agent shifted his gaze toward the other monitor, which now displayed gray snow. No discernable image. He instantly realized what had happened.

CHAPTER 15

Barrett moved on to the next lead provided by Dooley. The other address on Barrett's list resided in the Southern Commercial Center Industrial Park in Central Sofia. Due to the compact nature of Sofia's design, he crossed the city in very little time.

The warehouse district included a lot of drab, communist-era, one-story construction, which Barrett had expected to find in an old Eastern bloc country, the type used to contain needed materials so the communist machine kept humming along. Only a few of the cookie-cutter-type structures had been changed in the years since the Iron Curtain came down. Now, these buildings served a new purpose: to hold and ship consumer goods and supplies in order to drive their capitalist economy. Sofia's industry and the Black Sea town's tourists made Bulgaria an envious free market to the rest of Eastern Europe. Not to mention the influx of currency from the crime lords who called Sofia home.

The agent spotted the next address on his list. The building turned out to be one of the handful with recent modifications. Barrett parked a block away from the warehouse and approached cautiously, slowly walking past the building on the opposite side of the street, conducting his reconnaissance.

The large, brown-bricked warehouse stood out from the others nearby thanks to all the security modifications. A twelve-foot-high fence corralled the facility, while a security gate blocked the only driveway to the main road. Barrett noticed no buildings lay close enough to the warehouse to cross over from, and there was no available cover to avoid the external cameras if he wanted to climb the fence. Of course, these were the security measures he did see; he had no doubt a few surprises waited for anyone daring enough to enter uninvited. If he ever kidnapped someone, this would be a great place to stash them. *This is not going to be easy.*

Barrett needed to find a weak point in the building's defenses. The agent enjoyed what was termed in his profession a "sneak and peek." He relished the challenge of getting in and out without being detected. Barrett suffered from an uncontrollable attraction to places he wasn't supposed to go. Although if the President's daughter was being held here, this would be more like a "sneak and peek" plus "snatch and grab" along with the old "run like hell" type of operation. Not exactly a challenge one looks forward to, but he didn't have a lot of options.

The American agent knew in a perfect world his superiors preferred for him to locate the President's daughter then keep her under surveillance until a full special operations team got deployed. The team would, after careful planning, perform a proper takedown. But time was not on his side, and other than McKenna, who in the chain of command could he trust? He pictured Foresky sprawled out on the street, dying. No, this was his op, and he needed to see it through to the end.

Barrett desperately needed to get inside. He didn't speak Bulgarian, so any confrontation at the gate had to be considered a last resort. He grabbed his phone and attempted to reach Wright. No answer. Barrett wanted to report in to McKenna but felt it better to wait till after he checked out the warehouse, deciding it best to limit contact with his agency for now.

He noticed the trucks bearing the same logo as the building were not searched upon entering the complex, which was odd considering all of the other security precautions being taken. This was Bulgaria, after all. Barrett began to formulate a plan. It wasn't a great plan, but it was all he had.

Barrett had been observing some of the workers walking in and out of the compound, probably on break since it was a little after midday. He knew Europeans took their lunch breaks later in the day than Americans, so he followed a group of exiting workers to a nearby restaurant. He waited outside, pretending to talk on his cell.

Time to make his move. Then a cargo van with two employees from the warehouse pulled in and parked. *Even better* ...

***

Tiago Iresma placed the call out of fear more than anything else. He considered himself a prudent man and no dummy either. He saw the men who came to and from the hangar. Scary, dangerous men. Iresma has been the assistant manager for the airfreight company for five years. With the hangar gone, he hoped he still had a job.

Iresma had been on the phone in the first workroom with a representative of an engine manufacturer discussing fees due to his company when all the commotion started in the open bay. Once the shooting started, he ran for his life out the back exit.

"Who are these men?" asked Andrei Kovlor after hearing Iresma's story. Iresma passed on what he saw and what he was able to gather from one of the mechanics. He'd wanted as much information as possible before he made the call. Kovlor intimidated him. Hell, he intimated everybody. Iresma had heard all the rumors; Kovlor had connections with the Russian Mafia, he sold arms, contracted out assassinations, and had his own private army. The assistant manager didn't care to find out if any of it was true. He had six mouths to feed.

"Airport security."

"Portuguese locals?"

"Yes, I overheard one speaking and he definitely is Portuguese."

"And their story checked out?" Kovlor began to believe this was just a badly timed coincidence. His own calls to highly placed sources mirrored what Iresma had just told him. The wealthy Russian businessman wanted to hear the story from someone who was actually in the hangar at the time of the incident.

"Yes, the authorities confirmed this earlier, but they are holding some of our people because of the shootout. Anything I can do to help?"

"This is none of your concern." Kovlor planned to have a talk with the man he'd placed in charge of the mission about the

120

guard's quick trigger finger the next time they spoke. They'd almost blown the entire operation. "Have your boss call me when he is released." Kovlor hung up before Iresma responded, the Russian now convinced what happened at the hangar had no relation to any of his operations. However, the incident did demonstrate how fragile the situation was becoming.

***

After the van's driver and passenger went inside, Barrett strolled to the back of the vehicle. He quickly picked the rear door and looked inside. The van contained a few boxes and some blankets, which he assumed prevented the cargo from being damaged while in transit. More importantly, this left plenty of room to hide one American operative. He placed himself between the blankets and a box so as not to be visible to the van's authorized occupants. Barrett knew most people wouldn't even look in the back unless they were making an actual delivery. He hoped this was just a lunch run and that the men from the van planned on going straight back to the warehouse. If not, things could get messy.

CHAPTER 16

Silence enveloped the White House's Situation Room.

"What happened?" asked the President, who, like everyone else in the room, existed in a semi-state of shock. The ground video feed from the Moroccan street was gone, the monitor playing static. The Predator's feed now put on the two front screens showed white over the target building and surrounding area.

"Finding out now, sir." Shay worked feverishly over a laptop. "Get our man on the line. Get our video back up." Shay began pacing between stations. "This is serious, people. I want no excuses."

The building had been blown. McKenna didn't need any confirmation on what he saw. He almost felt bad for the CIA director, but the man had sacrificed a number of real good men to score some points with the President. *Politics* ... He turned and made eye contact with the Secretary of Defense before moving toward the door. McKenna had to go back to work; he was now sure the girl had never been in the building. Besides, this was Shay's mess; let him deal with it.

***

Barrett preferred to be chauffeured into the secured compound, but, if necessary, he was prepared to hijack the van and force the employees to drive him inside. He spent his time learning some basic Bulgarian on his phone to help him get by once he penetrated the warehouse. He also studied a map of Sofia to plan out possible escape routes if needed.

His patience paid off. A little over an hour later, the men left the diner and returned to the vehicle, neither looking in the back. Barrett had barely enough time to learn some simple words in

Bulgarian along with two possible ways he would take out of the city. The men in the front of the cargo van seemed to be having a casual conversation, their guard now down since they were fat and happy from lunch. He intended to give the van's driver a few minutes to determine what direction they would be headed before he made any moves.

He wouldn't have to; the van headed straight back in the warehouse's direction. Barrett was thankful for the ride. About time luck joined his side.

The van passed through the gate without being stopped then parked in a lot on the east side of the warehouse. The men left, never having looked in the back. Barrett waited a few minutes before letting himself out the passenger door so as not to attract any unwanted attention.

Thankfully, the van sat in a regular parking area and not in some designated loading or delivery section, which would have meant a lot more people around. Barrett saw a group of workers coming back from lunch walking toward him, so he joined them, blending in as they entered through a side door. His luck appeared to be holding.

***

Kovlor unmercifully berated the waitress. She felt hopeless, having tried everything to please her customer, but nothing worked. She couldn't know that Kovlor's irritable demeanor was not so much a result of his plate of fettuccini di scampi not being prepared to his liking but frayed nerves due to the ongoing operation. The last call from Lisbon had not helped much either.

Kovlor's phone danced on the table. He pawed it in one swoop and looked at the caller ID. The screen showed the call was from his most trusted subordinate, so he greedily answered. The conversation didn't last very long. His subordinate informed him of their progress. *All is going well*. His betters would be pleased. Kovlor tried another bite of the scampi and noticed that it was indeed prepared the way he had requested, although he did not let the waitress off the hook.

***

Barrett made it inside the building. He had entered through a side door used by the employees he joined coming in from the east side of the parking lot. Barrett looked up and down the brightly lit hall, scanning first for guards then for cameras, but he didn't see either in this section. No security setup to check IDs inside either. *Guess they left that for the guards at the front gate.*

Barrett observed a number of the returning employees head into a room up the hall and followed them into what passed in Bulgaria as an employee lounge. The area was comprised of a kitchen, living room, and locker room all in one. He smiled in turn and nodded at a couple of workers who passed by. Barrett poured himself some coffee to buy time until the workers left. He didn't have to wait long. Finally alone in the lounge, Barrett went to the lockers, examined a few, and quietly picked one of them open. The American retrieved a jacket and hat with a company logo on each. Though big, they worked, and he put both on.

Now sufficiently disguised, Barrett began to wander around the large building, trying to get his bearings. Most people would be surprised to learn the trick with a great disguise is not in how an individual makes themselves look, but in the way the person acts. Barrett kept this in mind as he continued to search the building. He walked around as if he belonged. He didn't try to make eye contact with anyone, but he didn't avoid it either.

Barrett made his way from the office section toward the more Spartan, warehouse side, glancing into a number of rooms and even entering a few of the vacant ones for a closer peek. In some of those rooms, Barrett noticed a lot of handguns and fully assembled AK-47s and 74s. Some of the other rooms that he strolled through held extra parts for the weapons, but so far, he hadn't seen any manufacturing facilities. The agent deduced the warehouse must be used for storage and as a shipping point for weapons and parts. Regardless of what the rooms held, one thing remained constant: everything had been stacked nice and neat. The place radiated order.

Barrett also kept a lookout for any escape route maps hanging on a wall to help guide him as he walked around, but he found none. This was Bulgaria, after all, and not a warehouse in the States. He would have to improvise. Barrett grabbed a clipboard with an attached legal pad and pencil from an empty office and began to scribble the layout of the warehouse on the second page. Like an obsessed artist, he didn't want anyone to sneak a peek at his artwork.

Walking around with a clipboard also helped with his disguise; it not only gave the appearance of him working but, because normally those who held clipboards in a warehouse signified some sort of authority figure, Barrett reckoned in a ordered place like this it meant no one would ask him any questions.

Barrett continued on, searching more of the warehouse till he found his way to a locked door near the back of the building. The secured door had a lot of warning signs. *This could be interesting.*

The writing in Bulgaria's Cyrillic language forced him to pull out his phone and use its translation program again. *Damn.* He noticed the low battery signal. The converted words read out like a movie: "Restricted Access," "Authorized Personnel Only," and the ubiquitous "Keep Out." This was a good sign, since what could be so sensitive that it had to be restricted in a weapons warehouse? He looked down both sides of the hall to make sure no one was paying him too close attention.

The door had an electronic lock, which used an access card. Barrett had forgotten to ask for one at the gate, so he casually opened the back of his phone and pulled out a plastic credit card, which he then connected via a small wire to the phone's USB port.

Barrett didn't dare to glance around again since he sensed this particular door had to be monitored by a hidden camera. He slid the card through the slot of the reader. The trick here was his phone's decryption software had to decode the lock in almost the same amount of time as an authorized card worked. Anyone standing there for more than a minute would surely raise suspicion. He finished sliding the card and waited. Above the slot, a green light blinked. Barrett turned the handle, opening the door while calmly placing the card and phone into his pocket. He entered the restricted area, not knowing what lay beyond.

***

"We will do whatever we can to help." Director Conley had called the Black Wolf's commanding officer to privately convey his thanks for the unit's support his people received during and after the ambush. The Secretary of Defense had given him McKenna's direct line, handwritten on a piece of paper, after their last meeting with the President. All the head of the Secret Service knew was that McKenna ran some military intelligence unit, but nothing more. In fact, he didn't even know McKenna's office location; he only had McKenna's name and number. Normally, there were many well-placed buffers between units like McKenna's and the civilian agencies. These days, after 9/11, there were so many intelligence agencies Conley had trouble keeping them all straight anyway. But now time was critical if the President's daughter was to be found alive, so Spencer had agreed to pass on the number. The Secretary of Defense also liked Conley and wanted to help him get the apology off his chest as well. As for any more information Conley might want on McKenna's group, he thought it best not to ask.

"Thank you."

"My people aren't exactly trained for a missing person's search, but she is still my responsibility."

"Who is? But between all of us, we will find her." McKenna did his best to try cheering the director up. "How is your team in Nigeria holding up?" He knew the pain Conley had to be feeling after the loss of his agents over in Port Harcourt. McKenna had gone through the same thing more times than he cared to remember since receiving his commission after graduating from West Point. You never got used to losing people under your command even though it was part of the profession. He wrote the letters, attended the funerals, then moved on, though every single one of them had stayed with him in one way or another.

"Good as can be expected. I sent a second team over to assist, and they're working with the locals to find out who conducted the ambush. This tragedy will hit home when they return to the States."

"It's good to keep them focused." McKenna kept the conversation generalized since he wanted to work with the Secret

126

Service, but at this point, he didn't perceive how they could help him any further. Besides, he wanted to keep information about Barrett's actions limited to a few people outside his own unit. A very tricky situation for all involved.

***

Barrett entered a short hallway with doors on either side and one straight ahead. Proceeding down the corridor, he realized the doorway on his right actually led to an even smaller offshoot hallway. It held one open doorway on the left side, and the passageway itself ended a few yards beyond. He saw clearly into the room from his current position. Through the open doorway, he caught sight of three guys. All looked seriously well-developed and out of place in the warehouse. They were even dressed like his two friends back at the hangar. Definitely mercenaries. He even noticed one of them had the same tattoo on his forearm! Getting warm.

The men appeared to be in a deep discussion, speaking what sounded like Serbian to Barrett. While he wasn't fluent in the language, he did pick up the words "bomb," "Turkey," and a demeaning word for Muslims. Strange, since he remembered finding the Muslim prayer beads back in Nigeria. He continued past the short, branched hallway, walked to the end of the original corridor, and peered through the small window in the door.

He had found the garage section of the warehouse. Barrett spied trucks being loaded up with boxes, and in the far corner, he saw a couple of men prepping two Mercedes-Benz sedans. The cars sat low to the ground. *Armored.* Vehicles like those meant one thing; someone important would be moving soon. *Maybe even the PD.* They looked almost finished. Barrett needed to confirm whether the President's daughter was in the building, and if so, the agent would need to act fast.

Barrett backtracked down the hallway. He stole another glance into the room the mercenaries had been in, noticing a fourth man coming through an adjacent door with a full plate of food. All three men stopped their conversation and looked at the incoming guard, who just nodded, shrugged, and locked the door from his side. *What are they guarding?*

127

After another pass down the hall and seeing no other mercenaries around, Barrett determined that if the President's daughter was here, she had to be somewhere behind that inner door. It was as good a guess as any, and he was running out of time. If they moved her again, he would lose all track of her. The agent needed to get in the room. Barrett went out through the restricted door and back to the lounge. The agent searched through the pantry until he found what he needed.

***

Scarov closed his eyes, letting the darkness take over and relax him. He had pushed his men to finish their preparations quicker than originally planned. The transfer was not scheduled for a few hours, but the experienced soldier always liked to be prepared. He wanted to move under the cover of darkness to a secret compound in the low-lying mountains in the central part of the country, which guarded an impregnable complex owned by his master. A place no one would dare look for his captive or even think of attempting a rescue.

Still wary of the Americans' satellite capability, Scarov planned his next move to happen at night. He would not underestimate them. Once at his destination, the final phase of the operation could begin. What happened after that he had not been told, nor did he care.

***

Cleaning supplies. Barrett's excitement grew as he uncovered a few containing ammonia and detergent. Barrett did some quick calculations in his head; he needed just enough to create a little chaos but not enough to blow up the whole room. He measured and mixed before placing the concoction in a small, metal can. Timing was also going to be critical. He took out his Berretta four-inch retractable knife and punched a small hole in the can then set the leaking container on top of a rag. He lighted the end of the rag, which he had soaked in alcohol. Not the type of timer he preferred, but it would have to do. Barrett's experience had taught him that the simple stuff always worked ... mostly.

128

Barrett figured he would need enough time to get in, retrieve Sara, and be on their way outside before the fireworks started. Any sooner, and his enemy might reinforce the security on the girl. In Barrett's experience, diversions on a real world hostage rescue operation hardly ever worked. If someone was protecting something valuable, then as soon as anything out of the ordinary took place, a prudent leader reinforced what he or she was guarding. He preferred to get in and out quietly, but without backup and being outgunned, he planned for the worst. If anything went wrong, and since no plan survives first contact with the enemy, he figured he'd be outnumbered at least ten to one and dragging a civilian along for good measure. Once he recovered the hostage, his options became limited, so he had to work it out now. The idea was to use the ensuing chaos of the employees evacuating as cover for their escape. *As long as everything goes to plan ...*

He finished up his homemade flash-bang contraption and did his best to disguise the device. The science experiment should be all bang with no real collateral damage unless someone was unlucky enough to be standing over the device at detonation. *Oh well; these people do work in a weapons facility,* he justified to himself.

Barrett headed back to the secured area of the building. He used his phone/card combo to unlock the door again and proceeded through the doorway. He took a few steps into the corridor when he suddenly heard a loud bang followed by alarms. Barrett's head dropped. *I always sucked at math.*

CHAPTER 17

Nothing. McKenna leaned back in his chair, more frustrated than he ever remembered. He had spent the last few hours calling contacts all over the world, and other than the recent intelligence he'd received from Barrett in Bulgaria, he knew as much now about the kidnapping as he did when he started.

His acquaintances at MI6, the Mossad, and South African Intelligence, who all had good resources on the continent, were in the dark as well. None of them had uncovered any recent chatter or additional information on the ambush in Nigeria. The other intelligence services assumed the attack had been a local matter.

McKenna obviously couldn't divulge the kidnapping, but he hoped to gain some nugget of information that would help them. If not for the luck of having his team present at the actual ambush, even the Americans would be at a loss. The kidnappers had been unusually successful at covering their tracks. He got out from behind his desk and moved toward his closed door as he switched gears, wondering how Barrett was researching the Bulgarian lead.

**

Barrett turned, surprised, as two mercenaries ran out of the room and passed him without even a glance. He couldn't believe his luck. Well, like Napoleon said, "Do not disturb your enemy when he is making a mistake."

"Now the fun part," he muttered to himself as he put the silencer on his SIG and prepared for his next move. Barrett took two deep breaths, attempting to calm his nerves. His heart always pounded during situations like this. It was a wonder no one else heard it. He thought, *Dominate the room.* He let out the second breath and strolled in.

He marched right up to the closest mercenary, who had his back to the door and was checking his rifle over. The man began to turn, but not in time. Barrett positioned the suppressed pistol six inches from the man's body and squeezed the trigger. Barrett knew he couldn't get too close or the blowback from the bullet impact might cause flesh and blood to jam his sidearm. The SIG coughed twice. The bullets plowed into mercenary number one's side.

As the first mercenary started to fall, Barrett used his left hand to throw his knife at mercenary number two, who stood by the inner door. The blade reflected light as it spun through the air, hitting the well-built soldier right in the throat before he could get out of its way. Startled, he attempted to pull the knife out. Barrett closed in while putting a round into the man's heart, causing him to crash back into a filing cabinet before dropping. Barrett knelt next to the merc and pulled the blade out of his still-twitching body then wiped the blood off on the man's sleeve.

He scanned around to make sure he hadn't missed anyone or anything. The room was clear. Barrett hadn't had time to check for cameras beforehand, but now he couldn't see any. The mercenaries probably didn't want the regular security guards to view their actions.

The up close and personal killings he'd just executed were the only way Barrett could keep his shots from possibly missing their targets, passing through the wall, and hitting someone in the next room. If one hit the President's daughter, his mission would be over. Barrett wiped the men's blood splatter from himself with a hand towel he stored in his jacket. Then he removed his bloodstained jacket and wiped most of the blood off the cheap polyester shell. He would need the jacket for the next part of his plan. As for his plan … so far so good. *Now, what is behind door number one?* He crouched to make himself less of a target, reached for the knob, and slowly opened the door.

Barrett's eyes took a few moments to adjust to the darkness. He scanned the area with his gun acting like a third eye. Other than a couch, the room contained only a chair, floor lamp, and plant in the far corner. *Not real cozy.*

Something stirred on the couch, catching Barrett's attention. He cautiously approached it to get a better look. A dark figure sat motionless. Barrett found the switch for the floor lamp and flipped it on. He waited, gun ready as the light fell across the figure's face.

***

The imposing leader of the mercenaries heard the thud and the alarms before staring at the man at his side. His subordinate immediately got on the radio to find out what happened. He turned to face his boss. "A small explosion in the workers' locker, most likely a case of incompetence." Scarov shook his head. He had concerns about the people here. He felt they posed a risk and had argued to shut down the warehouse during this phase of the operation; of course, Scarov had a low opinion of most eastern Europeans outside of his own kind anyway. His master disagreed.

"Send Milo and Kuvic to help. We do not need any unwanted attention right now. Tell the others to remain and stay aware."

"Yes, sir." The subordinate nodded before issuing the commands into the radio.

***

Sara Hanson had also noticed the alarms and wondered if her day could get any worse. She had been feigning sleep for a while in an attempt to learn more about her situation. Terrified and confused, Sara couldn't sleep anyway. Spying on her kidnappers wasn't easy. They spoke a language she didn't understand, but once in a while, the big one spoke French into a phone, which happened to be the only language other than English she understood. None of what they said made any sense to her though.

Sara had studied French in college to prepare for a summer in Paris after her junior year. God, she wished she was there now: the shops, the cafés, dinner at Le Senderens. *What was that cute guy's name I met while strolling the Champs-Elysees? Jean?* Her thoughts were interrupted when the door to her room opened. She watched it swing inward very slowly.

132

Barrett briefly examined Sara; she didn't appear to be any worse for wear, no visible marks on her face or body. "You okay?"

"Yeah," Sara answered, tight-lipped, while looking Barrett over, shocked to see the producer from the documentary crew walking through the door with a gun drawn. *What's he doing here?*

"Can you move?"

"I'm not dead," she fired back, still not sure if Barrett was one of the bad guys.

Barrett handed her the jacket and cap. "Put this on." He noted the kidnappers had made her change clothes, and she now wore a blue jumpsuit. Sara put the jacket on over her top. Though even bigger on her than Barrett, it would do the job. Barrett looked her over. Outwardly, she appeared calm. *If she's scared, she's doing a good job of hiding it.*

He opened the door and peeked out. The guards' dead bodies still lay as he'd left them. Barrett told Sara to focus on the door in case anyone came in. He wanted to give her something to concentrate on other than the carnage he'd created. Barrett surveyed the front room. He spotted some documents and notes strewn across the table along with a map for Istanbul. The agent pulled out his phone and took a few pictures. He needed to keep some juice in reserve. His charger waited for him back on the jet. It would have helped if Barrett had remembered to charge the phone more than once since he'd left the States. "Seems like they're planning something else," he muttered. "But what?"

"I overheard one of them talking to someone on the phone in French when they were bringing me here." She looked back at him, getting a full view of the room, realizing for the first time that dead bodies lay around them. "Oh my God."

Putting the phone away, he started back for the door. He looked out in the corridor. Empty. He turned to Sara, who'd started to shake. Barrett grabbed her shoulders. "Focus. You're gonna be okay." He paused for a second, studying her. She nodded. "Stay on my six." Barrett tucked his SIG under his shirt then picked up the clipboard he'd dropped outside the office; he needed to keep up appearances for just a little longer.

Sara finally began to realize Barrett might not be a bad guy after all. "Is this a rescue?" she whispered as Barrett led them down the hallway toward the restricted door.

"Depends."

"On what?"

"Whether we get away." Barrett opened the door, motioning for Sara to follow into the unrestricted section. He led her through the building while stealing glances at his impromptu map. The two got closer to the same outside door Barrett had first used to enter the warehouse, so he shoved the map into his pocket. *Almost home.*

Suddenly, one of the mercs appeared in front of them, coming from the same door the pair was heading toward. Just as he marched past, he took a second glance at the pair. His mistake. Barrett caught the man's head turn out of the corner of his eye and didn't hesitate. He spun, stepping toward the man and ramming the wooden clipboard into the merc's throat, crushing his thorax. Barrett then side-kicked him in the back of his thigh, wrapped his arms around the man's neck, and dragged him through the nearest office door.

Once inside the room, which luckily turned out to be empty, Barrett put the man's head in a vice made up of his arms, putting pressure on the carotid artery: a blood choke. In a few seconds, the mercenary stopped struggling and passed out. Barrett left the unconscious man lying on the floor, closing the door behind him.

"Let's keep moving." Barrett kept his voice smooth and calm.

Sara stood still, staring at him, wild-eyed. He ignored her and kept moving toward the door. She followed.

***

"What do we do about the insider threat scenario?" Janice Dooley asked. She occupied the same seat in McKenna's office that Max had sat in only a few days earlier, but without the fidgeting. She never suffered from nervous energy; she was always calm and collected, which helped make her such a good analyst. Dooley had made the trip back to Virginia right after the Nigerian mission went sideways.

SHADOW HUNT

Dooley admired a picture of her boss' family on the credenza behind his desk. The two kids had great smiles, and his wife looked so happy. She knew the colonel to be a very private man. This single picture was the only personal item he displayed unless you counted the blue coffee mug he always used that had an outline of a yellow triangle on it. The personable McKenna never divulged much of his background to anyone. *Such a shame.* His military exploits were a different story. His actions before and during the Afghanistan invasion had made him famous in the special ops community. As she recalled, he'd made quite a name for himself in Afghanistan.

While in the north of Afghanistan, the northern alliance banded together to help America rid the country of the oppressive regime of the Taliban. No such alliance existed in the south. The badlands between Afghanistan and Pakistan were so dangerous even the Taliban had a problem maintaining a tight grip on the region. So right before the American invasion, McKenna led a pathfinder team into southern Afghanistan to develop relationships with the warlords who exercised ruthless control over their dominion. After he accomplished this feat, he directed those same groups into battle against the Taliban and Al-Qaida.

The situation proved difficult at best, but McKenna kept the different factions together and molded them into effective fighting units, all the while leading from the front lines. Through hard work and ingenuity, the ad hoc forces were able to achieve most of their main objectives. McKenna moved up the ranks quickly after the expulsion of the Taliban from power in Afghanistan.

The Army promoted McKenna to light colonel, making him deputy of operations for the unit. He took charge of all Middle Eastern operations and oversaw the unit's participation in Operation: Iraqi Freedom. After living in the Green Zone for two years, he returned to Virginia, and in a short time, McKenna received promotion to full colonel and was more importantly assigned command of his current unit.

Dooley was pulled from her musings by McKenna's voice.

"First, I ordered Barrett to communicate only with the two of us from here on out, and second, I need you to get with the Secret

Service and work up a possible list of individuals who knew about the trip." McKenna leaned forward. "But keep our reason for wanting the names quiet. Let's not tip our hands yet."

"Already done, sir." She placed the list on his desk in front of him.

McKenna should have expected this. In all his years, he had never worked with someone so able to anticipate what needed to be done next. McKenna vowed to never bet against her in a poker game.

The colonel's eyes made quick work of the short list. "How far have you gotten?"

"Through most, but everyone seems clear so far." A little of Dooley's Boston accent came out. This occurred whenever she felt extremely frustrated.

"Keep going. Neither of those two will be safe until we figure this all out."

She nodded in agreement. "Speaking of threats to the President's daughter, how safe will she be with Barrett?"

McKenna smiled slightly. He knew full well of Barrett's reputation as a womanizer. "He's a professional. He can handle himself."

***

Barrett and Sara exited the building and were halfway across the parking lot when movement behind them caught the American agent's attention. The plan was to walk out the gate just like he'd observed other workers doing. Only he expected people to be filing out due to the fire alarm, but that wasn't happening. *Guess they react differently to fire alarms in Bulgaria.*

He should have considered this a possibility when devising his plan, since worker safety wasn't high on the priority list yet in the ex-communist country. Being late afternoon, Barrett thought they might be able to pass themselves off as workers leaving early. Most importantly to their cause was that, in his experience, these places were usually harder to get in than to get out. Besides, Barrett figured that whoever had set up this operation didn't tell everyone in the building who they had locked up in the back room. He planned on using the enemy's operational security against them.

136

Intense-sounding voices reached Barrett from behind them, and he realized something was up. The language clinched it. He didn't know Bulgarian, but he identified the languages uttered now as a mix of Russian and some Serbian spoken with assertiveness, which meant one thing: the mercenaries were hunting them.

Sure enough, when he turned around he saw two of them walking quickly across the parking lot toward the gate. They must have used the same side door to exit the building. Before he had a chance to warn Sara about making any identifiable gestures, she turned around to see what had caught Barrett's attention. The mercenaries immediately recognized her. *Guess the hat and jacket camouflage only went so far.* The two men instantly started to jog toward the gate, calling after the pair, trying to cut them off.

So much for plan A!

CHAPTER 18

Barrett and Sara cleared the gate ahead of the two men, but their pursuers were quickly closing the gap. Only about thirty yards separated them. Barrett could almost feel their breath on the back of his neck. He heard one of them talking on a radio. Time was running out. They turned at the gate and walked swiftly along the sidewalk on the same side of the road as the warehouse, heading toward his borrowed Skoda.

The pair passed a few parked cars with Barrett using every mirror, window, or polished metal he found on those cars to keep an eye on their pursuers. The reflections provided the agent with a good idea of the gunmen's movements, especially how close they were getting. *Too close.*

Barrett grabbed Sara's arm and pulled her behind a small box truck. He drew his SIG then took a slow peek around the side. The mercenaries had split up, with each one taking a different side of the parked cars. Barrett decided to engage the one walking down the street-side of the vehicles since he could box them in between the road and fence that surrounded the warehouse. He motioned with his hand for Sara to stay put while he began to step up and out from the front of the truck.

He rose with his weapon, firing twice before his target had time to do the same. The mercenary's body twisted violently as rounds slammed into his torso, knocking him down. Barrett pointed to the Skoda and whispered for Sara to cross the road and head for the car. He was hoping to use Sara to draw out the other mercenary. He knew the mercenary wouldn't shoot her since her value lay in her being a living hostage. *I hope.* Sara reached the car without incident.

The remaining mercenary didn't bite. *The merc is good.* Barrett waited a few more moments before heading to the Skoda. No shots interrupted his short trek. The agent took his time in the driver's seat of the sedan.

The merc finally appeared across the street, directly parallel to them. Barrett's show of slowly settling into the car had paid off. He sat in the driver seat with his SIG's muzzle resting on the door with the window down. Barrett let loose with two rounds that dropped the man as he tried to cross the street. Barrett's two shots didn't kill him instantly. The mercenary's body flexed while falling forward. This caused the man's finger to squeeze the trigger on his non-suppressed assault rifle. Two loud rounds popped off harmlessly into the street, but the damage had been done. The loud retorts reverberated loudly down the street.

The American agent engaged the clutch and pulled the car out of the space and into the road before suddenly stopping. Barrett jumped out and ran over to the body now sprawled dead in the middle of the street; he grabbed an arm and, using what little juice remained in his phone, took a picture of the tattoo.

Suddenly, rounds started to skip and dance around him as another mercenary joined the party. He fired from fifty yards away by the gatehouse—too far for his shots to be accurate with a pistol. Barrett raced back to the car. While jumping in, he heard Sara exclaim, "You're crazy." He ignored her, backing the Skoda away from both the gate and the firing gunman.

"Hold on." Barrett put the car in reverse, gunned the engine, pulled the parking brake, and, with tires squealing, performed a reverse one-hundred-and-eighty-degree turn. Once the car straightened out, he headed through the intersection and melted into the traffic on the highway.

***

The cool breeze blowing off the water always helped Johan Kress stay focused during his afternoon game of chess. He enjoyed nothing better than to get bathed in wind and sunshine while on his yacht taking on a challenger in his favorite pastime. Chess told him plenty about a person. Right now, his opponent, a potential new business associate from Spain, was making a lot of hasty moves; no planning or real foresight seemed to precede his actions. Realizing this with the game almost over, Kress had already decided to forgo any dealings with the Spaniard.

Johan Kress, an Oxford-educated Austrian, had served some time in his nation's military before realizing his future lay in the arms trade. *Much better to be the one who supplies the weapons than the one who has to use them*, he always thought. He also lived a very expensive lifestyle, which few careers supported so well.

His business acumen and ruthlessness helped him carve out a lucrative thirty-year career. While successful beyond his dreams at selling arms, he also found other ways to make even more money. One of his mantras was never deviated from. *Empty space is wasted space*. Whenever his planes would fly arms in, they would always move some form of other cargo out. His transports, whether by plane, boat, train, or truck, never returned empty, thus he always generated revenue. This helped in providing an excellent cover for them as well.

Another important attribute was in the acceptance of clients. He knew in order to have a long career in his chosen profession, one not only had to always deliver as promised, but also needed to choose the right sides. Kress, aware other arms dealers traded indiscriminately to both sides of the same conflict in their chase for money, realized early on Western countries were the better bet. They had more money and stability than the others. Although the west could be very fickle, he figured that was the price of doing business.

Through his dealings, Kress became very useful to some of the Western powers, who in certain situations could not publicly support certain regimes. In these cases, he would help to facilitate the movement of people and arms covertly so the countries involved remained in the background and anonymous. These transactions not only brought him great revenue, but also helped Kress accumulate a lot of favors from the respective governments. Those favors were more valuable to him than any amount of money he made during the arrangements.

The arms dealer's hundred-foot yacht *Zephyros* sat anchored in a cove overlooked by his estate on the island of Amorgos in the Greek Isles. The jewel of the Cycladic set of islands, Amorgos provided Kress with the perfect sanctuary. First of all, the island was not easy to get to; ferry and catamaran services were only plentiful in the summer months. Even then, when tourists flowed in, the craggy mountains still gave him a strong sense of privacy. But if he felt bored, Amorgos supplied Kress with some outdoor activities like hiking and world class scuba diving sites, though the Austrian never understood other people's passion for mountain climbing. He also had a variety of good cafés and bars to visit should he decide to venture out at night. Kress kept entertaining others at his home to a minimum, preferring to meet on more neutral sites.

While his estate contained every possible convenience a successful arms dealer desired, it was on his yacht Kress enjoyed spending the bulk of his time. As he moved his knight to finish off his opponent once and for all, the subtle warning tone of an incoming email grabbed his attention. Kress turned toward his phone, read the name on the display, and smiled.

***

"I cannot stress the importance of finding her," Kovlor snarled at his subordinate over the phone. "They must still be in the country."

"Yes," grumbled his subordinate.

"Failure is not acceptable." Kovlor made his point with as much venom as possible before hanging up.

Scarov grunted, not needing the threat. He gazed around the garage in the warehouse where the President's daughter had been held. He was not happy either. *Someone is going pay.*

***

Barrett kept checking his rearview mirror. So far so good as they continued to make their escape. He drove as normally as possible, doing his best not to attract any attention. Like most of his assignments, the key was blending in.

Sara stared at Barrett and said, "You're not a documentarian, are you?"

"No." Barrett continued to concentrate on driving.

"So you some kind of Special Forces guy or what?"

"Just consider me a friend." Barrett turned to look at her. Paused. *Here we go.* "I need you to take off everything you are wearing."

"What!" She stared at him in horror.

"Please." He was trying to be as polite but also direct as possible. *We could be getting tracked right now.* "Take off your clothes and any jewelry then grab the bag in the backseat and put on the clothes you'll find inside. Once you're done, place all of your old stuff in the bag so we can dispose of it. They may have planted a tracking device on you, and I don't want to take any chances." He nodded toward the bag of clothes he'd bought in a boutique shop after he used the ATM. He did give some thought that her captors might have implanted a device internally, but he discounted the possibility because that type of scenario would leave evidence behind if she ever got examined. Alive or dead, the U.S. government would never stop looking for the body. These men were professional enough to realize that.

Barrett had convinced her. She stopped staring at him as if he had three heads and crawled into the backseat to comply with his request. A tight squeeze. "Don't you dare look." Barrett shook his head. *Now, the hard part begins.*

***

Secretary of Defense Spencer didn't make many trips down to the Black Wolf's control and command center at Fort Belvoir. The command center, or CCU, was located in the basement of the unit's headquarters. From here, any direct action mission considered vital could be monitored in real time via satellite. Aerial or human-provided imagery was displayed on a silver screen in the front and on consoles in individual workstations, which ran the length of the sides and center of the room. For some operations, there might be only an audio feed for the CCU's occupants to hear.

The center was only staffed during these operations with analysts to review the information and if needed provide immediate assistance to those in the field. Right now, the two men stood alone

142

inside. When not in use, the center provided a great place for a private conversation.

"So no further information other than Barrett's following up on the intel in Bulgaria?"

"Correct." McKenna wished he had more. "It's the best lead we have right now, though we've not received any further intel from him since 1630 hours."

"What about the transport?" Spencer sat down on the corner of an empty desk.

"The jet's been released. I've ordered Major Wright to fly to Cyprus and hold fast till we know more." McKenna paused, preparing his next statement with care. "There is an additional item I want to talk to you about."

The Secretary of Defense grinned. "I wondered why we were meeting here."

McKenna went on to discuss the theory of a possible insider that had been developing over the course of their investigation.

"Okay." Spencer sighed when McKenna finished. He was no longer grinning. "I will update the President. A separate, discreet meeting will be needed to discuss the insider theory with him. In the meantime, I will make JSOC deploy a special ops team to Cypress in case you need them for additional support." He then picked up the secured phone in front of him, dialed the White House and, as usual, was put on hold.

***

"Who were those guys?" Sara asked, settling back into the front passenger seat after changing her clothes. She was surprised everything fit, but remembered the Secret Service had her vital statistics in a database somewhere, which she assumed was where he gotten her information. But still the jeans, blouse, and shoes were made of good quality and comfortable. *This guy has good taste.*

"Not sure."

"What did they want with me?"

Barrett shrugged his shoulders. "Other than the obvious?"

143

"You don't know much, do you?" She let the sarcasm flow. Barrett answered her with a cynical gaze. "Well." She turned to face Barrett. "Thank you."

Barrett gave her a nod then glanced in the rearview mirror. He saw cars moving toward them at high speed. Barrett kept his own speed steady, hoping it was just someone trying to get to their destination in a hurry. *Maybe some gangster in a rush to whack somebody.* The car, a new Mercedes, got to within a couple of car lengths then began to slow.

"Crap." He recognized the car as one of the two being prepped back at the garage in the warehouse. They must be using a tracking device after all, which Barrett hadn't gotten rid of in time.

"Hang on." Barrett knew the Mercedes had a lot of straightaway speed, but he hoped the recent modifications kept the German car from being nimble. He was going to test this theory. Barrett stepped on the gas and began to weave in and out of traffic. He did keep his speed manageable. No point in losing control and careening off the road. The Mercedes tried to match his moves, but the American soon became aware the other car was reacting a little slower. *They probably armored the vehicle. Now how to take advantage?*

He started to hear popping noises in the background. Gunfire.

"Down." Barrett tried to weave the car even more to lessen the odds of their attackers' bullets finding their targets. The gunfire, however, continued unabated, but so far, nothing had hit the rear window or penetrated the vehicle. These guys were too good to miss with all of those shots. *They were going for the tires ...* It made sense if they wanted any chance of getting the girl back alive. Taking out the rear tires or engine while leaving the driver somewhat in control of the vehicle was their best likelihood of success. He hated ops when his opponents had been well-trained.

A black and red Kawasaki Ninja speed bike that had initially been hanging back started coming up alongside his car. Barrett hoped it was just someone trying to get out of the way of the two crazy drivers zigzagging down the road. His eyes followed the motorcycle as a hunched driver swung closer. *Crap.* He had a passenger hanging on with one hand and holding a machine pistol in the other. The two vehicles were trying to box in the Skoda. He swerved, causing the speed bike to back off a bit and slow down.

The Ninja must have been employed as a scout to chase down the signal of the tracking device. *Smart.* Now, they used the bike to help control the Skoda's direction while the gunmen attempted to disable Barrett's Skoda. The maneuver had a chance if both vehicles had been Mercedes or any car for that matter, but a motorcycle? This meant one thing: desperation. The bike couldn't weigh more than five hundred pounds, no match for Barrett's sedan. If he could get rid of these two quick, then they might actually have a chance of getting away. *One problem at a time,* he thought, gripping the steering wheel a little tighter. He chose the motorcycle first.

Barrett could eventually lose the Mercedes, but the Ninja with its twin engines displacing six hundred cc would be a different story. It was faster and more agile than his sedan. On the flip side, the speed bike should be easier to dispose of. Barrett now focused completely on the motorcycle, waiting for the driver to make another move to get alongside. He obliged.

Barrett spun the steering wheel in the direction of the oncoming motorcycle, turning the car directly into the bike's path. The Skoda's front right end slammed the speed bike, sending it careening off the road, spilling the driver and shooter over the embankment. Both riders went flying through the air, spinning like gyros before they came crashing down to earth. One problem down.

CHAPTER 19

Barrett and the Mercedes driver tried to outfox each other with sporadic gunfire and screeching tires serving as the soundtrack to the chaotic scene. Barrett likened the whole affair to a high-speed game of chess. Thankfully, their attackers wanted the girl alive, so no bullets were fired into the cabin of their car … yet. The mercenaries were still attempting to disable his car by trying to take out the engine and tires, but Barrett wasn't making himself an easy target. The two cars continued to cut in and out of traffic when Barrett realized they were coming up on a passenger bus.

How could he use the slow-moving bus to his advantage? Barrett scanned the highway. A narrow underpass loomed a short distance ahead. He took a quick peek down at the map on his lap then at Sara still crouching low in her seat. "Get in the back, put the belt on, and stay low." Sara gave him the deer in the headlights stare, but it only lasted for a few seconds before she crawled over the middle console into the backseat. He heard the click of her seatbelt.

Barrett's side of the highway narrowed to one paved lane with a gravel track on the inside ending at the underpass. He maneuvered the Skoda behind the bus then cut over onto the gravel. The car began to vibrate. Barrett hoped the Mercedes driver would be too preoccupied with following the Skoda to look ahead.

Barrett massaged the steering wheel. He would only get one chance at this. The agent stepped on the accelerator, matching the bus's speed, and the Mercedes took the bait. The mercenary driving the other car accelerated, staying right behind the Skoda. He watched as the Skoda abruptly swerved over in front of the bus, cutting right in front. The driver of the Mercedes continued to follow the crazy maneuver of the American with his eyes, thinking the driver had to be some sort of cowboy. Suddenly, something dark invaded his peripheral vision. The driver turned his attention back to the road ahead. His eyes widened. The concrete pillar filled his vision.

The Mercedes rammed the concrete barrier. The hood crumpled, and the vehicle flipped sideways. The car rolled violently four times, being crushed smaller and smaller with every roll before finally coming to a stop. The smashed vehicle was no longer identifiable as the Mercedes Barrett had first spotted back in the warehouse. Barrett didn't slow down to admire his handiwork. He pushed the Skoda hard to separate them from the accident site for as long as he dared before slowing to a normal driving pace, blending in with the traffic once again.

In case he was wrong about there being a tracker inside the President's daughter, Barrett pulled the car over, opened his door, and went to the back seat. He took out his knife and cut open the cloth netting protecting one of the rear speakers. He unscrewed the casing on the speaker to remove its magnet. Magnets worked wonders in disrupting electrical signals and damaging electrical devices as a whole. Just ask anyone with a pacemaker. He had Sara rub the black cylinder all over her body like soap while he cut the second magnet out. This would have to do till they got somewhere she could be inspected more thoroughly. He made her place both magnets on her person as she sat in the front passenger seat. Barrett now followed the escape route he had worked on while hiding in the van.

"So, Mister Not-a-Documentarian, where are we going?" Sara was still recovering from the car chase.

"The coast."

"Why? Isn't there an easier way out? Can't you just call someone to pick us up?"

"No. This has to be low key and free of any international incidents. Your father kept your kidnapping a secret." Sara displayed no reaction. She had been the President's daughter long enough to know how these things worked. "Since neither of us hold proper IDs, public transportation like trains, buses, and planes are out, as is any type of official border crossing." He continued to keep an eye on the rearview mirror. "There is a small U.S. presence at a NATO base here, but it's mostly for show and probably the first place those guys will stake out. I doubt we will even make the gate. Our best bet is to find a private boat and charter it to Turkey."

Barrett figured their enemy had to have a reason for bringing her here, and one of the main ones might be connections in the government. How high they went, he didn't want to find out.

Barrett planned to stay off the grid and avoid places the enemy would expect, so the base outside of Burgas was out, as was trying to catch a ferry from Varna. The agent also considered heading directly to the Greek border a no-go as well. He wanted to take the longer—but in his mind the safer—way out of the country. Plus, the fact he'd discovered a lot of Turkish information in the mercs' possession back at the warehouse made him very interested in the country. Barrett didn't think he should bring the President's daughter in yet, so they had to hide out from everybody. *Might as well put our time to good use.*

He also chose not to alarm the young lady with the idea of a possible inside connection to her abduction. He'd ask her later at a better time. Barrett hoped Sara would become more relaxed and forthcoming once she got to a certain comfort level with him. He needed time.

The sun began to set as the Skoda headed east along the Sofia-Varna Road. Barrett wanted to make Varna soon. He desperately needed to dump the car. Not only could the bad guys ID the sedan, but someone must have reported the auto stolen by now. Also, traffic began to thin as the hour got later, making it easier for them to be spotted. Barrett studied a Sveti Kirov-created map he'd obtained from a gas station to guide them along in lieu of scarcely placed road signs when the car passed a large number of tall, whitish-yellow pillars spread out like trees.

"What's that?" Sara stared out the window. Barrett turned his head toward her, catching sight of the natural phenomenon.

"The Stone Forest. I read an article in a guidebook. Apparently they are made of sandstone."

"Cool."

Barrett planned on putting in for the night at Varna before heading down the coast to the port city of Nessebar. At Nessebar, he hoped to find a boat to rent and a captain who didn't ask too many questions. If that didn't work, he figured they could always borrow one.

**

"You have failed at your job." Scarov scolded the sweating man standing in front of him inside the warehouse's garage. The fat man, Demeter Nagy, couldn't stop his body from shaking while he stared at the Makarov pistol in Scarov's hand.

"You are head of my counter-intelligence team. It is your responsibility to keep me apprised of any operations directed at us."

"I do not know what ha—" Nagy's excuse was cut off by the loud retort of the Makarov. The round blew open the back of the man's head, silencing him forever. Scarov watched, emotionless, as the body fell. "Find her." He left the remaining men standing around as he marched away. *That should motivate them.*

**

Barrett and Sara entered the coastal town of Varna just after sunset. Barrett found a quaint little bed and breakfast to crash for the night. Their sanctuary was a typical ninetieth-century, Bulgarian-built house painted yellow and orange on the outside with an ornately carved, wooden ceiling on the inside. The home's second floor extended out over the first, running the length of the front supported by wooden pillars. This made for a grand covered porch where most of the guests liked to spend their leisure time after a day of activities at the beach.

Barrett liked the place. Cozy with no other guests lingering around. He passed the two of them off as Brits taking a late vacation. The elderly couple who owned and ran the establishment, being typical Bulgarians, didn't ask many questions. Barrett's eyes lingered on an older office phone on a corner table in the living room. Afraid to give his location away and not sure how connected the bad guys were, he turned down the strong urge to use the lobby phone to report in. He knew that a country like Bulgaria probably still used the old, centralized router boxes for outgoing international calls from landlines, so any call to a U.S. number might be flagged. How he loved communist paranoia. Besides, he still had the thought of an insider playing in his mind. He even began to question using his own phone if he ever got the thing recharged.

With no other guests in the bed and breakfast, Barrett had his pick of the rooms. As they toured the second floor, the wooden planks under their feet creaked with every step. Good. This would give Barrett plenty of warning should anyone attempt to sneak up on them. He chose one at the farthest end of the hall right next to the bathroom. The room only had one window and, short of a ladder, nothing could help someone climb up the side of the house—definitely the least approachable spot in the place.

Barrett refused to let the President's daughter out of his sight, so both of them made a supply run to a nearby grocery store. The small, family-run business had a limited number of products, but he found some food for them along with hair dye and scissors for Sara. Barrett worried as much about Sara's celebrity as First Daughter as he did the kidnappers. The agent wanted her to become as anonymous as possible. There is an old saying: "Anonymity has stopped more bullets than all the protective armor in the world put together." Experience had taught him to agree with the sentiment.

Back in their room, they both showered and ate. Sara used a mirror to look over her body for any signs of a surgical procedure. She saw no evidence. The tracker must have been attached to her clothes. Both remained quiet for a while. Sara still appeared a little shaken from the whole ordeal, and Barrett wanted to concentrate fully on the task at hand.

"You can have the bed." He pushed the wooden desk in front of the door. The antique writing desk barely blocked it. *Old habits are hard to break.*

"You don't talk much." Sara studied him, still trying to figure out the stranger who'd saved her. She studied the toned body, the power emanating from his movements, and the confidence radiating from his dark eyes. *He has potential.*

Barrett answered her with a shrug while he prepared a spot for himself in the corner of the room. This position provided him with a good vantage point, allowing him to cover both the door and window at the same time. Barrett wasn't in the mood for any small talk. His mind stayed totally focused on keeping them safe, or so he told himself as he avoided eye contact while preparing for the night ahead.

***

President Hanson had been having trouble focusing on his agenda lately. As President, he knew that he could be a potential target for terrorists and others trying to make a name for themselves, but he'd never thought this could happen to Sara. The guilt ate away at him minute by minute. He sat alone in his private office on the second floor of the White House, trying to get some work done when the Secretary of Defense entered, escorted in by one of Glavine's deputies. Unlike the more famous Oval Office, or "the Oval" as it was referred to by White House staff, which sat in the adjoining West Wing, this office was located upstairs right next to the private residence of the President and his family, making it much more conducive for the country's chief executive officer to do his work.

Of course, on this occasion where the Secretary of Defense requested a private meeting with the President, the location worked out well. The Oval sat not only in the busier annex of offices with people coming and going at all hours in the West Wing, but the office always had a guard posted outside who signed in every guest that entered the famous workplace.

"Good evening, Will." The President's welcome was filled with his usual warmth. He stood up to shake Spencer's hand and then motioned for him to sit down on the chair across from the Victorian desk Ulysses S. Grant had bought for his cabinet so many years ago. Hanson tried to put on his best front, but Spencer could see the pain in the other man's eyes. President or not, the man was still a father. In the short time they'd worked together, the Secretary of Defense had come to respect and admire Hanson even though they had their differences, especially on how the War on Terror should be fought.

"Same to you, Mr. President, and thank you for seeing me in this manner." Secretary Spencer steeled himself in preparation for the discussion ahead.

"Welcome to the Treaty Room. This is where, after the Spanish-American War, the peace treaty was signed, which ultimately gave the place its name. I'm not sure if you have been in here before?"

"No, first time I've had the pleasure, Mr. President." Spencer looked around the office, seeing pictures of the President's family and extended family along with some of the President's personal memorabilia.

Anywhere else in America, all the old furniture and art would be behind ropes or glass, but here in the Executive Mansion on Pennsylvania Avenue, the stuff was actually being used. The Treaty Room also displayed the disparity in time that paralleled the existence of the republic with a grand, old clock, which Spencer figured must have been as old as the mansion itself, sitting on the floor directly across from a new LCD television. The private office definitely seemed the most personal place he had ever met with the President.

"I hoped you had good news on Sara when you requested this meeting, but from your demeanor I imagine that is not the case." The President shifted in his chair, looking across the room at Chartran's large portrait of the men signing the peace protocol between the U.S. and Spain. The Americans, dressed in black formal wear, looked so happy and dignified, having just accomplished a major undertaking. Nothing like how he felt on this night.

"No, sir." The Secretary of Defense didn't even want to think how he would handle a situation like this if one of his three children had been kidnapped. Regardless of one's position in life, it was one of a parent's worst nightmares. He took a breath. "Mr. President, there is a possibility your daughter's kidnapping might have had inside help. The execution of the ambush was too well-planned to be spur of the moment. The people responsible most likely had advance knowledge of both her visit and individual movements."

"I can't say this hasn't crossed my mind as well. Although I was hoping it was a father's overreaction." The President sighed. *The most powerful man in the world they say …*

"I have a list of officials who were aware of Sara's trip. We are looking into them right now, but is there anyone else that might have had knowledge of the trip not listed that you can think of, sir?" Spencer passed him the copy.

The President reviewed the printout. "Not at this moment, but I will give it some thought. Let's keep this info tight." The President reverted back to using vernacular from his flying days. "We know how this town can be." Hanson still dreaded having to tell his wife what had happened, though it would be much worse if she found out through the media. If this went on any longer, he wouldn't have a choice.

"Yes, Mr. President."

***

The next morning, Barrett and Sara woke refreshed and ready for the next phase of Barrett's rescue plan: a forty-mile trip down the coast to Nessebar. The uneventful night in the barricaded room had allowed Barrett to sneak in a couple hours of much-needed sleep. They borrowed a Saab sedan that happened to be parked a short walk from the bed and breakfast and headed south.

Barrett first thought he would "borrow" a Porsche 911 parked next to the Saab, but figured with his luck lately the sports car probably belonged to a gangster. He had enough trouble already. At least Sara seemed better today. She appeared to embrace her shorter and darker hairstyle, which she said was symbolic of her no longer being a victim even if her rescuer didn't see it that way. The change invigorated her. Before the pair departed, Barrett did risk a call to someone he hoped could help without attracting attention.

***

Johan Kress looked at his dancing phone, not recognizing the number displayed on the screen. The arms dealer considered not bothering to answer when he remembered how few people actually had the number to his private cell. *Who could it be?* Kress finally decided to answer the call to satisfy his curiosity and was glad he did.

153

"Max, my friend, where in the devil are you calling from, and don't tell me you lost that fancy phone of yours?"

The paths of the two men had crossed for the first time two years before when Barrett was deployed on a mission for the unit. Barrett had been assigned to a small task force that included members of Britain's top secret intelligence unit, 14Int Group, or what was now called the Special Reconnaissance Regiment. The combined British/American team attempted to track a shipment of weapons in Hong Kong believed to be on their way to North Korea. While monitoring the cargo container full of arms housed in a warehouse at the port, the communication specialist picked up chatter about a future hit on a Western businessman. The team leader assigned Barrett to investigate the potential target. The target turned out to be Johan Kress.

Barrett spent the next week studying every detail about the man, peeling away layers of corporations and front companies. Information gathered from all the sources at the combined agency's disposal. The more he learned, the more he realized he didn't know about Johan Kress. Something wasn't right.

Kress immediately became aware of the task force's surveillance. His contacts in both governments had apprised him of the situation. They had the right people send communiqués to shut down the investigation. As for the probable hit, both governments knew Kress would be capable of taking care of himself. The order to back off made Barrett more interested than ever.

Barrett still wanted to get a better sense of Kress, so against his commander's objections, he approached the Austrian at his hotel and boldly challenged him to a game of chess. Barrett had learned through his research how much Kress loved the game and thought this was his best way in. Unfortunately, with Barrett being a novice at chess, the Austrian crushed him. During the match, each man sized up the other. They philosophized about governments and religion, discussed each man's passion for history and art, and ended up creating a rapport that had lasted ever since.

Kress didn't like many people. Most he considered either dumb or boring, not worth his time and effort. But something about the American intrigued him. The young man was confident enough to humiliate himself for his mission and never backed down during their disagreements, all the while remaining a good sport. His arguments had been well thought out, displaying a bright and educated mind. He'd earned Kress's respect.

"Bulgaria and no, phone's out of juice." Barrett kept looking over his shoulder to make sure no one overheard the conversation.

"I'm sorry you are in such an awful place." Kress never was one to hold back his opinion.

"You don't know the half of it."

"Well, I imagine you're not calling about the weather."

"No. Any ideas on the tattoo pic I sent you? I've run a dead end everywhere else." He couldn't shake the feeling he had encountered them before.

"It's interesting," responded Kress. "I've seen pictures of men with these tattoos who are part of Andrei Kovlor's organization."

"Andrei Kovlor?" Barrett repeated, wanting to make sure he got the name right.

"Yes, he came out of nowhere in the early part of this century. The Russian started moving arms and drugs into Africa from Eastern Europe. As you know, when the Iron Curtain fell, this left a lot of unused weapons available for the right price. The glut of weapons drove the prices of arms so far down that I almost got depressed." Barrett smiled. Kress continued his lecture. "He uses a lot of fellow Russians and Eastern Europeans for muscle, as you Americans like to say, and is especially fond of surrounding himself with ex-Spetsnaz members. The man is known to have hired plenty of them over the years." The Spetsnaz were the special forces of the Russian army, the most highly trained soldiers in their arsenal.

"After communism ended and the Russian army fell into such disarray, it became easy to recruit them. With all the problems in Russia during the '90s, many of them were just glad to receive a paycheck. He also hired a number of ex-GRU agents to help expand his business, using their contacts in various governments and rebel factions across Asia and Africa. This group is very well financed, organized, and ruthless."

Barrett thought Kress would have made a great professor. "So you know them?"

"Max, my dear boy, they are my competition!"

Barrett knew this meant his enemy had to be taken seriously. While there were a lot of arms dealers operating in the world, Kress considered only a few to be his actual competition. Not many had the connections, money, and manpower to rival the Austrian. A well-connected and financed organization with Spetsnaz soldiers and ex-Russian military intelligence agents was the last thing Barrett wanted to hear. *What did I get myself into?*

CHAPTER 20

The drive down the coast gave Barrett and his passenger a chance to take in the beauty of the Black Sea and the old towns dotting the coastline. Leaving behind the city nicknamed the Pearl of the Black Sea, though Barrett thought it looked more like a run-down old port, they began to see the golden beaches and blue-green waters, which for many were the main attraction of the Bulgarian coast. Once Barrett guided the Saab past the town of Obzor, they came into the more populated and growing areas along the coast. The first area was the section known as Sunny Beach, a popular destination for Europeans, especially Brits, who were responsible for buying most of the seaside villas that had sprung up in this part of Bulgaria.

Barrett decided now was a good time to question the President's daughter about her kidnapping. "Ms. Hanson."

"Sara."

"Okay, Sara, did you tell anyone about your trip other than those cleared by your Secret Service detail?"

"No, they were real strict. If I did, I wouldn't have been able to go. I so wasn't going to jeopardize this trip. My life's been pretty boring since my dad became the President."

"So you didn't tell any friends or boyfriends by accident?"

"No, and I don't have a boyfriend."

"You are absolutely sure."

"About telling someone or if I have a boyfriend?"

Barrett gave her the "I'm serious" look, doing his best to ignore how cute she appeared when she slightly tilted her head downwards.

"Yes, and why so many questions?"

"I believe someone who knew about the trip gave the details to your kidnappers."

"Oh my God." Her jaw dropped. He didn't say any more, letting the information sink in.

They sat in silence as the car continued to pass more construction sites sprawled out down the seaside, which reminded both Americans of a lot of beaches in the United States where demand for cheap, scenic vacation spots ate away at pristine coastlines. Seeing some of the construction sites abandoned didn't help. In Barrett's eyes, the coast appeared to be overdeveloped and on the way to being ruined.

They made Nessebar by late morning. The popular tourist town sat on a large, rocky peninsula jutting into the Black Sea; the small peninsula provided a scenic backdrop of water from almost everywhere. Barrett parked the car two blocks from the harbor, so he and Sara walked the rest of the way. Barrett figured with Bulgaria's reputation for smuggling, they shouldn't have much difficulty finding a boat to take them to Turkey without a lot of questions asked.

The town's port was lined with a number of seafood restaurants in and around the small passenger terminal. Thankfully, things were quiet this time of the year. With the summer onslaught of tourists over, now only a trickle of visitors remained. The congestion at the port normally caused by the numerous taxis and buses fighting over tourist dollars was a distant memory.

The Americans quickly cut through the terminal and started to head for the docks. The slips were lined with private vessels. Barrett peered back over his shoulder toward the terminal. A man who seemed to be asking a lot of questions grabbed his attention. *A coincidence?* This didn't matter since Barrett never believed in them anyway. Looking closer, he noticed a slight bulge in the man's jacket. He definitely was carrying a weapon and not doing a good job of hiding it. The guy also never pulled out any identification when he approached bystanders like a policeman would. *One of the mercenaries involved in the girl's kidnapping?*

"How did they find us?" Sara spotted the same mercenary.

"They haven't found us yet. I bet they're just covering their bases." Barrett searched around. "Come on."

He led Sara toward one of the fishing boats he'd noticed on their way toward the wharf, a common-looking thirty-footer with a covered fly-bridge. The vessel looked beat up with its white paint flaking off and rust showing throughout. But the agent knew the reputation of Bulgarian smugglers; some of these boats were probably a lot more than they showed. He simply needed to find the right one.

On one particular boat, Barrett's eye caught how clean and ordered the tie ups and decks had been kept. This meant that the captain took pride in his work. Barrett bet that the engines and other mechanics of the vessel were well taken care of too. Plus, he liked the name painted on the back of it. *The Lone Ranger.*

Barrett strolled over, crossing the gangway. The older gentleman Barrett approached was on the boat's stern, lying back on a chair with a hat and dark sunglasses, taking in the morning sun. Barrett got his attention and worked to find a common language. The man, who told Barrett just to call him Roy, spoke a little English. The two began to negotiate. Barrett could tell Roy had done this before. His confidence in the captain went up. The American agent and Roy settled on a price, and he agreed to transport them to Istanbul. Barrett used most of his remaining cash to secure Captain Roy's pricey services and waved Sara over to the boat. *The Bulgarians seem to be taking well to capitalism.*

***

Kress sat behind his seventieth-century mahogany desk back in his office at the Amorgos estate. The antique desk had once been used by a member of the ruling Hapsburg family in his native Austria. Kress believed money along with a person's deeds made them noble today, not blood; therefore, he thought the desk represented him perfectly well.

Kress couldn't get the question out of his head. *What is Kovlor doing that would attract the attention of the Americans and in particular a unit so highly placed as Max's?* Kress didn't know the exact agency his American friend worked for. Even he didn't have those kinds of

159

connections, but the arms dealer still had his assumptions. His American friend was too well-trained to be with the FBI or DEA, and too worldly seasoned to be CIA. He had the confidence and experience that only came from specialized military training.

The arms dealer had also heard the rumor late yesterday about a prominent American being kidnapped somewhere in Africa, but this was not the sort of thing Kovlor or his organization would get involved in. It would be much too high profile and attract a lot of unwanted attention. That was never good for business, and for all his shortcomings, Kovlor always demonstrated good business sense. The Austrian was now too distracted to get any work done. *Something definitely smells rotten in Denmark.*

He rang the bell on the table in front of him. Kress liked tradition. The only modern items on his desk were his cell phone and the laptop he was currently using. The rest of the office came right out of a Victorian-era picture. Books covered the walls, padded ornate chairs sat on the other side of the desk, and a super-sized antique globe stood on a stand in the far corner of his office.

"Yes." Graham, Kress's tall, English-bred butler, seemed to appear from out of nowhere. Kress considered him indispensable.

"Call Frederick, I need to take a quick trip."

"Right away." Graham disappeared just as quickly as he arrived.

***

Since it would take a few minutes for the captain and his one crewmember to get the boat ready, Barrett stood guard on the boat's stern, observing the approaches from the dock.

He used *The Lone Ranger's* sidewall for cover from anyone strolling down the slip. After a while of keeping a lookout, he came to the conclusion that the preparations for their departure were taking too long. Not that he could be considered an expert on boats, but this was a small one, and they planned on a relatively short trip.

Barrett left his observation post and went looking for Captain Roy. He discovered him playing with some gauges on the bridge. "What's taking so long?"

"Waiting for my first mate to give me the status of the engines."

"Tonto's not here. He headed onto the docks a few minutes ago." Barrett pointed with his thumb in the general direction of the marina terminal.

The captain looked genuinely shocked at hearing his crewmate was no longer on board.

"I thought you had sent him on an errand." Barrett's gut began to churn. This was not good. "We need to leave right now." He immediately headed for the stern's line. As he bent over to untie the line, he caught sight out of the corner of his eye of someone heading toward them, someone who moved with the swagger of ex-military. *Great ...*

Barrett kept low, creeping back in the direction of the covered bridge. He drew the Sig, keeping his eyes on the mercenary. Before he made it to the bridge, a loud thump startled Barrett, followed by the boat rocking. He turned just in time to be rammed to the ground by another merc.

While the first mercenary deliberately allowed himself to be seen, the second one had snuck around to catch the agent by surprise. Their plan worked well. The second mercenary had Barrett pinned to the deck on his back and while on top started to work over the American's midsection. Classic ground and pound action.

Barrett, frantically searching with his fingers for anything that would help him get out of his predicament, discovered the bottom of the deck mop. He gripped it tight, swinging with all the strength he could muster. Barrett didn't have great leverage, but the handle hit his enemy across the side of his face with more force than he hoped for. With his opponent momentarily stunned, Barrett leaned up and gave an uppercut. Then, as he slid to his left, he twisted, grabbed the mercenary's hair with his left hand, and pulled down the man's right arm with his other hand. While still pulling the arm, he pushed the merc's head down to the deck floor. He continued to pull the arm up until he heard a solid crack. Then he slammed the mercenary's head down, knocking him out cold. With this attacker out of action,

Barrett turned his attention to the other mercenary, who had just leaped onto the boat.

The man stood less than six feet away with his G36 pointed at the American's chest. Barrett scanned around for his SIG; the gun lay on the deck, out of his reach. There was nothing the American could do but surrender. Barrett winced as his hands went up, feeling again all of the blows to his midsection. He was also mad at himself for being so easily tricked.

The mercenary addressed Barrett in broken English, asking about the girl. *Guess they think I'm American. Why make it easy on him?* Barrett glared at the man, whose hawkish face reminded him of a picture he'd seen of Dracula somewhere. He replied with a shrug, pretending not to be able to understand the question. Barrett examined his foe from head to toe. He discovered the gunman also had a scorpion tattoo on his arm.

The ex-soldier had no patience for Barrett's antics. He motioned with his assault rifle, asking Barrett again when a loud report interrupted their conversation. The mercenary's body blew back, hitting the rail of the boat. The G36 tumbled to the deck and bounced overboard. Bright red crimson flowed from his abdomen. The mercenary gasped a few times, trying to breathe. Barrett moved quickly. He launched himself at the wounded man and rammed into him, driving the bleeding man over the rail and into the water.

Barrett, still trying to catch his breath, turned to see the captain holding a still-smoking, old-fashioned, all-American six-shooter. A .357 Magnum, to be exact.

The captain processed Barrett's expression, stating with a wry smile and heavy Bulgarian accent, "I always wanted to be a cowboy."

Barrett shook his head. *Explains the name of the boat.* "Thanks, Dirty Harry." Barrett dragged the other mercenary over to the side and dumped him into the water too. "Can we go now?" The captain didn't need any more convincing as he rushed to the controls, revved the engines to life, and started to make way.

With the sun burning off some of the crisp, autumn cold, the old boat cleared the harbor and began its trip down the coast to Turkey. The occupants of *The Lone Ranger* now settled in for the short cruise on the calm waters. Barrett stood next to the captain, rechecking the charts to make sure they were headed in the right direction. While some said paranoia was a side-effect of his chosen profession, he thought of it as being careful. Barrett didn't get many second chances.

Sara, seated in the rear, was still trying to put all the events of the past two days in some sort of perspective when she detected a speck in the sky that, over time, kept getting bigger and bigger. Finally she stood, putting her hands above her eyes to shield the glare of the sun. Realizing the object might be heading their way, she called out to Barrett, "Max, can you come back here? There's something I think you should see."

The agent put down the maps and quickly made his way to the back of the boat, wondering what needed his immediate attention. *Can't she sit and be quiet?* When she gestured to the sky, Barrett pulled out a pair of binoculars, studying the ever-growing object for a few moments.

"You must be kidding," he proclaimed over the growling of the boat's engines.

CHAPTER 21

"We got company." Barrett studied the approaching threat through his binoculars. It was a helicopter and, from what he could determine, the aircraft was on an intercept course for their boat.

"Bulgarian military?" Sara asked hopefully. The captain joined them.

"No." Roy shook his head.

"He's right," agreed Barrett. "There are no government markings. The bird is your friends coming to say hi." Barrett second-guessed himself. Should he have brought Sara right in and not worried about a leak? He discarded the thought after a moment. Now was not the time for regrets. Barrett needed to fully concentrate on defeating the new threat. His weapons were ideal for a close quarters fight, not engaging a helicopter in the Black Sea. He would have to improvise.

Barrett noted the helicopter was a civilian model with no mounted rocket pods or external machine guns. He only located a single person leaning out the open side with a long-barreled sniper rifle, still too far away for Barrett to identify the type of rifle the man held. The agent did have one advantage: his enemy needed the girl alive and should avoid destroying the boat. *I hope ...* He advised the captain to start a zigzagging course and not make it predictable. He assumed the sniper would target the boat's engines in order to disable them, because that's what he would do. Once *The Lone Ranger* sat dead in the water, their enemy could swoop in, take the girl, and finish the two of them off. A surgical operation, very professional.

"Guess we can't call for help," muttered Sara. Barrett ignored her as he began to search for anything to pile on top of the engine

164

hatch in order to harden the casing against the enemy rounds. *It won't make much difference, but why make it easy?*

Once Barrett finished piling everything he could find on top of and inside the engine hatch, he readied himself on the back of the boat by laying out his assault rifle, pistol, and a box of flares provided by the captain. He peered through the binoculars again, trying to figure out what other kind of weapons his enemies had brought to the festivities. This would give him their distance ranges, which would let him know how much time they had. "How do I get into these situations?" Barrett muttered to himself.

***

The experienced pilot of the silky Eurocopter AS555, Captain Francis Delpoix, did his best to anticipate the target's constant turns. The boat's captain was not making it easy, even for someone who used to fly for the Belgian Air Force. Delpoix wanted to give his shooter, who hung out the side of the helicopter, a clean shot of the engine casings.

Strapped to the side of the helicopter, Niko Baikov cradled an OSV-96 Russian-made sniper rifle loaded with thirty-caliber ammunition, a weapon he had used many times without fail. Baikov started to line up the shot through his scope, putting the rear of the boat in his crosshairs. Not an easy task considering both the helicopter and boat were moving at a good clip, which also caused the boat to vigorously bounce up and down on the water's surface. This all made for an extremely difficult shot. Baikov relished the challenge.

Delpoix had feared they wouldn't be able to find the vessel; the man who radioed in the request for support back at the dock had gone missing along with his partner. Therefore, the chopper had spent the last few hours chasing down every craft they came across on the water until finally spotting *The Lone Ranger*. Baikov informed him as soon as he had confirmed through his high-tech binoculars that their target was indeed on board the boat. Now, all they had to do was stop the ten-ton moving craft.

Baikov opened fire.

***

Bullets began to hit the engine casings. "You want to do what?" The captain, taken aback, stared at Barrett. His English wasn't very good, but it couldn't be this bad either. The captain started to regret his decision to accept this job and seriously considered jettisoning the cargo overboard. Good thing the captain considered himself a man of honor in the old traditional ways of smuggling, so he felt duty bound to complete the job. Plus, Barrett scared him.

"Listen." Barrett crouched low as bullets began impacting around them, savagely tearing into the defenseless boat. Since their enemy had experienced trouble knocking out the engines, they'd decided to take out the controls on the bridge instead, the pock-marks growing by the minute on the bigger target. It was as if the boat was being chewed by an invisible monster.

"They have the advantage. They can sit at a safe distance and either pick us apart or follow us to wherever we go and report our location to their friends. We need to get rid of them now. Besides, if they keep shooting, we won't have much of a boat left anyway." The other two still eyed Barrett like he was nuts.

"So you want to do this?" The captain tensed up, still not believing what his client had proposed.

"Yes." Barrett used his tone and facial expression to convey his seriousness.

"Will this work?" Sara asked, wanting to believe in the plan. She had more experience with Barrett than the captain, although she was beginning to wonder when their luck would run out.

"Don't know, but I'm out of ideas." Barrett shrugged as bullets continued to eat away at their boat. A round slammed into a life preserver only inches above his head, splitting the floatation device in two. A near miss, but the bullet made its point; they were out of options.

***

"Mr. President, the Russian president thanks you for the statement you sent out condemning the terrorist attack in Moscow, but he also requests that our government publicly support his renewed efforts to go after the Chechen terrorists." The Chief of

166

SHADOW HUNT

Staff read from the communiqué just received from the Russian embassy.

"You mean his eradication of any Chechen opposition to Mother Russia," the President sarcastically responded from behind his desk in the Oval Office. The two men were alone, so he stood to stretch. It was another long night. The President felt the stress all over his body, and he wanted to take full advantage of his brief moment of privacy. The daily grind kept him extremely busy and his mind occupied. *Sara …*

"They also want to know what we are going to do to try and stop the flow of weapons and fighters into Chechnya from the Middle East, specifically Afghanistan and Pakistan."

The President shook his head. "He is trying to deflect from their domestic problems with the economy." Hanson turned to look out over the rose garden. Even though it was a gray morning in DC, the well-manicured garden had a calming effect on him. "Get President Nabokov on the phone."

"What are you going to tell him?" Glavine asked, keeping his doubts to himself. He wondered if the President contemplated increased military action. He shuddered, considering what an escalated U.S. position toward the Middle East would do to America and the world after all the years already spent fighting over there. Glavine picked up the phone to have the White House switchboard set up the call between the two leaders.

***

Barrett signaled to Sara, who steadied herself on the deck with her left hand and used her right to fire a flare directly toward the chasing helicopter. The flare went up and missed, arching wide to the right. Next, the captain put the engines in reverse without slowing and felt the jarring motion as the old boat jerked forward with its bow going under the water line, almost causing the vessel to capsize from the sudden change in momentum.

Barrett and Sara held on as everything not tied down went flying to the front of the old boat. The agent just hoped that *The Lone Ranger* would survive the drastic maneuver. The boat's movement

167

caught Delpoix by surprise as the pilot continued to fly straight toward the boat.

Delpoix turned to the sniper and smiled, amused by the boat's occupants' utter desperation in firing a useless flare against their high-tech aircraft … though it served its purpose and kept the pilot and sniper distracted. The helicopter continued to fly a chasing course and passed over the boat, forcing it to make a looping turn to get back into attack position.

When Delpoix completed his turn, putting the boat back into their view directly in front of them, he noticed smoke beginning to escape from the engine compartment. The escaping smoke grew quickly into a large plume, hiding *The Lone Ranger* behind a thick curtain of black smoke. It looked like all of their shooting had finally paid off. The ship appeared to be drifting with its engine compartment on fire. *Time to extract the girl.*

The pilot positioned the helicopter directly over the boat, wanting to use the rotor wash to clear the smoke and give his sniper a clear view to dispatch any survivors other than the girl. After the threats had been cleared, Baikov planned to repel down to the deck and retrieve the target. Hovering around thirty feet above the boat, it took only a few seconds for the rotors to clear the air. Delpoix scanned the deck, his eyes wide in wonder. An alien-like figure now stood on the boat's deck.

Barrett, wearing a scuba mask he'd found in a locker and with a damp towel wrapped around the lower part of his face to protect him from the smoke, strolled out onto the exposed back portion of the deck. With the downward wash of the blades pounding him, he aimed his assault rifle and fired. He had changed out the barrel on his rifle to the longer, twenty-inch one in order to increase its range, using it now to engage the suddenly vulnerable helicopter.

The 7.62 heavy rounds, when grouped tightly together, punched through the bottom front glass on the helicopter and penetrated the cockpit, hitting Delpoix's feet and legs. The last rounds not only took out some of the canopy but also hit numerous components on the pilot's control panel. Barrett thumbed his weapon to full automatic and opened up with it.

He raked the open side of the helicopter. Baikov never even saw him. The sniper's body shot upwards as the rounds slammed into him, punching the life out of the experienced soldier and knocking him out of the open door. Still attached to the safety harness, Baikov dangled lifelessly a few feet below the wounded helicopter.

Barrett reloaded and continued to pound the helicopter with relentless fire. This was their only chance, and he had to take full advantage. Dark, gray smoke began to fill the inside of the Eurocopter. With warning alarms wailing, Delpoix had a hard time controlling the chopper, let alone getting away from the boat to avoid any more gunfire. The pedals useless, he had no rudder control and no real way to stabilize the aircraft. The control stick vibrated between his legs. The pilot responded by gripping tight with both hands, squeezing with all his might. The swaying body of the dead sniper didn't help as the pilot continued to struggle to keep the helicopter airborne. Grimacing, Delpoix tried to restore control over the sick aircraft, but the experienced pilot lost the battle. The whole helicopter shook violently, going into a death spin before it turned over and fell like a dead pigeon, smashing into the sea. The Eurocopter tore apart as it hit the water, sending debris and spray in all directions.

Barrett stood up on the deck, stunned his idea had worked … But his plan wasn't done yet. The agent picked up the oil can he'd used to douse the outside of the engine, which had created the smokescreen, and tossed it overboard. He hoped the engines had not been badly damaged as a result of being temporally turned into a smoke machine. Barrett ordered Sara and the captain to throw everything not essential into the water, especially anything that could be used to identify the boat. They threw a few clothing items over the side as well and any personal effects they could spare. He then took a fire ax and chopped some pieces of the boat's deck free so they could be tossed overboard as well.

Roy cringed as each of Barrett's swings made contact with the deck, cracking through the wood, but he understood that his own neck was on the line too thanks to his former crewman's betrayal. The captain, who couldn't bear to watch Barrett hack away at his beloved boat, went to check on the engines and gave them a thorough examination. Covered in a layer of burnt oil sludge, Roy reported the engines still functioned. Barrett let out a breath he didn't realize he'd been holding.

The kidnappers were eventually going to send someone out to investigate the missing helicopter. Therefore, Barrett wanted to give the impression that the boat either sank or had been so badly damaged in the confrontation that it couldn't go far. Searching either their wreckage or the nearest marinas should tie up their pursuers for a while, buying all three of them some much-needed time to make their way to Turkey.

CHAPTER 22

Dave Kelner liked visiting the Pentagon. In his mind, it was a place filled with men and women who had made many sacrifices for their country and who followed orders to get things done.

"Glad the President brought you in on this." The Secretary of Defense continued, "We need somebody to keep some egos in check." Both men still fumed over the fiasco in Morocco.

The two men sat at a small conference table in Secretary Spencer's office, taking a quick lunch meeting consisting of a couple of salads Kelner had kindly picked up from the Subway downstairs.

"Will, sum up what you think so far." Kelner liked Spencer's straightforward manner.

"We think European-based white Muslims are conducting this op."

"Which makes sense since they can operate more freely." Kelner coated his salad with fat-free ranch dressing. "If that's the case, where would they stash her?"

"Not sure. These groups have tentacles everywhere."

"I will check with the NSA. Besides their data collection capability, they also have a listening post over in Hungary. I'll see if they can come up with something." Kelner became serious. "Let me know if you need anything. A crisis like this brings a lot of politics. We don't have time for any of that slowing us down. We must bring those two home."

"I know." Spencer recalled Secretary Shay's behavior over the last couple of days. *We all need to work together.*

***

The Lone Ranger wound its way down the Bosphorus amid a wide variety of seafaring vessels. Everything from rowboats to cruise ships navigated the tricky currents of the narrow, snake-like waterway that connected the Black Sea to the Sea of Marmara and ultimately the Mediterranean. The American noted the number of new blue, white, and red catamarans acting as sea buses racing both ways. Barrett watched all of the crafts, taking comfort that their boat would disappear among them as they cruised down the channel.

Traveling down the seaway was like a trip back in time, with both shorelines dotted by structures that spanned over two thousand years of architecture and history. Barrett and Sara saw ancient forts, castles, and historical waterfront mansions speckling the shoreline. Nestled among these architectural wonders lay the oil pipelines and the modern radar stations which helped monitor the boat traffic on the heavily traveled strait.

Barrett, like so many before him, stared in awe as the edges of the ancient city of Istanbul began to appear on either side of the Bosphorus. There at the crossroads of Europe and Asia, the great metropolis rose up like a timeless monument to man's glorious past. He shielded his eyes, peering through the powerful sunlight at the European side of the city rising in full splendor up ahead on their right.

The boat now paralleled the old government assembly buildings. The three long, yellowish structures built in the 19th century had housed a parliament that advised the Ottoman rulers until World War One, when their centuries of reign finally ended. Sara decided to give her eyes a rest from the abrasive sunlight, choosing to cross the boat and look over the growing residential areas of the Asian side of Istanbul instead.

Istanbul, originally a Greek settlement thousands of years ago, came into its own when Emperor Constantine the Great moved the capital of the Roman Empire there and renamed the town Nova Roma, Latin for the New Rome, in 333 AD. The city served as the capital for the Christian Byzantine Empire, or to be more accurate the Eastern Roman Empire, for a millennia. The term Byzantine didn't come about until a French architect coined it in the eighteenth century.

Once the Eastern Empire fell, the ancient city became the capital of the Ottoman Empire for another five hundred years and was still one of the most populated cities in Europe with over fifteen million people, the bulk of which were of the Muslim faith.

Barrett thought about what it must have been like on that final day in May of 1453 when the citizens of Constantinople held out one last time against Mehmet II and his overwhelming army. To those courageous defenders, failure would not only mean their deaths but also the end of the fifteen-hundred-year-old Roman Empire! Talk about a heavy burden to bear.

The Lone Ranger passed under the Bosphorus Bridge, one of two suspension bridges that crossed the strait connecting the Asian and European sections of the grand city, arriving at the Besiktas Harbor on the more crowded European side in late afternoon. Not a moment too soon for Barrett's liking, since he was positive the boat couldn't last much longer.

The boat docked in the fishermen's section of the docks and, with the captain's help, Barrett and Sara were able to secure a ride on a truck full of fish heading into the city. After saying their goodbyes to the captain, both crammed themselves in the back of the front cab as it rolled out of the marina and into the city proper. They avoided Turkish Customs, and this solidified Barrett's belief that Roy was indeed a smuggler and thankfully a good one!

***

The orbiting helicopter guided the recovery vessel to the edge of the debris field, and their comrades on the surface still couldn't figure out what had happened. Pieces of the boat and the helicopter's twin covered a square mile. The searchers had pulled out of the water everything from parts of a rotor to a woman's shoe.

"What have you found?" Scarov spoke into his headset from the co-pilot's seat of the Eurocopter, his patience running thin. The helicopter had just returned to the wreckage area after heading back to pick the mercenary leader up. Scarov wanted answers. *Where is the girl, and what caused the crash?* If the girl had died, then they needed to recover the body. Scarov also knew the pilot of the crashed chopper and held his flying skills in high regard. This added to the mystery.

"Pieces of both our helicopter and the boat." Captain Donsin held a piece of a floatation device with the name *The Lone Ranger* still visible on it. He tossed it on top of the helicopter's fuselage debris pile, which continued to get bigger on the back of the ship. "But no bodies yet."

"Did the boat sink?"

"Sonar hasn't picked up the major parts of the hull yet. But if she didn't sink," he looked at the debris, "they couldn't have gotten far."

"Keep looking." Scarov nodded to his pilot, and the chopper made a turn, heading to shore. There were a number of nearby places the boat could have limped to that they needed to check out.

***

Barrett and Sara found one of the ever-emerging mobile phone shops in the city after the fish truck dropped them off. The agent bought a universal charger to replace his damaged one, along with a new, prepaid cell phone, or burn phone as they were commonly called in his profession. Although Barrett now had the ability to charge his assigned cell, he still dared not use it.

Barrett still thought there might be an insider somewhere in his government, so he wasn't sure if he or the phone had been compromised. Though his smartphone possessed the capability of running a self-diagnostic to detect and fix any internal intrusions, the software still couldn't tell him whether the calls themselves were being intercepted or monitored in any way. This was especially a concern if the insider had access to the Unit's technology in electronic monitoring. *Better to stay a ghost for now.* This was why he preferred to use a burner phone instead. By using cash to purchase the phone and its pre-paid minutes, his calls would be virtually impossible to trace unless he got sloppy. So he decided to leave his high-tech gadget and the GPS tracker it contained off for now. Barrett explained some of this to Sara as they left the store, looking for a quiet place to collect their thoughts. He used general terms since she didn't have the proper clearance to know how the phone's technology worked.

After a few minutes, the pair realized "quiet" was a relative term in Istanbul. The city seemed to be on permanent rush hour. The recent government protests didn't appear to have had any lasting effect on the city's vibrancy. Barrett decided to use the hustle and bustle to his advantage. Stopping at an empty bench in front of a nearby bus station, he removed the burner from its package. Barrett doubted anyone could overhear him with all the background noise going on around them. He just hoped the person on the other end did. "Time to discuss your homecoming."

"What about you?"

"I still need to figure out what those guys are planning next."

"I want to help."

Barrett was taken aback. "No way. You are too valuable. You are going home if I'm ordered, and that's final."

"You realize some things are coming back to me now. More stuff I overheard when those bastards had me." Sara inched closer, defiant.

Barrett lowered the phone. "Tell me."

"Only if I get to stay. Besides, you said yourself there may be an insider. It would be too dangerous to go back now."

"You serious?"

She glared, arms crossed.

Barrett took a long breath; the salty air and fishy smell reminded him that they both needed showers. He dialed a number he'd hoped never to have to use. The recorded voice of a woman sounded in his phone's earpiece. "Thank you for calling Globalmax. Please enter the extension number you want to be connected to now." He inputted the extension and waited. Beeps sounded, and he tapped in his ID number. Again, he waited. Finally, he heard a familiar voice answer on the other end.

"It's me, Boss." Barrett would not formally identify himself over the backup line.

"Good to hear your voice." McKenna sounded relieved.

"I have …" Barrett looked at Sara. "My vacation ticket."

"How is it?" McKenna sat up a little straighter in his chair.

"A little ruffled but otherwise still useable," Barrett informed him. Sara frowned.

"Great, but we're not finished on our project yet, so I'm not sure about the vacation yet."

"Any ideas when can I go? It's an expensive ticket." The President's daughter shook her head in disgust then turned away.

Silence dominated the connection as McKenna thought for a moment. The reminder of how perfect the kidnapping had been planned and executed would not go away. "Not yet, but I don't think we have a choice; give me twenty-four hours." McKenna didn't see any other options. "Can you sit tight till then?"

"About that," sighed Barrett, who now felt he had no choice but to break protocol. "Sir, I think this next event is even bigger than the kidnapping, and it's going down soon."

"Not the priority. We complete this task, get you both debriefed, then move on the information."

"I know, but I've got an idea."

"Alright, let's hear it before I get with the Oval and see what they want to do."

***

The President was in turmoil. He was elated at the news his daughter had been found alive and a national crisis so far had been averted, but was frustrated that her safety could still be at risk. Hanson put McKenna on hold and addressed his Chief of Staff, who was sitting across the desk from him in the Oval Office. "Why did she have to go in the first place? She's just like her mother."

"Actually," Glavine produced a slight grin, "she kind of reminds me of you."

"Are you enjoying this?"

"No, Mr. President, but please consider why she went to Nigeria. She wanted to help someone, to serve something bigger than herself. Until we find out about the leak, this may be the safest option for her." The President knew his friend was right. *So much for being the most powerful man in the free world.*

"She's exactly like someone else I know." Glavine watched the President punch the mute button on his phone.

***

Barrett and Sara had a day to kill. Barrett decided they use it trying to decipher the documents found in Bulgaria and the next phase of the kidnappers' plan. After checking into a motel under assumed names, since most didn't ask for passports in Istanbul, they purchased new clothes to replace the ones they'd tossed overboard back on *The Lone Ranger*. The Americans planned on making their way to a restaurant down the hill at the Spice Bazaar, one of Istanbul's oldest markets. Heading to dinner, the pair passed a crowded street market where every shop seemed to sell books. Barrett wondered how all the merchants stayed in business while they wove their way through the maze-like bazaar. Barrett observed even more book sellers around a tight corner then remembered the university was nearby, so the vendors had plenty of potential customers.

The situation made the American agent uncomfortable as they pushed through a heavy throng of young people; for one, he didn't like crowds, and two, he felt vulnerable with the President's daughter so exposed to the masses. He grabbed her arm to keep her close. She slid closer, not resisting. *Focus, Max,* he kept thinking to himself. The other stalls in the market sold a variety of framed calligraphy, and some even pushed ancient coins. He would have loved to stop and browse, but he didn't have the luxury of time.

Leaving the Book Bazaar behind, Barrett and Sara crossed a small, park-like area filled with backgammon players. A wave of apple-scented air hit them as they passed a group of men huddled around the tables smoking water pipes, a common habit among older Turkish males.

Reaching Beyazit Square, the pair viewed some of the ruins from the old Roman forum, which used to dominate the area in ancient times. Some of the once grand columns had been stacked on both sides of the tram tracks that ran along Ordu Caddesi. Today, the large, open space held vendors selling various items, especially carpets and silks from Asia, along with a number of street performers

177

preparing for the evening ahead. The smell of spiced mackerel in the air emanated from the food venders selling the balik ekmek, grilled fish sandwiches, made from fresh fish delivered by fisherman earlier in the day. These caught the attention of a hungry Barrett. The square with the fortress-like entrance to Istanbul University standing guard on the northern end began to fill with tourists and students as the Americans cut through, heading in the direction of the Spice Bazaar.

The smaller, more manageable market as compared to the Grand Bazaar resided near the coast, where their final destination, the Pendali restaurant, was located. The restaurant got a strong recommendation from the receptionist at the hotel, who informed them they had gotten lucky since the place rarely opened at night. The Americans decided to give it a try. The excursion gave them a chance to briefly explore the Bazaar Quarter of the ancient city while Barrett made it a point to avoid the Grand Bazaar with its maddening, maze-like design, packed crowds, and pushy traders.

The pair left the busy square, walking downhill past the wall of the university and the magnificent Suleymaniye Camii. Both gawked at the sight of the grand, sixteenth-century mosque and its four minarets with balconies overlooking the Golden Horn. Sara admired the well-manicured gardens that surrounded one of Istanbul's most revered religious sites. Regrettably, the couple couldn't stop and visit, so they continued on their trek. Barrett and Sara squeezed through a few cramped alleys filled with aggressive vendors until they saw them. The pigeons.

The wild birds were everywhere. This was how the receptionist told them they would find the Spice Bazaar and the restaurant at its entrance. The Americans pushed past more vendors. The smell of spiced meats and coffee began to become unbearable for the starving agent. With great relief, they entered the market hall, immediately taking the tiled stairs up to the second-floor restaurant.

**

The President sat in deep thought while alone in his private office. He'd really learned to appreciate solitude since being elected. The conversation about his daughter had snapped something in the President's mind. He now remembered a phone call with Sara about

178

her going on the trip in the first place. He'd been in a meeting in the Oval Office. Due to time constraints, he'd taken the call from her right then and there. The President leaned back in his chair. Who had he been meeting with? Then it hit him. He couldn't believe it. *No way.*

CHAPTER 23

Barrett and Sara settled themselves inside the restaurant that once served as an old guardhouse to watch over the Spice Bazaar and ordered their dinner. The President's daughter enjoyed an eggplant with lamb dish, while Barrett had the more traditional chicken kabob. They ate with a vigor created by hunger and nerves, quickly cleaning the local cuisine off their plates.

"How's your tea?" Barrett sipped his own cup of high-octane Turkish coffee while looking over the blue, ceramic tiles that covered the floors and walls of the restaurant.

"Tastes like Earl Gray." Sara seemed to have almost forgotten that people might still be out to kidnap her. She felt the confidence reverberating off the man sitting across from her. It was contagious. Sara felt secure every time her eyes met his. Barrett strained to hear her among the chatter of other patrons as the place began filling with locals and college students from the nearby university for dinner. Again, the upside to all of the ruckus going on around them was that it now would become extremely difficult for them to be overheard. Barrett thought about the old football proverb. *Take what the defense gives you.* Barrett reached into his pocket and took out the pictures he had taken of the documents back at the Bulgarian warehouse.

"Okay. Sara, can you tell me anything about your kidnappers?" Barrett flipped through the pictures, trying to see if he could make sense out of them. She sat back, trying to recall all that had transpired during her kidnapping. She did her best to keep her emotions at bay.

180

"A couple of them spoke French. The big guy with the scar, who I think is their leader, spoke French to someone a few times on the phone. I overheard their conversations while I pretended to be asleep."

"You speak French?"

"I took it in school."

"What did he say?" Barrett asked, trying to be as nice as possible. This was going to be part friendly conversation, part interrogation. She might be the best lead he had to figure out what was going on. *And she chose to stick around.*

"Something about a success in Moscow and other stuff I didn't understand." Barrett stayed quiet, letting the silence nudge her on. "Well, what I heard directly translated means 'where the servant lays.' Of course, it all depends on the context."

"Whose servant?"

She shook her head. "No idea. The big guy mentioned the letters DGSE a lot. What do they stand for?"

Barrett took a few moments to process this new information. "French Intelligence." He leaned back in his chair, crossing his arms, bewildered by how French Military Intelligence would be involved in any of this. Though it only mattered if the young lady heard right.

***

The Maybach glided through the wet streets of Old Paris like a black bird of prey on the prowl. Kovlor sat in the back seat of the high-end Mercedes in a dark, custom-tailored Armani suit with a cell phone jammed in his right ear. His face flushed red with frustration as he spoke about the missing President's daughter. The fuming Russian decided against threatening the person on the other end, so he abruptly hung up on him instead. The plan was not going his way, and he detested when things didn't go his way.

First, the rain had drenched Paris, and now, the search for Sara Hanson seemed to be getting nowhere. It all put a damper on his night, a night he had been anticipating for weeks. Kovlor had plans of taking his new mistress to dinner at the discreetly elegant Taillevent restaurant to enjoy one of his favorite meals followed by a walk on the Champs-Elysees. Then, as the night wound down, he planned on retiring to his palatial suite at the Hotel de Crillon, a palace once occupied by Louis the Fifteenth, where he aspired to partake in his favorite kind of dessert.

***

The two Americans pored over all the information they had gathered in Bulgaria, coming to the conclusion that whatever was going to happen next most likely had to involve a mosque. The pair narrowed the potential targets to a place of worship, since the notes mentioned the word numerous times, although they never specified which one.

"If these people who kidnapped me are Muslims, why would they attack their own kind?" Sara finished her tea.

"If they are? We shouldn't conclude anything yet. This happens all the time. Remember the news reports from Iraq during the war. How many mosques did the insurgents blow up trying to rally support for their cause?" Barrett sounded like he wanted to convince himself too.

"That's crazy."

"It's why we call them fanatics." Barrett paid the bill. Time to find a quieter place to continue their investigation. Besides, he wanted to head back to the motel before the streets emptied.

***

"Serbians, mercenaries, all hogwash. I'm telling you, this has been a Muslim terrorist op from the start," Shay pointed out to Dave Kelner from his office phone in Langley. "Spencer's man is in over his head. He's chasing ghosts."

"Possibly." The Deputy National Security advisor knew Shay all too well; his ego still appeared bruised after the fiasco in Morocco.

"It's probably part of their grand plan. My sources at the White House tell me the President thinks she has been located, but no rescue is yet planned."

"Think this is some kind of setup?" Kelner fumbled with papers on his desk.

"You saw what happened to my people, and Barrett is going to blindly lead Hanson right into something worse."

***

Barrett and Sara had picked up some travel books about Istanbul on their return and used them to look up mosques in the area. They discounted the Hagia Sofia for its importance to both Christians and Muslims; plus, the structure built by Emperor Justinian was being used more as a museum these days. The Blue Mosque was also disregarded for it had six minarets, which some Islamic circles consider blasphemy. They then went over the history of the two mosques, which seemed to be the most likely targets: the Suleymaniye, which they'd passed on their way to the restaurant, and the Eyüp Mosque. But with the time constraints, they would need to choose correctly the first time. Something had to stand out between the two remaining mosques.

Barrett read aloud the history of the famous Suleymaniye from a guide book. "The Mosque was built in 1557 and is one of the most important mosques in Istanbul, more so than the now turned into a museum Hagia Sophia or the Blue Mosque with its controversial and considered by some sacrilegious six minarets. The mosque complex is a great monument to its founder Suleymaniye the Magnificent, under whose leadership the Ottoman Empire was brought to its zenith in the mid-sixteenth century. The renowned Imperial Architect Mimar Sinan designed the mosque and built the shrine to overlook the Golden Horn on the site of the ancient Eski Saray Palace." He finished no closer to an answer.

Sara took her turn to read from one of the recently purchased guidebooks. "The Eyüp Camii, or mosque in Turkish, is one of the holiest sites in Turkey. There is a saying: 'The Suleymaniye is glorious, Sultan Ahmet is beautiful, but it is the Eyüp which is holy.' The mosque was built on the outside of the Theodosian Wall where the Standard Bearer of the Prophet Mohammed, Abu Ayyub al-Ansari, fell during the Muslim's failed siege of Constantinople in 688 AD." She continued, "The tomb of the Prophet's companion is also on the grounds of the mosque situated in the Eyüp section of the city. The historic mosque also served as the place where the sultans held their inaugurations in the glory days of the Ottoman Empire. The site is still a place of pilgrimage for Muslims from all over the world and is considered the fourth holiest in Islam behind only

Mecca, Medina, and Jerusalem." She continued to scan down the page and paused. "Get this; the tomb of Mohamed's servant is a revered place for worshippers."

"That's gotta be the place," Barrett interrupted. "Where the servant lays ... that has to be a reference to the standard bearer."

"Ansari."

"Yes, him. Plus, it's the fourth holiest site, right? I don't think the guys we saw will get very far in Mecca or Medina. They don't strike me as the religious type. Jerusalem is also another site important to more religions than just Muslims."

"Makes sense." She met Barrett's eyes. "If we are right and this is only an attack against Muslims."

Barrett hadn't realized how much Sara agreeing with his conclusion meant to him or her smile. The damn smile. *Stay focused.*

***

"How's the project going?" the Secretary of Defense asked on the video teleconference from his office in the Pentagon. The Secretary noticed McKenna appeared calm on the screen. The previous couple of days had been long and were wearing on everybody, but this guy looked like today was just a normal day. *Man's a machine.*

"It's moving. Our analysts are backtracking the Turkey connection." Best to hold the information tight. The Secretary of Defense didn't need to know all the details anyway.

"Good. Keep me informed." Spencer understood the brevity behind McKenna's answers. He trusted the man's instincts.

***

The Eyüp section of Istanbul lay near the upper portion of the Golden Horn and ran down to the Black Sea. The district was a conservative Muslim place of worship and burial, with mausoleums lining the streets surrounding the ancient mosque while gravestones of ordinary people dotted the hill that overlooked the area, sometimes called a village of tombs.

"First, we will go up there." Barrett pointed to the top of the hill as she followed him. "Let's take the funicular up to the Pierre Loti café."

"Why?"

"Old habit."

Barrett strained to look up the hillside as he began feeling the effects of another restless night. The Americans were staying at an obscure motel in the Sultanahmet section of the city, with nice rooms tucked away from the hustle and bustle of the tourist areas but still within walking distance of the main attractions in the district. All the employees were friendly while not being intrusive. Mainly, the motel was a place where once again, the young pair wouldn't attract attention.

Even though the agent considered the motel relatively safe, he didn't let his guard down. Barrett felt more emotionally vested in this mission than any other he had been on in his career, and couldn't figure out why. This was not like him. He had always been able to separate himself from missions before.

After studying his travel guide, Barrett reported in to McKenna.

"We're still here, Boss."

"I need you to sit tight for a few more hours to finalize the extraction. We're going really far off the books here."

Barrett used the opening the delay had caused to tell McKenna about their thoughts on what the kidnappers might do next. He kept the specifics on the Eyüp mosque out of the conversation. "We want to check a few sites out."

"Negative. Sit tight."

"I want to conduct a few quick drive-bys. This may be our only chance to learn what's going on."

"Your mission is done." McKenna wasn't happy; he knew the guys on the ground should always be listened to. It was all about context.

"Copy ... Any update on Prague?" Barrett wanted to change the subject, and the previous mission still nagged at him.

"The analysts from crypto extracted partial data from the info you brought back. We haven't put all the pieces to the puzzle yet, but Foresky had obtained solid information on a group of Serbs running guns through Eastern Europe."

"Seems I'm attracting lot of them these days." Barrett didn't believe in coincidences. Then it finally hit him about where he had seen the tattoos before. *Prague.* The mercenaries chasing them operated with the same boldness as those in the Czech city.

"One more thing: The Prague police discovered a bomb under Foresky's car. He was doomed before he ever set foot in the bar." McKenna attempted to alleviate Barrett's feelings of responsibility for the Polish agent's death. Having one less burden to carry may help Barrett get through his current situation.

"I'm just glad he never offered to drive."

CHAPTER 24

In an effort to hedge their bets, McKenna, after finishing with Barrett, placed a courtesy call to his counterpart at the Mossad. He kept his information vague in order to keep Barrett's investigation secret, but did pass on a warning about a possible threat to holy sites in the city. Maybe if they were wrong and the bad guys attacked Jerusalem, the Israeli intelligence agency might discover something of value.

Of course, there was no guarantee the Mossad would ever share the information with McKenna and his people. The Israelis were notorious for keeping everything close to the vest, only providing vital information to other nations if it also helped Israel. *Just need to know how to deal with them.*

***

Barrett finished his conversation with McKenna then made one more call before tossing his burn phone away in a street-side trash can. He picked up another one just to be safe. *I miss my phone.*

Posing now as a Canadian couple from Vancouver, complete with newly acquired wedding bands, Max and Sara strolled to the funicular station near the waterfront and boarded the car that would take them up the hill to the café. Barrett had spent some time during the night giving Sara a brief tutorial on their new cover. She was a quick study. Both of them were conservatively dressed, with Sara wearing a scarf to cover her head. It was the respectful thing to do and helped her blend in better. "I thought your superior said we were supposed to stay in the room?" The couple filed in along with other tourists and locals who were visiting the graves of loved ones; it would be a somber ride up to the top.

187

"No chance. Besides, we're safer on the move." The thought of sitting around and waiting for the cavalry abhorred Barrett. "This may be our only shot at stopping these guys."

The café, which overlooked the Eyüp Cemetery, was named after the French novelist Pierre Loti, who had once lived in the area and wrote about the café on top the hill, bringing notoriety to the place. It shared the same location as the one frequented by the Frenchman, but was erected after the author's death, though Loti would have recognized this cafe decked out in ninetieth century décor and furniture just like during his time. The café also provided its patrons with a grand view of the Golden Horn. This meant that Barrett and Sara could use it to observe the mosque below it as well. "Who was the second call to?"

"Personal contact, definitely out of our loop." The duo gazed at all the gravestones on the hill as the car rose past the Eyüp Cemetery to the top. The Americans observed the variety of gravestones, including some of their distinguishing features, including turban-capped ones for gentlemen and the flower-topped markers for women, with tall cypresses standing guard over them all. Before entering the café, she looked to her right and saw a couple of tall, worn, uninscribed tombstones that marked the graves of Ottoman-era executioners. Sara felt a chill run up her spine.

"What are we looking for?"

Barrett answered by pulling out his new burner as they took a table on the shady terrace, which provided them with an unobstructed view of the religious complex below. The waiter, dressed up in a Turkish outfit from the ninetieth century, in keeping with the theme of the restaurant, stopped by to pick up their tea order. After the conversation with his boss, Barrett had placed a call to the one other person who could help shed some light on what the mercenaries might be up to. Time to see if that call paid off.

***

I hate warehouses, thought Petrov. Back in the old Soviet days, this was where a lead brought you, during which you would get ambushed, shot in the back in most cases, for getting too close to someone connected in the politburo. Good thing times had changed.

Petrov still fumed at being cut out of his investigation. A few of the details bothered him, and he couldn't let them go, so the seasoned inspector decided to check some out. He had gotten nowhere so far, and now he wanted to start over, retrace his steps.

He learned that the concrete truck was titled to a business based out of the warehouse. He knew the truck had been reported stolen, but Petrov wanted to talk to the owners anyway. The inspector first planned on peeking around in the early morning before anyone showed for work. He lived by an old saying: 'Nothing in Russia is as it seems.'

He jimmied the back door while Litenko covered him. The pre-dawn hour kept them both cloaked in darkness, especially after Litenko broke the single light hanging over the door. Petrov used his body to shield the light emanating from the penlight dangling from his mouth, which guided his hands. The door cracked, and Petrov pushed it fully open. Litenko entered first, followed by his partner. A minute later, the building flashed orange, followed by an enormous roar. Smoke billowed everywhere as the warehouse collapsed in a heap of rubble.

***

"I don't have time for this. Send me what I requested NOW." Kelner hated bureaucrats, particularly those who thought they'd achieved their positions on their own merit. His cell buzzed a number from the Deputy Director of the National Reconnaissance Office. "Thanks for getting back to me quick, Vince."

"No prob, Dave. I got the images you wanted. Can you tell me what I'm supposed to see on these?" Vince Nolan was a team player and somebody Kelner liked on a personal level.

"Sorry, I can't right now."

"I figured. Still thought I'd ask. Not many requests come through here on a higher clearance level than my own."

"Thanks again. I owe you one." Kelner hung up, not wasting time downloading the pictures on his secured drive; he forwarded the message, hoping they would be analyzed in time. The data needed to get to the right analysts ASAP. Time was critical, and lives hung in the balance.

***

"This doesn't make sense." On the phone, Barrett argued with Johan Kress, who was in his Greek estate's garage carefully caressing his Koenigsegg CCXR. He massaged his hand over the black, stealth-looking Swedish supercar, whose 1,000 horsepower engine ran on bioethanol fuel—the pride of the arms dealer's car collection even though the man rarely drove the exotic sports car. Ownership was satisfaction enough, like a piece of art. A piece of two-million-dollar art!

"My dear Max, if your conclusion is correct, then one must remember who their target audience is. Not educated Westerners like us, but borderline Fundamentalists who just need a push. And in their extremely limited minds, this is actually more of a shove." He continued speaking of Sara's kidnappers' possible desire to do something to a mosque.

"I'm tracking. Why do this in the first place?"

"That is *the* question, my young friend. You find the answer and this whole mystery is solved."

"Any ideas about the possible French involvement?"

"That's tough to answer as well. We know the French are still upset over their loss of importance in the world," Kress explained, "and we all are aware how they feel about America. Jealousy. When one sets the pace for a while, it becomes difficult to get in the back with the rest of the pack."

***

While Kress continued to lecture Barrett, a tall, heavyset man with jet-black hair and green eyes appeared on the hilltop café's terrace, confidently striding directly to the Americans' table. Barrett gave the man a careful once-over before deciding he matched the description Kress had given him earlier. The man, dressed in slacks and a long-sleeved, button-up shirt, was a trusted associate of the arms dealer and, more importantly, out of the normal channels. Barrett thanked Kress then hung up.

"Mr. and Mrs. Brady?" the newcomer asked in very good English with almost no discernable accent. "I am Emre Hamit." He displayed a warm smile as he shook both of their hands. The man towered over Barrett even though the American stood fully erect to greet him.

"Max, and this is Sara." Barrett pointed to the President's daughter.

"Pleasure." The Turkish agent's narrow nose didn't quite match his round face. "I'm sorry," he continued. "Our mutual friend told me to meet with you but nothing more. He told me this situation is something only for my ears right now and not my superiors." Hamit finished as Barrett motioned for him to sit down.

Barrett lowered his voice. "That's because what I am about to tell you is a theory. We have no real proof." The Turkish agent was on an obvious need-to-know basis. "We believe that a terrorist group is targeting a high-value mosque in Turkey, more than likely the Eyüp Mosque due to its value to Muslims worldwide."

Hamit's eyes widened. "The Kurds?" he asked, referring to the ethnic minority that resided in the eastern portion of Turkey. The Kurds had for years been fighting for an independent state.

"No, Russian and Eastern European mercenaries, I think. We do not know who they are working for yet or what their religious beliefs are either."

"So it could be the Kurds." Hamit began to get fired up.

"I doubt this is their play. They usually do something like this themselves, and this is an attack directed to Muslims both in and out of the country."

"Yes." Hamit seemed to calm down. "This is not how they operate. If true, this is very bad for everyone. An action like what you propose will greatly increase anti-Western sentiment all across the globe, destabilizing much of the hard work done by moderates and Westerners alike. The Arab states themselves are in disarray these days, changing governments by the week. This would lead to war across the region."

Barrett nodded his agreement and explained they needed to get inside the ancient mosque and take a look around. Hamit offered to make a call. He told the American he could arrange an audience with the Imam.

With the meeting set, Barrett handed the waiter some Turkish lira to cover their bill, though he gave the small sheet of paper a good look over per Hamit's advice. "This is an old custom," he had told the Americans. Barrett carefully scanned the invoice and, seeing nothing unusual, he put down enough liras on the table to cover the cost and the tip. With that tradition out of the way, all three headed down the hill.

The trio decided to return to the mosque, using the steep, cobbled path and stairs, taking them about fifteen minutes to make their way down to the mosque complex. All the while, Hamit played guide as he explained the differences in tombstones and pointed out a few other interesting tidbits about the cemetery. He told them that back in Ottoman times the graveyards were not a morbid place but were where the living happily strolled and celebrated the dead. This explained a lot of the ornate decorations and lavish tombstones populating the cemetery. Sara pointed out a cute white and orange cat using one of the pole-like tombstones as a backscratcher. Hamit also informed them the original mosque had been damaged in an earthquake, forcing a rebuild by Salim III in the eighteenth century.

They exited the stairs right behind the religious complex and headed toward the nearest gate. Most of the northern side of the complex was dominated by the largest Baroque structure in Istanbul, the Valide Sultan Mirisah. This edifice contained the tomb of Mirisah, who was the mother of Salim III, and was a still in-service soup kitchen for the poor.

The trio entered the mosque complex through a large gateway with beautiful, gold calligraphy above them as they stepped into the courtyard under the shade of a huge plane tree. The Servant's Tomb was on the left and the mosque on the right. A long line of worshippers already in place obscured a lot of the blue tiles that decorated the outside of the tomb. Max, Sara, and Hamit continued through the octagonal-shaped courtyard; the going was easier on the smooth, stone floor beneath them as they passed the water fountain and up a step to the doorway of the Eyüp Mosque.

Gold leaf designs on white marble highlighted the entrance. As the trio removed their shoes, a gray-bearded man in a simple cloak approached Hamit, and they hugged like old friends. Hamit then introduced the newcomer as the Imam who, due to his lack of English, greeted the Americans politely with a slight bow and smile.

Barrett did his best, trying to remember the proper protocol for behavior in a mosque. He respectfully kept his voice down, addressing Hamit. "Has he noticed anything unusual, or have any strange people been around lately?"

Hamit conferred with the Imam. "No."

"Please ask if anything has shown up or needed to be fixed recently."

The Turk complied and, after conversing with the older man, turned to Barrett. "My friend informed me the only thing out of the ordinary occurred when they received a clock from an obscure Muslim foundation no one here has heard of before."

"Interesting. Can we see it?"

"Yes." Hamit had anticipated Barrett would want to inspect the clock and had already asked for permission.

Sara, being a woman, could not follow the men, and with no desire to go to the area reserved for female worshippers, she stayed right inside the doorway. Now with her head and mouth covered by a silk scarf, Barrett didn't need to fear that she would be discovered. Hamit assured him she should be safe in such a holy place of worship.

The older gentleman led them toward the back of the mosque. Barrett gazed over the beautiful, gold-and-red-colored carpet with black-and-gold artwork that covered the main worship area. He looked up at the colorful, high arches holding the roof in place before passing under the cupola with its mini-stained-glass windows under the dome, giving the roof a grand presence. The Eyüp was impressive. The men did their best not to bother worshippers who knelt on the carpet with their palms up, praying in Arabic.

The group entered a small alcove near the back separated by a silk curtain. The Imam walked directly over to a table sitting in the middle of the room, which the clock and some other trinkets rested on. The caretaker swung his arm toward the gift, inviting the two to take a closer look. Barrett and Hamit walked up, examining the clock. The timepiece was made of teak and had a round, gold-etched clock face that sat on an eight-inch-high base that was three inches wide. It was beautiful in a plain kind of way. Barrett looked it over, but he didn't notice anything. He decided it would be best to get a look at the clock's insides, so he pulled out his government-issued phone.

Feeling this was worth the risk, he pressed a finger against the screen, turning the smartphone on. *Hello, my old friend.* Barrett held his cell up in front of the clock, snapping a picture. The older Muslim didn't look too pleased since pictures were not welcomed in the mosque. Barrett apologized with his facial expression then walked over to the corner of the room, where he studied the image in private.

His phone was equipped with a special filter, which had the ability to render an x-ray-like view of an object. The techies back in Virginia had tried to explain how the app worked, but Barrett couldn't remember the details. It didn't help that one of the techs happened to be a very pretty blond Barrett felt deserved more of his attention. When it came to gadgets, he only cared about the end result anyway. The image flashed up on the small screen. Barrett squinted and held the phone closer to his eyes.

"Oh crap."

CHAPTER 25

"What is going on?" Hamit looked on with serious concern as he approached the American, who still stood off to the side of the room, working the touchscreen on his phone.

"She's pregnant." Barrett forwarded the picture back to Dooley in Virginia for further analysis. This was no time to worry about leaks. Turning to the other men in the room, he said, "The gift may have a bomb inside." Hamit stood speechless for a minute before recovering enough to translate Barrett's discovery to the Imam. His eyes said everything. All three became silent … waiting.

After what seemed to be an eternity to the men in the mosque but was really only a few minutes, Barrett received an answer. His screen read: *Centex, timer detonator with possible backup phone trigger. DO NOT USE PHONES.*

Barrett absorbed the message. *Great, this just keeps getting better and better.* He now wondered why someone couldn't think to put a jammer app in his phone. He only needed a device to match the frequency of one of the two cell signals, incoming and outgoing, a phone uses to make calls, thus blocking any incoming transmissions. *Damn thing had everything else.* He relayed his phone's message to Hamit, who in turn informed his Turkish friend.

Barrett returned to the clock, pondering his next move. "Here goes," he spoke softly to himself while slowly running his finger over the clock's back. The Imam bowed his head, murmuring prayers in Islam as Barrett removed the back plate, smiling grimly. "Well, we could use all the help we can get." Barrett placed the plate down and got his first good look at the inside of the clock. *I know that clocks can be a sign of death in some Asian countries, but this is ridiculous.*

195

Barrett found the packed Centex rather quickly since the timepiece had limited internal space. The majority of the clock's insides had been taken up by the mechanisms that kept time. Then he saw what he feared the most.

Barrett's silence was far too much for Hamit to bear. "What now?"

"The bomb contains an anti-handling device, so there is no way to disarm it."

"These people are professionals."

Barrett continued to study the device. "A bomb with C-4 is very simple in creating and disarming. It uses blasting caps, which are the charges that, once they blow, ignite the C-4. So in reality, all you need to do is remove the blasting caps to disarm it, unless …"

"Unless they put in an anti-handler mechanism?"

"Yes." Barrett picked up his phone. While not a bomb disposal expert, Barrett, like many soldiers, was trained in the basics of explosives thanks to all the IEDs, or Improvised Explosive Devices, that had killed and maimed American troops in Iraq and Afghanistan over the years. Something else gnawed at him. The Imam turned paler as Barrett kept studying the bomb.

"Don't worry; I'm not going to try and disarm her. That only works in the movies." Barrett dialed his cell again. "Look at the bright side; if she goes off, we won't even feel it." Hamit frowned, not looking too comforted by that statement. Barrett turned his attention back to his phone, waiting impatiently for the other end to be picked up.

"I thought you were not supposed to be using the phone." Dooley's concern exuded from her desk in Virginia. She had been the one to forward the analysis and warning by their ordinance expert to Barrett. He knew his modified phone worked off a satellite network, not regular cell phone towers, so the risk was minimal. Or so he hoped.

"You know I have trouble following instructions. Please pull up the info on Foresky and tell me about the bomb in his car."

"What are you thinking?" Dooley began to retrieve the data on her computer.

***

The President was sitting in on an early morning meeting with his national security advisor and his deputies in the Oval Office when Glavine interrupted. "Excuse me for a second." President Hanson rose to meet him in an attempt to hold a semi-private discussion next to the couch where his other guests were seated. Time seemed to be of the essence for the impromptu meeting.

They spoke in low tones so the others in the room could barely make out what the discussion was all about, but it was clear the President appeared happy if not joyous at the end. One of those in the meeting did pick up a few words, and those, he understood, would make him very rich.

***

Barrett grabbed a pad and paper and started writing down the information provided by the senior intelligence analyst.

"I thought you couldn't use your phone?" Hamit looked horrified as Barrett hung up. "If the bomb can't be disarmed, then we cannot stop it."

"Not exactly. The device is not armed yet and probably won't be till the next call to prayer. I'm betting she will go off right in the middle of the service."

"The sermon starts in twenty minutes. What are we going to do?" The sounds emanating from the main hall signaled that the mosque was already beginning to fill up. Time was running out.

Barrett finished his writing. "You need to get some people on the radio—these three frequencies to be exact—and keep the radios on." Barrett handed Hamit the list of frequencies. "We are going to try and jam the device manually." He continued to explain the low-tech solution to their current dilemma.

"This will work?"

"I hope. The back-up trigger mechanism works by receiving a pulse sent from the bad guys on either a radio or cell phone. The pulse contains a two-digit or four-digit code to arm or detonate."

"So we need to block the code from getting to the clock."

"Right. As long as your men keep those frequencies tied up and we don't tamper with the bomb, we should be okay. My guess is once we mess with the device, we may have only two or three minutes before the fireworks start."

"We will also shut down the nearest cell towers."

"Good idea, but still stay on those frequencies because these guys won't leave much to chance."

Hamit got the Imam to show him to the closest landline. Barrett was surprised that one was hanging on the wall right outside the small room. After a few minutes, Hamit put the phone down and walked back. "My men are using those frequencies now, but the towers will take a little longer. There are two that provide coverage for the area, and the owners are dragging their feet. They are afraid to upset their customers, but they will be shut down soon."

"Good. Now you can request an ordinance disposal team."

A minute later, Hamit finished his latest call and put his hand on the American agent's shoulder. "The local authorities are on their way."

"Great. They can play with this thing from here on out." Barrett pointed his thumb at the clock while taking what he hoped would be his last peek at the deadly device before walking out of the room. He wanted to update Sara. Hamit advised the Imam to evacuate the mosque and prepare for the bomb squad's arrival.

"Where is Sara?" Barrett called back to Hamit as he glanced around the entrance to the mosque for the President's daughter and noticed for the first time she was gone. The main hall was beginning to fill up as the evening prayer was getting closer.

"I don't know." Hamit joined in the search for the young lady.

"She needs a leash," Barrett muttered to no one in particular as he left to find her. After not seeing Sara inside the doorway of the main hall of the mosque, Barrett slipped his shoes back on and headed outside. He finally spotted her next to a wall, where she was staring intently at something on the other side of the road; Sara didn't even notice Barrett pull up next to her. She appeared to Barrett to be on edge. "You trying to get lost again? Because if you do, then your dad is going to send me on assignment to the Arctic!"

She rolled her eyes. "You're lucky; he's always too busy for me."

"He's kind of got an important job." Barrett stared in the same direction as Sara, trying to see what had been keeping her attention so focused.

"It's one of the guys who kidnapped me." She gestured toward a man across the street.

"Are you sure?"

"It's hard to forget them."

Barrett nodded in understanding, even feeling a little foolish. He probably would never forget anyone who kidnapped him either.

The person she alluded to wore Western-style clothes with a shawl wrapped around his neck. He appeared to be praying at a grave right off the road. Barrett noticed that the man, who had short, cropped, reddish-blond hair would look at the mosque very subtly every few moments. The man had picked a spot directly across from the main gate, and with this vantage point, he had an unimpeded view of the entrance. Barrett had been in this man's position before and recognized his actions. Covert surveillance.

The sirens for the bomb squad and police cars now filtered toward them from a distance. "Red," the nickname Barrett gave the man kneeling in front of the tombstone, began to look around. Worshippers started to empty from the mosque, filing toward the outside of the wall. Many of them appeared nervous; some even shouted at each other. Barrett watched Sara's new friend get up from the grave he was pretending to be praying over and march out toward the road. Barrett decided now was the time to turn the tables.

Barrett hailed Hamit and hurriedly explained that he intended to follow the kidnapper. Hamit agreed to stay behind and work with the locals in dealing with the bomb. Barrett and Sara followed Red out the gate and into the plaza, walking past some market stalls which dealt in religious paraphernalia. The shopping area seemed a little out of place among the serene atmosphere of the mosque complex itself.

They followed Red toward the waterfront, where he jumped into a waiting Mercedes SUV. Barrett needed a car. He scanned up and down the road in desperation then spotted a blue Renault sport sedan parked next to the street. The agent asked Sara to keep an eye on the kidnapper's boxy vehicle while he bent under the steering wheel to start the car. After fiddling with the ignition wires for a minute, Barrett got the Renault running and gestured for Sara to jump into the car; then he pulled out into the late afternoon traffic, trying to follow the Mercedes.

The Renault had gotten four car lengths behind the SUV when the sedan suddenly started chirping. Both Americans looked at each other. Barrett turned the dials for the air conditioning controls, and the noise stopped. "The belt is going."

"Will the car still work?"

"Yes, but it may get hot in here."

They continued following the Mercedes but had trouble keeping the SUV in their sights, with the other vehicle leading them along the Feshane Caddesi into the more populated part of the old city. Istanbul's notorious traffic congestion was going to be a problem.

***

The man riding in the front passenger seat of the Mercedes SUV noticed a blue sedan appear in the background the last few times he checked his rearview mirror. With all the traffic on the road, this would be easy to dismiss as coincidence, but his gut was telling him something different. He had been in the game too long, beginning with his days as a Russian GRU agent, to ignore it. Red told the driver to make a few not so obvious turns so he could determine if the blue car presented a threat. The driver complained the traffic on the roads would cause them to be late. The passenger ignored his protests. There had already been one failure on this operation, and he wasn't going to be a part of another. Somehow, the authorities had discovered the clock. He would now proceed very cautiously.

***

"They're turning up there." Barrett didn't like how this was playing out. He really couldn't keep a covert tail on the SUV in these conditions, but he wanted to find out where this guy planned on going. He believed the risk to be worth the chance of getting their

200

cover blown even as he cut off another car to make the turn just in time to see the SUV pull another one.

***

Two turns later and the blue car still sat twenty meters behind them. His gut was right.

"Do we double back to the highway?" the driver asked, coming to the same realization as the ex-GRU agent.

"No, that would let them know we are on to them. I have another idea." The passenger picked up his cell phone.

CHAPTER 26

Gunnery Sergeant Tom Donner was not happy. Donner, veteran of Iraq and Somalia and currently the highest ranking non-commissioned officer on the embassy's security detail in Greece, didn't like being kept out of the loop on a mission, especially one that might make him a target. The burly veteran, along with fellow Marine Corporal Anna Diaz, was driving one of the embassy shadow cars.

The car, a Toyota Camry normally used for quiet forays by the ambassador into the city proper, had been heavily armored with category three bullet-resistant windows, reinforced doors, run flat tires, and a steel plate that ran the length of the bottom in case of a potential explosive. Much more subtle than the limousine caravans the ambassador typically traveled around Greece in.

The experienced Marine had only been informed by his commander that intel had picked up chatter on a possible attempt on the ambassador's life. He had been ordered to bring a female to act as a passenger and drive a preset route toward the Embassy. The soldiers in the vehicle would also be supported by a Marine FAST team. Though not a fan of the intelligence community, Donner went anyway. Donner always followed his orders. At least until he felt they were not in the best interests of his men or himself. Then his superiors learned how stubborn the grizzly veteran could be.

Donner and Diaz rode to a safe house outside of Athens, where they picked up the Camry and began their drive back. The return trip to the embassy had been routine so far. The gunnery sergeant glanced in his rear-view mirror and noted the DHL delivery van a few car lengths behind, which contained the quick reaction counter-terrorist team. Or so he was told. The gunny did not recognize any of the men, and they sure as heck didn't look like Marines.

***

Tom Reirson cautiously navigated the yellow delivery van through the packed streets of the Greek capital, keeping the Camry in sight. Sitting in the passenger seat, Bellows let his H&K 416 assault rifle lay across his lap like a beloved puppy while he kept a sharp eye out with the help of binoculars for anything suspicious. In the back of the vehicle, the ex-PJ and now electronics expert Ron Kale sat hunched over a laptop, feverishly trying to absorb all of the intelligence gathered so far pertaining to the hastily prepared operation.

The team was on a fishing expedition and using the ambassador's Camry as bait. If someone made a move on the embassy car, the operators didn't want to just react; they wanted to have the time to set up a counter ambush and capture one of the attackers if possible. For the team members who had landed in Greece less than two hours ago after receiving their new tasking orders from McKenna, it was a game of catch up. The men in the van needed any advantage they could get.

"We should be coming up to the embassy soon." Reirson guided the van along Vas Sofias Avenue.

Kale chimed in, popping another pain pill in the process. "The compound will be on the right side. Get this, guys. The main building is a perfect square. The design is supposed to be a tribute to classical Greece." His eyes scanned the data off his laptop.

Reirson and Bellows turned to each other, each shaking their head. Youth.

"Keep the info tactical." Reirson knew if this went like they thought, there wouldn't be time to waste on any information not useful in the takedown.

"You sure you can still play with us?" Bellows asked Kale.

"Unlike you Navy squids, us Air Force guys can operate with a scratch." Kale moved his aching arm out of its sling. Bellows nodded. Kale was earning their respect. He hoped he would be able to back up his bluster when the time came.

The Camry began to cross the last main intersection before the embassy.

"Now or never," sang Bellows. The DHL truck snaked along, keeping the Camry in sight at all times.

"Eleven o'clock," Bellows shouted, pointing at a Peugeot sedan driving toward them and the Camry. He used one hand to balance the binoculars on his face. "I got a driver wearing a motorcycle helmet." He remembered the mercenaries' MO from the snatch and grab in Nigeria. "They're going for the ram again." Reirson stomped on the gas pedal in an attempt to intercept the Peugeot.

Damn, thought Reirson. He should have kept the distance between the two vehicles tighter. The rest of the team grabbed their assault rifles and prepared them for use. The metallic clicks of weapons being checked and cocked reverberated through the van.

Reirson pushed the truck to its limit, but they were not going to make it in time. The Peugeot veered at the last moment, moving almost head-on into the Camry. Both cars came to an abrupt and loud halt. Then a VW van pulled up next to them. Three well-armed mercenaries spilled out of the VW's side door. With weapons ready, they moved toward the disabled cars. The driver of the Peugeot tore off his helmet and joined them.

***

Gunnery Sergeant Donner recovered rather quickly from the impact. He began moving his extremities and running a hand over his face. The Marine had been in worse predicaments, so he proceeded calmly, without panic. He could move everything important, and other than a cut on his nose he had no injuries except maybe for being sore for the next couple of days.

Donner looked around outside the vehicle, taking in the situation. He eyeballed three armed unknowns approaching his vehicle. Two of the men had the ubiquitous shawls wrapped around their necks that Middle Easterners wore, and the other's face was unshaven. His seasoned eyes also discerned the assault rifles and side arms they carried. Good news because anything short of an RPG would not penetrate the vehicle. "Corporal." The GySgt scanned around the vehicle as their ambushers took up their positions. He repeated his call to the young soldier. "Diaz."

"Yeah, Gunny?" Diaz meekly responded, trying to shake the cobwebs, her mind still in a fog from the impact.

"Get your sidearm out. We have guests."

***

Reirson stopped the truck behind a couple of other vehicles that had been forced to a halt because of the accident in front of them. The mercs wanted to use the mayhem to their advantage. Reirson and his men planned to change all that.

Amid the chaos on the street, the ambushers never noticed the DHL truck pull up or the three armed commandos deploying from within until it was too late. As one of the mercs approached the passenger door, trying to place an explosive, his body suddenly shook violently, torn apart due to rounds from Bellows' assault rifle. The attackers didn't know what hit them. The Americans used sound suppressors and subsonic rounds while moving with tactical purpose to engage the attackers. The counter ambush was on.

***

Kress's short helicopter ride ended at his private pad on the outskirts of Athens behind a boutique resort he'd invested in years ago. The Austrian made his way through the small yet opulent lobby toward a set of tinted glass doors in the back. Through the dark partitions lay the sole reason he bought into the gaudy place: Café Ares, his office away from home. The great food and wonderful views of the water kept him balanced through tense and often laborious business meetings. Today, an old associate waited for Kress at his private table. "Hello, Nechy." Kress extended his hand along with a polite smile as he greeted Mikail Nechenko, or Nechy as Kress always referred to him.

The Russian passed himself off as the owner of a small tech company in Athens, but was really the senior agent of Russia's FSB station in Greece. The FSB was Russia's new and improved version of the old Soviet KGB. Nechenko had fallen in love with Greece; he even married a Greek, and his children grew up in the country. Kress had been doing business with Nechenko off and on for over twenty years.

Both men sat. "What do you want?" The fat and sweaty Russian didn't like small talk. He was a straight-to-the-point man with no imagination, whom Kress considered quite boring. The Austrian, dressed smartly as usual in a custom, tailored gray suit and matching handkerchief with nothing out of place, answered the Russian's question by sliding the picture of the scorpion tattoo across the table. He watched as Nechenko picked up the photo, looking for any subtle sign of recognition. He didn't need to. The Russian quickly crumpled up the picture then placed it on a side plate.

Kress contemplated the Russian agent's actions, raising his eyebrows. Nechenko grunted in response. "Well, that answers my first question, although not much of a surprise since the Americans didn't know anything about the men who wear this tattoo. I figured they must be from your side of the street as they would say," Kress said.

"I've got nothing to say."

A sly grin appeared on Kress' face. "Come now. Seeing as how I assisted you in that jam you got yourself into last year in South Africa."

***

The ambushers' explosives expert approached the embassy car to place his charge on the front passenger door, while the three remaining mercs formed a triangle around the accident site in order to create a secure perimeter. Once realizing they were under attack, each of them immediately tried to find some form of cover. The mercenary at the tip of the triangle and closest to the Americans actually moved closer toward his ambusher's position, paying the ultimate price. He received two rounds in the chest at close range from Kale. The merc was lifeless before his body hit the ground.

Reirson moved up to the VW van and engaged the mercenary who remained between the van and the mangled cars. The mercenary, smaller in stature compared to the others, proved to be a lot tougher as well. Reirson fired twice into the man's legs as he approached the van from behind then moved to the left. The man went down but continued to hold on to his weapon, returning fire toward Reirson. *Great ... This guy isn't going to surrender.* The merc tried to crawl back toward the Peugeot, firing in the general direction of the American, who ducked his head behind the front, driver-side wheel-well for cover. Rounds smashed into the other side of the car, flattening the front tire with a whiff as the air escaped. Reirson knew if the small merc got back to the Peugeot, it would present a problem.

Bellows, with his rifle pressed tightly against his shoulder, moved wide of the Camry opposite from Reirson's position, rounding the vehicle at a safe distance. He stepped past the sprawled corpse of the demolition man in the street, scanning for his objective, the gunman on the far side of the car. Barrett got a clear visual and moved behind an old Fiat sedan for cover. He peered through his sights, tilting his head every few seconds to increase his range of vision. His target, a tall, sturdily built man with a shawl wrapped around his neck, stepped back and turned to take a quick glance toward the VW van and away from Bellows. He looked around for his own men, confused. Bellows took advantage; he stopped, sighted, and depressed the trigger. The back of the man's head exploded, reminding Bellows of a grape being squeezed.

***

Reirson low-crawled under the van. The smaller merc, though bleeding out badly, still continued to hold down the trigger on his rifle, spraying some serious lead in Reirson's direction, hence the need for the American to do his best impersonation of a turtle. The gunman could be heard moaning. With their main objective met and the secondary proving impossible, Reirson had only one thing left to do; he radioed his teammates.

CHAPTER 27

Reirson opened up on his target. The wounded mercenary continued to move around the Peugeot to avoid Reirson's hail of bullets, which shredded the French-made car above his head. The merc pushed hard with his elbows, trying to make his way to the back of the car and away from the threat. He had a hard time focusing due to the loss of blood. His movements became slower and slower until he arrived at the Peugeot's rear.

The smaller gunman prepared himself by leaning back against the car, hoping to ambush his pursuer if he tried to follow. The volley of firing suddenly stopped. The merc thought he heard the soft thud of a footstep behind him. He turned his head, but before he got halfway around, the bright glow of a muzzle flash materialized in his peripherals, and everything went black. The agents would need to look elsewhere for someone to interrogate.

**

Bellows stood over the small merc's corpse and gave the all-clear signal. Reirson and Kale conducted a site exploitation, searching the Volkswagen for any possible intelligence while Bellows helped the two Marines get into the yellow van. The operators finished their fruitless search and joined them. The mercenaries had left nothing of use behind. The whole event from the car being rammed to their exfil took less than five minutes. The delivery van sped off, weaving its way through traffic, leaving behind the accident and mess of bodies.

**

"Why this direction?" Barrett asked while following their quarry down a side road adjacent to the Atatürk Bulvari, one of Istanbul's main thoroughfares.

"Maybe they are trying to avoid traffic."

"I hope so." They had been tailing the men in the Mercedes for over a half hour across the European side of the city. Now, the truck appeared to be headed southeast again.

His phone rang. *Crap, I forgot to turn it off.* He viewed the screen. *Kress.*

"I have learned some information pertaining to your new friends." Kress had on his lecturing voice, which annoyed Barrett.

"I'm all ears." Barrett tried to keep the SUV in sight.

"Kovlor is a chameleon."

"What?" Barrett really needed to focus on his driving.

"Our good friend Andrei Kovlor is actually, or *was* I guess is the proper term, Mirko Tolvic."

Barrett's eyes shot up at the mention of the name. He had a personal connection to the man. "He's dead?" Barrett referred to the worldwide belief that Tolvic had died when the helicopter transporting him to the World Court in the Netherlands crashed shortly after takeoff. His body reportedly had been recovered from the wreckage and a positive ID made. The Serbian general was in the Dutch country to face charges by the UN for the atrocities he'd committed as a warlord during the Yugoslavian civil war. Barrett couldn't believe it.

"Similar to many of the godlike figures in man's history, he appears to die before coming back to us transformed."

"It explains those tattoos." Barrett's memory now jarred. "The paramilitary group he ran in Bosnia, while officially called the Red Brigades, had an offshoot unit nicknamed the Scorpions." *How come that didn't come to me sooner? Could I have possibly forced back a lot of what happened back in Bosnia after Hanna died ...?*

"I remember now too. A horrible lot." Kress shuddered at remembering the stories of the group wiping out entire towns, including women and children.

"Also explains Foresky."

"Who?"

"A Polish agent Tolvic had assassinated, most likely to hide the fact that he was killing off some of his old cronies who could have blown his new identity."

"That makes sense, since it also appears he had help in his return."

"From whom?"

"The same people I fear maybe behind the kidnapping."

"You know?"

"Of course. I do have friends in low places although I am unaware of who exactly was kidnapped other than a high-ranking American. It appears, my friend, you are in a real-life Noir."

Barrett shouldn't be surprised. "Just what I always wanted. So who we talking about?"

"FSB."

"Russians? Why?" Barrett was not quite sure if he believed in his friend's proposed theory. "It's a big gamble for them."

"Not if you use a buffer like Kovlor. I have a feeling he received Moscow's support for his dealings."

"What do the Russians get out of all this?"

"The million-dollar question, my friend. Generally speaking, we know the jump in oil prices a decade ago gave the Russians an opening, and they have continued to manipulate the prices for their own gain. The increase in oil revenues has rescued them from oblivion. In fact, for a time, their economy was quite robust thanks to their revenues from oil and natural gas. With this, they have been rebuilding their government infrastructure and their military arsenal as well while tightening their grip on the populace. If they do conspire to do evil, who will stand up to them?"

Barrett sighed. He knew that if this was indeed true, then with Russia being a nuclear power, no one would do anything to stop them. Just like when they invaded Afghanistan in the 1980's, and more recently their actions in Chechnya and Georgia showed that most of the Western countries would huff and puff, but when push came to shove, they wouldn't act. Western-style democracies charged their political leaders too high a price for any action of this magnitude. He thanked Kress, promising to call him if he needed any more help.

"Looks like they are heading toward the Sultan Mehmet Bridge," Barrett told Sara, referring to one of two suspension bridges connecting the European side of the city to the Asian side. Crossing over should help them follow the Mercedes since the Asian side was more spread out, allowing the roads to be bigger, easing the congestion. Right before they got to the modern suspension bridge, the SUV ahead unexpectedly pulled off, making a right turn. Barrett sighed while turning the wheel to follow. *They never make this easy.*

The Mercedes finally pulled into a parking area adjacent to a large castle complex right on the Bosphorus. Max parked his car in front of a café across from the ancient, sprawling structure. The English part of the sign read "Fortress of Europe." Barrett remembered seeing the old, stone fort angling down the slope right to the Bosphorus edge on their trip down in *The Lone Ranger.*

He checked the guide map and learned the Rumeli Hisari was built by Mehmet II in the 15th century to control the defenders of Constantinople's access to the waterway, cutting off their ability to resupply during his siege. The fortress had been built on the narrowest part of the strait and used in tandem with a smaller version built on the Asian side to effectively cut off any relief from waterborne vessels. Once the city fell into the sultan's hands, the fortress was no longer needed for its original purpose. The Ottomans later used the citadel as barracks for their own troops and eventually a prison.

Barrett decided to report in. "I followed one of the mercs ID'd by Ms. Hanson to the Fortress of Europe."

"What's going on there?" McKenna's curiosity was piqued.

"Not sure. Guidebook says the place has a small museum and is used for public concerts and private meetings. I'm going to investigate."

"Max, that's a no-go. Stand down. Leave this for the locals. You stopped the bombing at the mosque. We heard they moved the device outside before it exploded. So apart from some gravestones, no one was injured. We also have to ID the source of the leaks.

That's enough work for one day. The analysts can put all this together now. Bring yourself and the girl in."

"Copy." Barrett hung up. He planned on following McKenna's orders, but first, he wanted to check out what was going on in the fort. Barrett also didn't mention the Russian connection because while Kress presented a compelling argument, he still was not convinced. He peered out at the ancient structure looming nearby. The attraction to places he wasn't supposed to go called to him …

He couldn't resist.

"Where are we going?" Sara asked.

"We are not going anywhere." Looking over at Sara, he said, "Sit tight for a few; I'm going to see what your friend is up to in there."

"Why can't I come?"

Barrett ignored her question. "I should be right back." He didn't want to get her hurt, and besides, she would only get in the way. He shot a quick text to Kress. Any more background info on the fortress would only help. Barrett slung his rifle across his back. He hoped he wouldn't need the weapon since he only had one magazine left. *This is my op, and I need to finish it.*

"Whatever." Sara fumed. She hated being ignored.

Barrett shoved one of the guidebooks in his back pocket and headed across the road. He located the shortest portion of the crumbling stone wall, which ran the perimeter of the complex nearest to him. A scan of the area revealed no cameras or sensors. "My door," he mumbled to himself. As he approached the wall, he glanced up at the lighted suspension bridge that provided a modern backdrop to the fortress. This would make for a nice postcard. Barrett used the stones to crawl up and over the wall. The protruding pieces held up well under his weight. They were much firmer than they appeared. Barrett cleared the top before silently dropping into the complex.

Crouched, Barrett took in his surroundings; the agent found himself in a park-like setting with ruins overgrown by grass and trees. Lights emanated from the nearest guard tower. The rotunda building sat at the highest point of the fortress on top of the hill. Barrett, still crouched, moved quickly to cover the short distance. Once he got near the tower, the ground sloped away, so he jumped over onto an ancient stone path. He was then forced to navigate steep stairs with no handrails. He spotted the open air amphitheater located a short distance away. The place appeared empty.

Barrett turned his attention back to the tower. It reminded him of those old knight-and-castle movies he'd viewed as a kid growing up. *How to get inside?* He walked around the stone structure and found the door. He tried the large, metal handle. Locked. The agent pushed on the thick, mocha-colored wooden door, but it didn't budge. He studied the lock then decided it would have taken him too long to pick even if he had the right tools. Barrett wasn't getting in that way. He looked up.

The centuries-old guard tower stood approximately four stories high, but he only needed to climb up fifteen feet to crawl through the open window, if he could call it a window. They were just glassless sleeves in the stone barely big enough for a man to squeeze through. He used the stones on the outside for handholds and footholds like he did on the wall. Barrett reached the narrow opening and peered inside. The fairly lit interior exposed empty space in the middle of the rotunda with stairs hugging the walls as they wound up and down. He squeezed through the window, lowering himself onto the stairs.

The metal stairs rattled when Barrett's feet made contact. He didn't move. Once they stopped squealing, Barrett used the silence to listen. Nothing. He carefully walked down the circular stairway. The Turkish government had placed the metal stairs over the old, stone steps some time ago to make them safer. Barrett preferred the quieter stone ones.

He came to the bottom of the stairs, which Barrett estimated was one story underground, and with no obvious door, he hit a dead-end. The American searched the area with his flashlight, and then out of the corner of his eye he noticed some disturbed dust in front of a wall to his left. *Interesting …*

First, he probed the wall with his light then with his hands. Barrett found an outline of a small door recessed into the wall matching the disturbed dust below. The entry appeared to have been used recently, possibly even tonight!

Barrett probed and prodded, trying to figure out how to access the stone door. He put pressure on both sides, first left then right. As he pushed on the right side, the left began to inch outward. Barrett pushed some more as the opening was gradually revealed. He opened the door just enough for him to fit through and stuck his flashlight in the opening. Barrett spied a metal ladder leading downwards. *How much deeper does this place go?*

He slowly descended, trying to keep the swaying and creaking to a minimum. His heart jumped with every clink, the noise echoing in the small space. Barrett bottomed out in some sort of dark passageway.

His limited light showed floors and walls made up of the same limestone and brick as those above. As Barrett walked forward, he saw that parts of the wall and floor had been reinforced with concrete so that in some places they actually became smooth. The musty odor of mildew attacked his nostrils while the warm, dead air enveloped his body. Barrett felt like he was in a grubby sauna.

Barrett switched to a blue filter on his flashlight to attract less attention as he moved slowly down the corridor. He continued down the passageway till he came to an intersection. Two tunnels appeared in front of him, both dark. He couldn't see far down either of them. He chose the one on the right. Barrett began to realize he was walking around in catacombs that might run under the whole of the fortress complex. *What is this place?* He started to make a mental map in his head while he continued to explore. Suddenly, he heard something up ahead, faint voices breaking the monotony of his search. He moved toward them, stopping at the next intersection. He listened. It was a mix of Russian and Serbian! He was close.

***

Sara Hanson loathed waiting around. She tried to keep herself busy by looking at one of the guidebooks she had picked up with Barrett earlier. She became so engrossed in the colorful history of the

Janissaries she failed to realize rain had begun to drizzle outside. A little later, she also didn't detect someone approaching her car. Startled, she jumped in her seat when someone rapped at the window. Assuming Barrett had done the knocking, she rolled the window down before looking up. With the rain coming in, Sara barely made out the face of the person standing over the car, but she was struck by the realization he had a gun pointed at her.

CHAPTER 28

Barrett continued his exploration through the underground labyrinth undisturbed. He had just searched some rooms where it appeared men slept. They were modest sleeping quarters, which included two bunk beds and one large, shared dresser. The rooms appeared to be used for temporary purposes since he didn't see any personal items in any of them. They seemed utilitarian, like on a submarine.

He also detected a few active leaks of water dripping in and places where the walls had already been stained. He considered that the Bosphorus might not be the best neighbor to have. *Did she even knock?* Through all this, he wondered if the electricity being used ran on generators. He listened intently, but didn't hear anything, not even a low hum. He trekked on.

The spider web of corridors led Barrett to a large bay. The main hall he estimated to reach twenty-five feet high in the middle of a dome-shaped, concrete ceiling. A metal catwalk circled the room halfway between the floor and ceiling, and he could see from his vantage point they included two small alcoves built into the wall. He figured a total of four alcoves since everything down there seemed to be built symmetrically.

The cavernous room happened to be crawling with mercs moving around crates and an assortment of equipment. *A storage depot?* The American consulted the map in his head, deciding to backtrack and search for a better way around. Barrett had no desire to relive Custer's Last Stand.

***

The President's daughter had been taken into the café and then led through the back to the café's storeroom before she descended down a set of stairs to a darkened basement. Sara didn't have time to look around; she and her captors immediately entered a hidden door embedded in the floor and down another flight of stairs into an old tunnel. Once inside the tunnel, the group walked in the direction of the ancient fortress.

"Where are we?" Sara stared down the long tunnel, fear about to overwhelm her. She received no answer. The mercs continued to lead Sara down the passageway lined by boxes, then after a few turns she was shoved inside a small, barely lit room. Losing her balance, she fell ungracefully to the floor.

Sara surveyed the room. The only light helping her came via two electric lanterns placed on either side. There wasn't much to the place: stacked boxes, a cot, and a few chairs.

Her attention was now drawn to the doorway as a large man strolled in, stopping a foot from her. "Get up," he commanded. "I need you to do something for me."

Reluctantly, Sara started to stand. "Sure, anything for you. But I have one request; where am I?" Her voice was sprinkled with as much defiance as she could muster, while she used her hands to wipe the dirt off of herself. Sara's retort did surprise her. Was she pissed at being captured twice, or was Barrett beginning to rub off on her?

"In part of a tunnel network built by the Ottomans before the final siege of Constantinople and fortified during World War I for their military. Now we use." The man sounded annoyed.

In fact, the room she currently occupied was part of a much larger underground complex built by the Ottoman Turks so they and their allies could sneak out under the cover of darkness and conduct secret raids against the residents still holed up in the city of Constantinople. The nightly attacks were an attempt to weaken the morale of the city's defenders.

The subterranean catacombs had been forgotten until the Ottoman government discovered them during WWI. They reinforced the walls and ceilings with steel and concrete as a bunker for the military to hide in case of Allied bombing. The place had since been abandoned with the fall of the Ottomans after the war until one of Kovlor's subordinates discovered the underground site. Scarov didn't know all the details, nor did he care to.

Standing upright, Sara still had to turn her head up to meet his eyes. Annoyed, she didn't want to give him or anyone the satisfaction that they intimidated her. But what stood in front of her didn't just scare Sara. He terrified her. First his body, the size of an Olympian; then his face, emotionless, dead eyes staring right into her soul. Did he realize how frightened she felt? The eyes and scar intimidated; she would never forget him.

"You have a new purpose." She couldn't find her voice to respond. "I want to meet your friend Barrett." She stayed silent. How did he know Max's name? Maybe Barrett was right, and an insider was helping her kidnappers.

One of Scarov's men stepped forward and slapped her.

"You are going to help me."

***

Barrett found himself on the edge of the underground complex's center hub again. All roads, or in this case passageways, met there. Crouching low to stay out of sight as workers milled about, he shuffled between crates, wanting to get a better picture of the whole situation, especially since every single person he had seen in the catacombs had been armed. He read the writing on the box closest to him. His Russian sucked, but these boxes definitely originated from the Russian military. Had they been provided officially or stolen? Barrett decided to go around so he could sneak some more peeks and not just "John Wayne" into the middle. *I won't last long if I charge in there.*

***

Sara, with no better options, spent her time in solitude searching the room that served as her jail. She looked at the boxes stacked against the back wall and began moving them around. Maybe Barrett's curiosity had also started rubbing off on her. She proceeded slowly, careful not to arouse the suspicion of the guard outside her door. Sara, thankful the sealed boxes were not heavy, pushed a few away from the wall until she heard a clang followed by a slight rattling noise. Sara finished sliding the last one aside and found the source of the noise: a piece of dark metal had fallen.

She picked up the mysterious object, giving it a quick onceover. The metal piece measured about ten inches long and three inches wide, with a sharpened end that looked to have been stuck between two boxes stacked on top of each other. A little smaller than a combat knife, the thin, metal object probably had been used to cut through the taped lids, a homemade box cutter Sara's captors must have missed before they put her in the room. She opened one of the boxes and found rifle magazines. Empty rifle magazines. The same held true for all of the others she opened, which explained why the containers were light. Unfortunately, none of them contained anything to help her escape.

Sara put the box cutter under her shirt and inside her jeans. Not a great hiding place, but what were the odds they would search her again? She continued to clear out everything until the wall lay bare in front of her. She now eyed a tiny door or more aptly a metal hatch near the bottom corner. The hatch wasn't locked, so she slowly opened the cover and peered inside.

A dark tunnel barely big enough for her to fit in if she crawled lay beyond. *Could this be any worse?* Sara prepared herself to crawl in to examine the passageway a bit further when she suddenly heard the distant sounds of mercenaries congregating outside in the hallway. She backed out, closed the opening, and started to shove the boxes back against the wall.

***

Dave Kelner was enjoying a late lunch at a nearby diner filled with staffers from the various government agencies when his cell phone beeped, grabbing his attention. He answered, expecting to hear good news and compliments, maybe even a bonus. Putting three kids through private school did drain one's bank account, not to mention his wife's freewheeling spending habits. What he gathered through the almost inaudible screaming made his blood go cold. This couldn't be. His mind spun with possibilities. It wasn't supposed to happen this way.

***

Barrett opened up with his assault rifle, his rounds sparking off the metal on the catwalk as he crossed the intersection, providing him with precious cover fire. *How had they seen me?* One moment, he had been quietly exploring the catacombs. The next, he was in a fight for his life. Barrett tried to pin the gunmen on the catwalk down as he changed position. The bastards found him pretty quick though. He slid across the slippery floor and rolled into the far wall as the return fire impacted all around him. Chips of stone and wood showered the American. Barrett low-crawled past the near corner, readjusted his sights, and steadied himself. *These guys are way too violent. Always willing to shoot first and never even bother with the questions.*

Suddenly, the firing stopped. Barrett didn't move. He tried to control his breathing. His heart still raced. The agent listened, but there were now no sounds at all. No footsteps, reloading, cocking of weapons, or even voices. The silence had become as bad as the staccato of rifles during the firefight.

Out of nowhere, a voice boomed through the halls, breaking the spooky silence. Barrett looked around and for the first time noticed the small speakers placed around the center walls. "Barrett, we should meet." A creepy, calm voice oozed in broken English over the loudspeakers. "I have the girl." Scarov put the radio up to Sara's mouth, but she remained silent. He grabbed her right arm and squeezed tightly, and she yelped in pain.

"I hope you die," Sara grunted as Scarov still held the microphone to her mouth. Barrett recognized the voice immediately. The realization of what he had done by not listening to McKenna and heading straight over to the Embassy stung him. He felt like he'd been kicked in the gut as the air rushed out of him. The agent now surveyed the situation and came to the only conclusion available, something that he'd never thought he would do. He'd had no choice back on *The Lone Ranger,* but here, he had to make one. Barrett yelled out, "Okay." With hands shaking, he dropped his rifle on the ground, put his hands up, and stepped out at his full height into the hallway.

A mercenary appeared from around the corner, his G36 aimed right at Barrett's heart. Another man joined him. The new one promptly proceeded to search Barrett thoroughly and relieved the

American agent of his pistol and knife. He also took Barrett's phone, which abruptly turned off when the man's finger contacted the touchscreen. He gave a nod to his partner, who motioned with his rifle for Barrett to move. Both kept a safe distance from him; the men were pros. Fuming, Barrett let himself be led through the main center of the underground labyrinth, down another tunnel to the small room where Sara was being kept. They stopped at the doorway; the lead guard pushed Barrett inside.

The American grimaced at Sara and then surveyed the box-filled room. Only one way in or out, he deduced. Barrett was greeted by a very large individual who stared at him without showing any emotion. Scarov didn't smile or gloat. This was business, and while Barrett was an adversary, he should be respected before being disposed of.

"You are done interfering, American cowboy." Scarov sized up his enemy, looking over the man who had caused him so much trouble. The American had an athletic build and average height; nothing else stood out to the Serbian. Scarov decided the man's physical attributes appeared ordinary at best. He figured that the American must be one of those strong-willed, never-give-up types, either that or just lucky. Either way, this made him very dangerous.

Barrett pondered the big man's threat. *Real original.* He studied the room, still trying to figure his way out of the mess he had gotten into. *This guy could play the defensive end in the NFL,* Barrett thought, looking back and seeing the sheer size of the man. He noticed the stance and facial expression of his captor who towered above him. The eyes sent a chill down Barrett's spine. They looked dead. Though the man had a calm and collected demeanor, Barrett wondered what went on inside. Was there a way to crack his outward calmness? Something he could use to his advantage?

"You know my name. What's yours?"

"Does not matter." Scarov stared into Barrett's eyes while maintaining the stone-cold facial expression.

"It does to me." Barrett tried to stall for time. "How 'bout I call you Hank and your girlfriends there Jane and Judy." He pointed out the other two guards in the room. Barrett's naming session was

abruptly interrupted when Jane stepped forward and punched him in
the sternum, knocking him to his knees. Barrett, holding his stomach,
struggled back to his feet.

"Okay, so you don't like Jane. How about Joan?"

Scarov had wasted enough time on the American and nodded
to his subordinate as he walked out.

What neither he nor Scarov realized was that while everyone
paid attention to Barrett, Sara had slowly pulled out the box cutter.
The President's daughter didn't need an interpreter to understand
what Scarov meant as he left their little cell. She waited long enough
for him to be a good ways down the hall then sprang like a cat. Sara
gripped the metal knife tightly and brought it down with all her might
on the guard nearest her. He cried out in pain as she drove the box
cutter into his collarbone. The guard next to Barrett turned toward
his howling comrade.

Barrett moved swiftly. He stepped forward while twisting his
torso sideways to lessen himself as a target in case the weapon fired
and palmed the merc's hands. He got control of the trigger finger
before turning his hips and flipping the gunman over his shoulder.
The man landed with a loud thud. Barrett now had control of the
rifle and fired point-blank at the man on the ground. A round drilled
through the man's forehead, closing his eyes forever. Barrett then
swung upwards and fired at the mercenary Sara had just stabbed,
sending bullets at his head, one crashing through the bridge of the
man's nose, silencing his screams. Barrett moved to the doorway and
peeked outside. The passageway was empty, but for how long?
Hopefully, the mercs had been ordered to carry out the executions in
the room, so the gunshots would be expected. If not, company
would be coming to check up on the guards, or the big guy may have
already sent extra help to dispose of their bodies. Barrett shuddered
at the thought. He needed an exit strategy fast.

"Over here." Sara motioned to Barrett, moving some of the
boxes over, revealing the hatch. She lifted up the hidden door,
showing him the entrance to the small side tunnel she'd initially
discovered when she had been left alone earlier. "Where do you think
this goes?"

"Don't care as long as it's not here." Barrett put his gun in his belt and motioned for her to crawl into the small space. They didn't have many options. She squeezed in, crawling forward for a few feet, then waited for him to follow. Barrett reached back, sliding a box over before closing the hatch to conceal their escape. Barrett couldn't see much in the tiny, dark tunnel. He had no idea where the two of them were going. *This is turning out to be the worst ever rescue attempt in history.*

CHAPTER 29

Barrett and Sara moved as fast as possible crammed in the tight, dark space. Sara led them deeper into the shaft. "What do you think this was used for?" Sara liked to talk when nervous. They had been moving at a good pace using mostly their hands and knees, which Sara felt being rubbed raw by the rocky floor.

"Maybe to drain some of the water out." Barrett eyed the severe water lines on the walls. The tight space would not accommodate a person much bigger than Barrett; in fact, his shoulders were touching the sides. He couldn't think of any other purpose for the small tunnels. He remembered seeing the leaks in the passageways and wondered if it ever did indeed flood up there.

The passage made a slight downward and left turn, toward the Bosphorus. Maybe he was right. *That would be a nice change.* They continued until they came upon another tunnel. While the one they were in seemed to be heading toward the river, the new one appeared to return back into the complex. Sara stopped. "What do we do now?"

"Let's stay on this one, but move into the opening of the other for a sec so we can switch places."

Barrett didn't know where this shaft actually led, but he wanted to get as far away from his captors as possible. Sara crawled into the new tunnel opening and waited for Barrett to crawl by and take the lead. *Men.* The duo continued, making their way down the tunnel, Barrett realizing the air was becoming cooler as the two moved forward.

The shaft finally ended at an old, weather-worn grate. Barrett held up his hand for her to stop so he could look and listen for what might be waiting for them beyond the metal grille. In his limited view, he saw some grass and light shimmering from the strait, but he couldn't see or hear anyone, which didn't mean someone wasn't out there guarding this part of the ancient ruin. At least the water did explain the cooling effect at this end of the tunnel. He pushed on the grate. The rusty metal didn't give. He shifted onto his back with his knees to his chest and kicked with all his might. The added force did the trick. With a screeching sound of defiance, the old, rusty grate gave way.

That's bound to attract attention, thought Barrett as he wiggled out of the confined space, landing on the grass. Barrett surveyed his position to get his bearings. He stood outside the wall of the fortress on a very short, grassy bank, which quickly sloped down to a rocky shoreline. Barrett turned to the right and discerned something unusual between some trees and the fortress's outer wall. The grass and rocks in front of him swayed. He stepped over and reached his arm out, feeling a flat, rubbery surface. *Camouflage!*

Barrett examined the tarp painted to look like the riverbank's foliage. *Curious* ... He pulled the side back to see what lay beyond. Inside, hidden by the tarp, lay a dock built into a natural, cave-like cove. Only someone standing right next to the entrance like Barrett had been would even realize this man-made dock existed. The dock appeared to be pretty new, just a few years old by his guess, so was definitely not part of the original construction.

Barrett spied a small, fiberglass boat moored inside. Next to the vessel lay an empty berthing spot capable of mooring a much bigger craft. The one now inside probably served as a patrol boat or escort. Peering back outside toward the bank, he noticed the rain had stopped.

"What is all this?" Sara examined the hidden marina, overwhelmed.

"Covert boat slips."

"I figured this part. I mean what is all this about?"

"Keeping us chasing our own tail. The Russians are still rebuilding their strength and want to keep America and the West focused on something other than them. The American public would be in an uproar if anything happened to their little darling." Sara scowled at him. "Our response would be swift and massive." Sara stared down, realizing she'd never thought about the consequences if something happened to her. "This way, America continues to spend all her resources on chasing Islamic terrorists around the world, giving them more time."

"More time for what?"

"Do you know why they're more dangerous now than at any time during the Soviet days?"

"Money. They didn't have much during their communist days."

Beauty and brains ... Focus, Max. "Give the girl a free ticket to Disneyland. It's much easier to spend huge sums of money than to use nuclear missiles. The Russians are buying their way into Western countries by setting up new businesses, investing in established ones, and contributing to political campaigns all across Europe and North America. Not to mention they are second only to Saudi Arabia in oil production. The Russians are using Western greed to divide and conquer."

"So why do this now?"

"With oil prices in decline, they may be getting desperate. Their economy is too dependent on the stuff."

"What do they get out of all this?"

"Their place in the world back. Pride. Who knows?"

An abrupt noise called his attention from inside the dock. Barrett turned to see that the sound came from someone running toward them and shouting. He squinted to get a better view. A merc.

Sometimes he hated being right. Barrett pointed to the small boat bobbing in the water, still tied to the dock. "Get inside."

Sara jumped in, ducking below the seats. Barrett faced the oncoming guard, who still shouted at them. He put one hand up like he wanted to surrender, while the right hand lifted the Makorov he had taken off his executioner in the catacombs and squeezed twice. The double tap blew the surprised guard back into the empty berthing space with a splash. The only reminder of the lone guard was the rippling water and reverberating echoes from the gunshots. Not quiet, but very effective.

Barrett returned his focus to their escape. "Get out." He jumped into the patrol vessel. Sara stepped out onto the dock, observing the frantic movements of her rescuer. The agent untied the speedboat before moving to the controls. Barrett started the engines and turned the boat around so the bow faced outward, a difficult maneuver in such a tight space. The boat squealed as its sides rubbed along the wooden planks of the slip. He pushed on the throttles, jamming the steering column in place using a life jacket he found behind the driver's seat. The engine went from a rumble to a roar.

Barrett took off his belt, tying the transmission gear control in place. He jumped out of the rumbling speed boat, giving a tug on the belt, trying to get the craft out of neutral. He pulled again …

The boat blasted through the tarp concealing the secret dock, shredding the cover to pieces as it raced out into the river.

With the cave now quiet, Sara stared at Barrett in bewilderment. "Why didn't we use the boat?" she yelled with their ears still ringing from the effect of the howling engines in such a confined space.

"A hunch." Barrett followed the runaway craft.

As if on cue, an alarm blared on a speaker against the wall, followed almost immediately by weapons fire. The sky filled up with tracers streaming toward the boat, tracking its every move. Soon after, a whoosh sounded overhead, causing them both to turn toward the sky, where a faint, reddish glow appeared, streaking after the vessel. The missile hit dead center. *Boom!* The speed boat exploded in a flash of bright orange, pieces of fiberglass and metal raining into the river. Reflex caused the pair to duck even though they were in no danger from the flying debris. Their nerves were now stretched to the breaking point, and the fireworks show wasn't helping. Barrett began to tire of these guys' penchant for violence, especially explosives.

"Bad guys' anti-theft device. A great deterrent, no?"

She stood speechless.

The alarm continued to howl.

"I think that's the dinner bell." Barrett scanned for a way out.

He realized the hidden dock was no longer a safe place to be.

"This way." Barrett led them out of the cave, up the grassy bank, and back toward the fortress.

"What are we doing?" Sara did her best to follow.

"Last thing they'd expect."

***

"We have confirmation of an attempt on the vehicle," McKenna reported to Secretary Spencer over the secured line between his office and the Pentagon.

"Casualties?"

"No personnel in the decoy car or assault team were injured."

"Good." The Secretary of Defense sighed with relief. "So Dave Kelner is the leak." It was stated more like an observation than a question. "No one believes it. The President really liked him."

"We all did, but this is the nature of the business." McKenna sounded disappointed. He had experienced plenty of betrayals in his career, though no one as highly placed as Kelner in the U.S. government, if Kelner was proven to be the mole.

"I don't envy you guys." The Secretary of Defense shook his head. "This is a tough way to live."

"For some, sir, it's the only way. You want him brought in or put under surveillance?"

"I will get the President and Attorney General on this, see what they want to do. Well done, Lance."

McKenna followed up his conversation with the Secretary of Defense by putting in a call to Dooley. "Do we have confirmation on Barrett and the PD arriving at the embassy yet?

"No."

"Let me know the minute they arrive."

Where are they?

***

Barrett knew they would have been sitting ducks trying to cross the river in the speedboat, so he decided the best course of action was to backtrack. He briefly thought about swimming across, but wasn't sure if Sara could make it. Now he planned on taking the long way around in an attempt to avoid their pursuers.

Back inside the fortress, Barrett and Sara did their best to transverse quickly through, but climbing over and going around some of the crumbling stone structures in the dark hampered their efforts. Barrett hoped the trick on the dock would work to throw the mercs off. He wanted to get out through the same part of the wall he had used to enter the complex, but in order to do that, they would have to go back via the enemy-controlled fortress grounds. "Do what your adversary least expects," was his motto.

The complex outside had minimal lighting even though their captors desperately searched for them. *Guess the mercs don't want to draw any more attention to themselves than we do.* With only the light from the moon, which now sat high in the sky as the clouds cleared to help guide them, the pair moved cautiously across the grounds. Barrett and Sara entered the amphitheater, crossing between the stage and audience section which afforded them solid cover in the shadows. They had barely cleared the amphitheater when Barrett heard the crunching of wet grass under men's boots, the warning providing them plenty of time to dash inside a small, stone structure before a trio of gunmen ran by. The pair waited a few moments for the mercs to get farther prior to heading out again.

They were now on the verge of making Barrett's planned destination that lay a little farther down the path. Barrett felt in his gut they might now actually escape. *Almost there.* He held his hand up for them to stop behind an ancient stone pillar across from the wall section Barrett had used earlier in the evening. "Ah, crap."

Four men had been posted by the shortened section of the wall Barrett wanted to climb. He had hoped to climb back over the wall and make a run for their car. Now, the situation dawned on him. Since he had walked into a trap, they must have watched him enter the complex. His stomach tightened.

"I got an idea." Sara broke the silence. Barrett ignored her at first, looking around. He needed a new plan, but was drawing a blank at a very inopportune time.

"I'm all ears," Barrett finally responded through clenched teeth.

"How did you get down to the tunnels?"

"Tower." He pointed to the same guard tower he'd used earlier.

"Follow me."

Barrett reluctantly allowed her to lead them back toward the turret. When they got there the wooden door stood ajar, left open by the searching guards, they both assumed.

Sara pointed down the stairwell. "This is where you came in, right?"

"Yes." Barrett looked at her, bewildered, before realizing what she planned. *And some think I'm crazy.* They snuck down the tower, retracing Barrett's steps, going through the secret door at the bottom, entering the catacombs for a second time. Back in the fire.

CHAPTER 30

"You sure this is the right way?" Barrett still couldn't believe he was following the President's daughter through the underground maze. He didn't remember this section of the complex, nor could he recall the area as part of his mental map either.

"See those boxes?" Sara gestured to the containers lining both sides of the walls. "They sat right near where I came in." Barrett continued to follow her lead. After another turn, she came to a stop and pointed to a set of stairs. "Those lead to the café upstairs."

Barrett would never doubt a woman's sense of direction again. He had been grateful the pair had been able to progress pretty far through the passageways without running into any mercenaries, especially since this seemed to be their main way in and out. All of a sudden, Barrett stopped and put up his hand. "Hold on."

The President's daughter kept walking toward the stairs; she slowed and turned back to Barrett. Too late.

Scarov appeared out of the dark shadows like a wraith and grabbed Sara's hair. She screamed, trying to pull away from his grip, but to no avail. The Serbian mercenary had anticipated their attempt at deception. They had tried to fool him once already in Bulgaria. Not again.

Barrett rushed him and slid feet first into the bigger man's legs, knocking all three of them to the ground. Barrett climbed on the Serb and started to work him over, but Scarov used his legs to kick the American agent off. Barrett crashed into some of the boxes along the wall, crushing them. The Serbian soldier possessed freakish strength.

Barrett attempted to regain his footing. "Run!" Sara backed out of the center of the room toward the stairs but stood, fixated on the fight between the two men. The concern she felt for Barrett staked her to the spot.

The mercenary rushed Barrett, using his long reach to grab Barrett's collar then jumped, reaching out with his leg, slamming his thigh into the agent's stomach. Catching Barrett like this, he twisted in midair, using his other leg to strike the back of Barrett's knees, taking him off balance and bringing him down. Scarov continued to turn his body as both men fell to the floor. Barrett recognized the scissor takedown. Classic Russian Combat Sambo move. *This guy definitely had Spetsnaz training.* He knew Russian advisors had trained Serbian soldiers in the later part of the twentieth century.

Barrett slammed onto the floor, his shoulder taking most of the blow. He let out a loud grunt as he bounced off the hard floor. The Russian did his best to control him, but Barrett twisted and spun on the ground to break free of the merc's hold. Barely. His opponent moved fast for such a large person. Scarov attempted to get on top of Barrett, again trying to grab and pin the American's arms. Barrett slithered out of the man's grip but took a knee to his ribs for his success. Barrett rolled on his back and swung his legs over his head, doing a kickup to get on his feet. Scarov likewise recovered and charged Barrett.

Barrett did a bullfighter's turn, giving the big man an elbow to the middle of the back as he passed. He left his leg out to trip the big man but failed. The Serbian just powered past the smaller man's attempt. Scarov turned at Barrett again, this time catching him around the waist and driving the American into the nearest wall. He threw punches at Barrett's torso, which the American tried to block with his forearms. Some connected. Barrett felt his body being pounded into minced meat. Scarov followed those up with a head bump, gashing Barrett's forehead, making him woozy. Scarov continued to work the agent over, connecting with pulverizing punches. Barrett did his best to avoid as many as possible, but his opponent's long reach made this difficult.

Barrett shook his head to try and clear the cobwebs growing inside. He had to do something. He couldn't get away from the other man's longer reach, so he did the opposite and slid forward, closing the gap between the two combatants. This limited Scarov's ability to connect with his big punches, and if he did, there would be a minimal amount of force behind them. Starting to tire, Barrett stamped down on his opponent's kneecap and felt it give. He followed up with an elbow to the man's chest. Both strikes hardly slowed Scarov down. Barrett knew the knee had to be dislocated, but the mercenary didn't miss a beat. The man seemed to be impervious to pain.

Even worse, however, was that exhaustion had begun to take a toll on Barrett. His arms and legs gave the impression that they were being weighed down by bricks. Fear also began to creep in. He couldn't afford any mistakes against such a bigger and stronger opponent. Thoughts of Sara, her smile, even Foresky lying there on the street had crept into his mind.

He couldn't fail …

The Serbian mercenary enjoyed his way with the smaller opponent; his confidence grew, maybe too much. The American had skills, but Scarov believed this was his fight to win. Barrett's desperate gambit on the knee had gained him a little time and space; he pushed the pain flowing through his body to the back of his mind and grabbed a piece of a broken box, which had previously broken his fall. The agent whipped it at the mercenary, but Scarov ducked, letting the wooden piece fly past his head and fall harmlessly to the ground.

With his opponent distracted, Barrett closed the distance between them again. Using the last of his reserves, the tired agent desperately threw a triple combo, which took the mercenary by surprise. First, an uppercut to the chin, then an elbow to his throat, and finally an old-fashioned punch to the sternum. Scarov thought he had Barrett on the ropes when the American surprised him with that lighting quick combination. Barrett took advantage of the move by continuing to pound away. He used desperation and fear to fuel his attack, utilizing speed over the other guy's brute strength.

Barrett pounded away on his opponent, trying to inflict as much damage as possible as quickly as possible. Scarov desperately pushed the American off. Barrett stumbled back, tumbling over next to the wall. The American agent lay between the mercenary and the end of the corridor, trapped.

Barrett slowly got up. He had almost nothing left. He looked at Scarov. The surprise strikes and quick movements had taken their toll on his enemy, the cool, efficient, killing machine gone, now replaced by a wild-eyed animal. With his back to the wall, he watched as Scarov, now sneering, pulled out a Russian combat knife, which he brandished at Barrett while smiling. Twirling the blade in his hand, eyes blazing, he charged the cornered American.

Barrett gained renewed vigor from what he saw in Scarov's eyes. The American crossed his arms at his wrists and struck down hard into the Serbian's knife hand as he tried to ram the blade into Barrett's stomach. Barrett slowed the mercenary's strike enough so he could grab his opponent's wrist. By turning his upper torso and pulling on Scarov's wrist simultaneously, Barrett kept the Serb off balance, causing his opponent's entire body to start leaning downward. Barrett had all the leverage. He attacked the man's weakened knee with a couple of powerful side-kicks. The big man started to fall. Scarov didn't go all the way down, but remained on his knees with Barrett standing over him in a death lock.

With Scarov still off balance, Barrett twisted and pulled the knife free, inching his body ever closer to the bigger man, who was now struggling and grunting in an effort to get up. Barrett drove the blade sideways between the man's ribs and into his heart. He took in a breath while manipulating the knife, looking straight into Scarov's eyes, which widened in fear, the life draining away. Barrett waited for those eyes to die.

Scarov's eyes rolled and his body went limp. Barrett pulled the knife out, stepped back and let the big man fall with a thump to the ground. The American looked him over, feeling for a pulse. He couldn't find any. Barrett never enjoyed killing anyone—it was an unfortunate necessity of his job.

The two Americans made their way up the stairs. Barrett, covered in grime and blood, yanked the doors to the café's basement open while Sara helped to steady him. Barrett felt like he had been run through a grinder. He didn't know how much more he had left in him. No one appeared in the basement, so the pair took the second set of stairs up to the café. They entered the storage room behind the seating area; no one was waiting for them. Barrett heard the distance rattle of gunfire and screaming originating from the fort. *Great, they're just shooting at everybody.* He imagined the pissed-off mercenaries firing at anything that moved.

They made their way past the doors and entered the cafe. The deserted dining room looked a mess. Tables and chairs had been knocked over. Food had been spilled all over the floor, along with menus and napkins. The area appeared to have emptied in a hurry. Had customers fled at the first sounds of gunfire? *But gunfire from where and at whom?* tugged at Barrett's mind.

They made their way through the chaos of the once-nice watering hole for tourists with the faint sounds of sirens now mixed in with the occasional retorts of assault rifles. The rain had stopped, leaving everything shiny. Barrett wondered if they should try and make a dash for the car. *Not that hanging out in a café run by your enemy could be any safer.*

Still breathing heavily from the fight and the stair climb, Barrett crept to the front door for a better view of the outside. Through the glass door, he observed two mercenaries across the street making for the café. He motioned for Sara to get behind a flipped-over table.

Here we go …

As the men reached the sidewalk tables, one of them abruptly turned, looking to fire back toward the fortress. His body shook as a couple of rounds punched through him, forcing him to crash against a garbage can, knocking it over. The other mercenary headed for the safety of the café, not even bothering to check on his buddy.

Barrett intercepted him as he came through the door. The gunman stepped into the café only to be surprised as Barrett grabbed him from behind, wrapping his arms around the merc's neck to put him in a choke hold. Within seconds, the man lay unconscious at the American's feet. Barrett quickly relieved his victim of his assault rifle and magazines. He dragged the body away from the café's entrance, sliding him under an empty table before heading back to the front door to assess the situation. Their car sat idling ... waiting. *Could we make it?* He examined the area between the fortress and the street out front one more time. Two other armed men ran toward the café.

You've got to be kidding ...

Barrett readied the G36 he'd just taken from the mercenary, pulled out the magazine to check for rounds, and emphatically slammed it back home with a large clack. In his condition, Barrett knew he was setting up for a last stand. He handed the Makarov to Sara, made sure the gun was loaded, and briefly showed her how to use the Russian pistol before telling her to get behind the counter.

"After I take care of these two, make a run for the car. I'll stay behind and cover you."

She shot him a look. Her safety was his only concern now. *Is this because of duty or something else?* He turned to avoid her gaze and ignored those thoughts to focus on the approaching threats. She leaned over, planting a kiss on his lips. Barrett reciprocated before tearing himself away.

The men, with their guns at the ready, cleared past the road. Barrett rechecked his assault rifle and put the closest target in his sights. As the two men got closer, he thought he recognized one of them. He blinked twice to make sure he wasn't seeing things. He sighted the man again, but his appearance didn't change. *No way.* Crossing the street toward him was one Emre Hamit!

Barrett opened the door slightly and called out to the Turk. The American was so beat up it took Hamit a few moments to recognize him. Hamit lowered his weapon and shook his head in relief. Barrett felt relieved as well, though a little bit confused. He braced the door open with his back, allowing the two men to enter the abandoned establishment. He kept his eyes scanning over toward the fortress.

Hamit stared wild-eyed at the punching bag that used to be Barrett's head and torso. His associate, who appeared to have had medical training, gave Sara and Barrett a brief examination. As the man fussed over Barrett, Hamit informed him that McKenna had asked him to look into the fortress since the pair had not arrived at the embassy as expected. *McKenna?*

"I have more than one friend," Hamit responded with a smirk. He continued on, telling Barrett that when he and his men searched the old fort, they'd encountered the armed mercenaries and a brutal gunfight ensued. His men followed the mercs into the tunnels while he and his deputy chased two others to the café. Barrett reciprocated by updating Hamit on all that had transpired at the ancient fort, though he still left out Sara's true identity. Hamit and his man's eyes grew wide as the American spun his tale.

After a few minutes, the firefight outside began to subside. The retorts of semi-automatic rifles become less and less frequent. Hamit's men were turning the tide on the mercenaries, who had become disorganized with the double whammy of Barrett killing their leader and the local authorities showing up in force at their previously secret location. It would only be a short time before Hamit's small force secured the whole complex. Barrett still didn't know who Hamit or his men were, but based on the fact McKenna knew him and due to their interaction with the local authorities, he assumed they were with Turkish Intelligence.

Thank goodness. Maybe I'll bring him back some raki.

CHAPTER 31

The TV at the far end of the grand lobby of the elegant Hotel Raphael was showing the breaking international news story of the day: American Deputy National Security Advisor Dave Kelner had been found dead in his car from an apparent suicide. His car, parked next to the Potomac River outside Washington, D.C. was discovered in the early morning by a jogger. The investigation was ongoing.

***

Kovlor and his new mistress headed back to their suite after dinner and the cabaret at the risqué Le Crazy Horse Paris. Kovlor loved the shows, especially the more erotic ones. Across the magnificent lobby, a small group of four men in overalls meandered around, entering and leaving through a back door to the stairs.

After Kovlor and his most recent conquest entered the elevator, additional men in maintenance uniforms positioned inside the stairwell on the top floor received a signal and quickly rid themselves of their outerwear. They now sported dark gray fatigues with the French flag on their left arm, the uniforms of the GIPN. Groupes d'Intervention de la Police Nationale was a specialized counter terrorist unit of the French National Police that normally operated outside the city limits of Paris. The men put on their Kevlar helmets and raised their H&K MP5 submachine guns, preparing to move.

The Russian millionaire and his date stepped from the elevator and strolled hand and hand like two teenagers toward their suite. Kovlor stopped to view his surroundings, making sure they'd disembarked on the proper floor. He pointed out a gold information plaque, confirming their location, so the giggling couple continued

238

across the hall to the door of their suite. This was the arms dealer's first visit to the hotel. He'd had so much bad luck lately he felt he needed a change. Maybe he was getting superstitious.

Just as Kovlor bent down to run his room card through the slot, the SWAT team burst from the stairwell, brandishing their assault rifles, and in a commanding tone their leader ordered the pair to get on their bellies. Stunned, Kovlor and his mistress complied; the policeman searched and flex-cuffed them rather quickly. Three members of the SWAT team peeled off from the group in the hallway and entered the suite, subduing the bodyguard posted inside.

Kovlor's other guard had stayed downstairs to park the Maybach. He would not make it back upstairs. The other GIPN team downstairs had already seen to that. The SWAT team members within the two-thousand-Euros-a-night suite rummaged through Kovlor's belongings, tearing the room apart. The men confiscated papers from the arms dealer's suitcase, along with his laptop.

The leader of the SWAT team approached Kovlor, advising him that he would be taken into custody for questioning, but not the young lady. The team led the arms dealer to the elevator. Kovlor quickly sobered, protesting his handling by the men in GIPN uniforms. He informed them he had a lot of connections within the French Intelligence apparatus, and someone would pay for this disrespect. He repeated over and over that Kovlor was not a man to be trifled with.

The group made their way to the other end of the hall, entering the service elevator. The occupants waited with one of the men, holding the doors open. Kovlor watched a man stroll toward them in an extremely well-tailored suit. *Armani or Hugo Boss,* he thought. As the man got closer to the elevator, Kovlor thought he looked familiar. He squinted, doing his best to focus through his alcohol-induced fog.

Then it hit him. This was the American agent who had ruined his last operation. He recognized him from the picture taken by the security cameras in Bulgaria. Once this realization hit Kovlor, his knees weakened, and he felt sick.

Barrett got in and turned around, facing out of the elevator. He smiled as the doors closed. "Mr. Tolvic." Barrett stared straight ahead as the doors slid shut. "There are some people who look forward to meeting you." The air rushed out of the arms dealer, and he collapsed in a heap on the floor. The rest of the tactical team members laughed as the elevator filled with six Americans disguised as French commandos and one ex-Serbian warlord headed down.

The doors opened on the ground floor, and the men carried Kovlor out the service elevator through a back door and into a waiting black SUV.

"We got our man again." The senior NCO on the assault team hung back, walking in stride with Barrett.

"Yes, we did, Brad." Barrett matched smiles with the CAG shooter, thinking about the mission when the two soldiers had first met. It seemed like an eternity ago.

"Try to keep a handle on him this time." Thomas secured Kovlor inside the SUV before getting in himself. Barrett closed the doors, pounded the window twice as an all clear, and watched the SUV take off down the alley.

He walked back into the hotel, crossed the lobby, and was out the front door, nodding to the doorman as he left the hotel. Barrett continued across the street toward a large blue delivery van parked at the side of the road. He opened the side door and stepped up into it, the modern, high-tech layout interior greeting him projecting a direct contrast to the plainness of the vehicle's exterior.

"Nice work." Barrett patted Kale on the shoulder while turning to Reirson, who'd just left his post outside of the hotel to join the others in the truck. Kale and Bellows sat in front of monitors displaying the hotel's front, the inside of Kovlor's suite, and the alleyway. The men monitored the hotel's own security system they had hacked into plus a few extra cameras the team had installed earlier. The van contained some of the most sophisticated surveillance gear in the U.S. arsenal. The guys inside were the eyes and ears of the operation.

"Anything for the First Boyfriend," joked Cruise with a wry smile. Barrett ignored him.

"We got the Serb arms dealer who tried to pass himself off as a Russian in custody, and we found the offshore accounts for Kelner, but what about the Russian connection to all of this?" Bellows asked, looking up from his station. The ex-SEAL never appeared comfortable sitting behind a computer screen. The boring part of the seasoning process to make him a better field agent one day. The others waited for Barrett's response. Barrett had let them in on the possible Russian connection Johan had mentioned, but that information was still being tossed around by the senior staff of the unit, the other intelligence agencies, and the White House. Beltway politics. Besides, none of the supposed experts knew what to make of the discovery.

Max Barrett looked back outside through the van's window toward the quiet French street and sighed. "Sometimes, gentlemen, you just don't get an answer!"

EPILOGUE

The rain came down in droves, slamming against the only window, creating a soothing staccato sound for the office's only occupant. The middle-aged man working behind his desk didn't mind the torrential downpour outside since it could be worse. *It could be snowing today instead.*

The encrypted cell phone on his desk lit up and began to beep, breaking into his trancelike state brought about by the rain. The man viewed the caller ID: an international number. "Yes," he said into the phone with much impatience. He was, after all, a very busy man. After listening to the other end of the call for a few moments, he finally spoke. "I see." He continued after a brief pause. "Terminate all contact."

He pushed the red button on his phone to end the call then turned the device over, opening up the back. He took out the SIM card and walked over to the fireplace, his only luxury, in the corner of his office. He tossed the card into the fire, watching the flames quickly consume it. The scene was a perfect metaphor for what he'd just learned. Turning away from the fire, he walked back to the window and looked out over the rain-soaked Kremlin.

Yes, things could always be worse.

###

Thanks for reading *Shadow Hunt*.
Please consider leaving your review at the place of purchase.

Max Barrett will return in 2016.

To receive the latest information on upcoming releases first, please
join my mailing list at www.michaelpedicelli.com.

ABOUT THE AUTHOR

Michael Pedicelli is a U.S. Army veteran with a B.A. in History and an MBA in International Business. When not writing screenplays and novels, he is a student of military history and works as a global business adviser in the private sector.

Made in the USA
Coppell, TX
18 February 2020